Aliege

The third book in the Hleo series

By

Rebecca Weller

Copyright 2017 © – ISBN 978-0-9950316-2-3

Paula,
thanks so much for
the support!
Becky W...

This book is dedicated to my family.
The people in my world I am
fortunate enough to spend my days
with. You offer endless, support, laughter
and love. This one's for you.

One

I never seem to know I'm making a mistake until I've made it. The thought continually played over in my head while I hurried down the sidewalk. I was in a part of Hartford that, if I was being generous, I would describe as badly maintained, looking to meet with a man I had only ever spoken to via email, and no one else in the world knew I was here. I passed by a pawn shop, a tarot card reading place, and a convenience store advertising cheap cigarettes. I quickened my pace as long shadows, cast by the setting sun, added to the already ominous feel of the area. Finally I reached the store I was looking for.

Milton's Oddities and Rarities was scrawled in gold lettering across a dark green wooden sign. It was the only shop on the street that didn't use flashy neon to attract the eye. Once the sun was down, the words would be almost impossible to read. I peered through one of the large picture windows of the store at a jumbled array of antique sofas, tables, china, and books, loads of books.

The cardboard sign on the door was flipped to *closed*, but I'd been expecting that. It was actually the reason we were meeting at this time. Milton, the owner of the store, had only agreed to speak with me after business hours. So there wouldn't be any interruptions, his words. I took a breath, bracing myself for the possibility that I would have to make a run for it if Milton turned out to be really weird, and knocked on the door. Through the small glass window, I could see that it was dim inside, and I pulled the collar of my jacket up around my neck as I glanced down the street. Had I gotten the information wrong somehow?

I frowned, about to give up and walk away, when a figure appeared on the other side of the glass. A man peered out at me, then turned the lock and inched the door open, just wide enough for me to see his face. "You are?" He stared at me with narrowed eyes. I knew from our predetermined online arrangement that he must be Milton Cambry, a heavy-set, mousy-brown-haired man with a thin moustache and thick glasses, who appeared to be only a few inches taller than me.

"Hannah Reed." I squared my shoulders.

"Yes, of course, Miss Reed, come in." His tone immediately became welcoming and he pulled open the door to the shop. I stepped inside, trying not to bump into a pile of leather-bound books stacked precariously on a three-legged side table.

"In this neighborhood you can't be too careful." Milton pushed the door shut and twisted the lock. I watched his fingers and swallowed the lump forming in my throat. *I'm sure he's innocent.*

It was hard to take everything in since most of the lights were off, but the store was jam-packed. Display cases, bookshelves, and tables were all covered with little odds and ends. Sofas, chairs, and other pieces of furniture were crammed between the display cases, making it almost impossible to walk around, but straight ahead of me was a narrow aisle that led to the back of the store. Light shone out from under a closed door marked *private*.

"Thank you for meeting with me." I stayed near the store's entrance, subtly sizing up Milton in an attempt to determine his threat level.

"I have to admit, I was intrigued that someone your age would have any interest in such an unusual artifact." Milton ambled towards the back of the store. When he was about halfway there, he stopped and turned to face me, as though expecting me to follow.

I closed the gap between us. "My father's a history teacher. He told me the story of the Glain Neidr once, and it stayed with me. I know it's probably ridiculous, but I sort of hoped I could confirm its existence and, I don't know, find it somehow." I shrugged as I repeated the story I'd first given Milton when I'd stumbled upon his Glain Neidr website.

I'd brought up looking for the Glain Neidr a handful of times to Ethan Flynn, the Hleo assigned to keep me safe, after we'd returned from Veridan, the Hleo's North American headquarters.

Every time he brushed the suggestion aside, maintaining that searching for the elusive stone with the mystical capability of giving the wearer unlimited power over his or her greatest natural talent was a lost cause. I'd let it go for a few weeks, but the failure to get any real answers at Veridan had eaten away at me. Then I had a string of four unpleasant images of protecteds—those who, like me, were destined to change the world in some way by making a seemingly meaningless, yet ultimately life-altering, decision—pop into my head back to back, and I got sick of waiting. Maybe this was all about some mysterious decision I had to make, as one of the Hleo's leaders, Miriam, had suggested, but I needed to figure out how to control my visions until that time came.

It had only taken me an evening of online research before I stumbled on Milton's website, devoted to his quest to track down the elusive gem.

Milton had been fairly open to meeting me, although I gathered from our correspondence that he was a rather apprehensive individual. The only real issue was that I had kept my meeting a secret from Ethan. He had been running over data about my latest images with his partner, Simon, and thought I was currently at the library in my hometown of East Halton.

"I wouldn't hold your breath on finding the Glain Neidr, but I admire your youthful ambition. And I'm more than willing to share what I know." Milton pushed the door of the back room open to reveal a small, cluttered kitchen. Given the papers and files scattered across the round linoleum dining table, and a filing cabinet shoved against the back wall, I guessed that the small space also doubled as Milton's office. Milton grabbed a cloth and swept the crumbs off the side counter area onto the floor, maneuvering carefully to avoid knocking over his toaster and coffeemaker. Then he went about gathering up an assortment of used coffee mugs from the table and counter, depositing them into a small sink before motioning for me to have a seat. He seemed harmless enough, but I still sank onto the high-backed wooden dining chair closest to the door, just in case.

Milton plopped down onto a vinyl, floral-patterned chair across from me, smoothing down the bulky sweater he had on as he settled in. "So, what do you know about the stone?"

"I've only been digging around for a few weeks, so I don't feel like I know very much. My dad told me the legends of Sir

William Gray, and Gwendolyn, but I don't really know where the necklace came from, or where it ended up after the story of Nicholas Rye running across Ireland." I glanced at the papers in front of me, subtly scanning them for any mention of the Glain Neidr.

"The necklace's origins are shrouded in mystery. If you know the story of Sir William, then you probably know he found the Glain Neidr on the Isle of Man. But there are different versions of exactly how he discovered the necklace. The most common account is that Sir William came across the stone, half-buried in the earth, when he was seeking shelter in the seaside caves. There are some fanatics who take this story further and allege that Poseidon, king of the sea, bestowed Sir William with the necklace after he rescued one of Poseidon's daughters when she ended up trapped in the caves.

"There are other, even more outlandish, stories too, but I have always put stock in the cave theory myself, except without the Poseidon aspect. Too fanciful for my taste. Others seem to agree with me. It's the most popular belief regarding the necklace's origin, in any case." Milton pushed his glasses up on his nose. I appreciated that his thinking lined up with Dad's; it helped his credibility.

"That's amazing." I shook my head. Although the history was fascinating, I wanted Milton to move on to the necklace's current whereabouts. I didn't have a lot of time and that was what I'd really come to learn.

"After Nicholas Rye, there are three other historical figures whose accomplishments have been credited to the Glain Neidr. The necklace actually disappeared after Mr. Rye and didn't resurface again for almost 300 years." Milton frowned, as though trying to make sure he had the timeline correct, and I realized that must account for the period the necklace had been in the hands of the Hleo, and then the Geltisians, a splinter group of the enemies of the Hleo, the Bana.

"Andreas Matisse, a wealthy socialite musician from the later 1700s, is the next historical figure believed to have been in possession of the Glain Neidr. It was alleged that he could play any instrument placed in his hands, particularly the violin, with such beauty that it would bring the toughest of individuals to tears. There are only two known references linking the Glain Neidr to Matisse; two separate newspaper articles mention a mysterious chain visible around his neck during every performance. It's not much, but enough for Glain Neidr seekers.

"From Andreas Matisse, the necklace ended up in the hands of Darcy Hammersham, a blacksmith and ironmaster whose intricate works can still be seen in areas of England and Wales. How that transfer of ownership occurred is not known. Hammersham's keen understanding of smelting and metallurgy led to advancements that helped pave the way for the industrial revolution. In a letter he wrote to one of his relatives, he mentions a stone he wore on all occasions. It was his firm belief that the rock had been forged by God's own hand. Hammersham believed this necklace blessed every piece of his work." Milton thrust photocopies of painted portraits of Matisse and Hammersham, as well as photo examples of Hammersham's ornately-designed fences, doors, and stair railings at me.

"After Hammersham came Esther Mantle, his beloved niece. She was a dancer, a ballerina, who built up quite the reputation for herself. In one magazine article she's described as being as graceful as an angel's descent from the heavens. She is responsible for bringing the necklace to North America, and was photographed on multiple occasions with a strange gold chain woven into the tutu of her costume, although the stone was never captured on film.

"According to official treasure hunters, the necklace vanished for good after Esther, but I feel I've actually solved the mystery of where it ended up. After decades of research, I discovered that the Glain Neidr did disappear from the hands of Esther Mantle. Years ago I found an old police report describing an incident that occurred in the household of Reginald Crockford, Esther's husband. One of their servants stole several pieces of jewelry from the home and took off, never to be tracked down. The document doesn't actually mention the Glain Neidr by name, but Esther retired from her dancing career right after the incident. It took a very long time, but I was able to piece together who that servant was, and where the stolen jewelry went, and to catalogue each piece, including a mysterious necklace that was sold for far less than its true value, a smooth stone, as black as night, with a perfect hole in its center, threaded onto a gold chain. It contained no diamonds or other precious stones, so it was sold in a hasty exchange, ending up in the hands of one Mr. Muirhead." The excitement in Milton's voice was mounting.

He paused for a second, his hand settling on a well-worn folder. "It was while in this man's possession that the one and only known photograph of the necklace was taken, and I just happen to have a copy of that photograph. Would you like to see it?" Milton's eyes were wide.

My breath caught in my throat. I had seen the Glain Neidr represented in different paintings, but never an actual image of the mysterious stone. "Yes, I would love to."

He slowly flipped the file open—obviously delighted by the suspense he was building—and there before me was an ordinary-looking dark stone on a gold chain, lying on a decorative silver tray. The picture was a photocopy, or maybe even a photocopy of a photocopy; the quality was pretty grainy. The image was black and white, and had the flat haziness of a picture taken during photography's infancy, but it was the Glain Neidr. I reached a hand towards the picture and traced my finger along the famous oblong hole as it peered out at me mysteriously.

"It's extraordinary, isn't it?" Milton clasped his hands together.

"I can't believe you have a photo of it. So what happened after Mr. Muirhead?" I kept my eyes on the glass-smooth stone.

"This is where the necklace's story gets even stranger." Milton lowered his voice, and I glanced up at him. "Mr. Muirhead was a very powerful, very wealthy man, but at the same time, a mystery. I haven't been able to find out much about him, but I was able to discern one very interesting fact. It seems that the intriguing Mr. Muirhead didn't age. Apparently he looked the same fifty years after obtaining the Glain Neidr as he did the day it first came into his possession. I'm not sure if his frozen age has to do with the necklace or not. It's the only piece of information I've been able to get on the gentleman."

My pulse raced as I met his gaze. "He doesn't age?"

Milton appeared pleased at being able to stun me. What he didn't realize was that my shock was based more on hearing that Mr. Muirhead shared one of the Hleo's standard traits, than on the idea of not aging itself.

"Crazy, isn't it? I'm actually expecting some very interesting news from one of my contacts. I expect to hear from him any day now." Milton leaned back in his chair, puffing up his chest.

"I would love to hear what you find out." I checked my watch. I could tell Milton wanted me to stay longer. I had a feeling he would spend all night spouting details about the Glain Neidr if he could, but I needed to get home. "I have to get going, but thank you for your time." I stood and gave him a warm smile.

"It was a pleasure meeting you, Miss Reed. I look forward to our next meeting." Milton ushered me back into the cluttered store.

The sun had set while we'd been talking, and now half of the stores on the street were closed. I thanked Milton again and strode back to my car, wishing I'd found a closer parking spot. I couldn't shake the feeling of being watched, and without Ethan close by, a sense of vulnerability enveloped me. By the time I reached my vehicle, my heart was pounding and I unlocked the door and jumped in.

I checked my phone before starting the drive back to East Halton, but there were no missed texts or calls. I breathed a sigh of relief. I didn't want to worry Ethan unnecessarily if he'd been looking for me at the library, but I appeared to be in the clear.

My relief was short-lived. When I pulled into my driveway, Ethan was sitting on the porch steps. I swallowed hard. *He knows.* I hated keeping anything from him, but I was convinced that finding the Glain Neidr was the only way for me to get the answers I needed, and unless he told me why we couldn't go after it, I had to keep digging.

"Hi." I got out of my car and crossed the lawn, joining him on the stairs.

"Hi." He watched me, a trace of a smile on his lips that didn't reach his eyes. I sank down onto the top stair beside him, rubbing my hands together. "How was your night?"

I looked over at him, trying to read his expression. "It was okay. I went to the library and—"

"Hannah."

My shoulders slumped. "I'm sorry I didn't tell you. I wanted to, but I knew you'd be against it."

"Going off to meet some random person you met online? Yeah you're right, I'd be against it." Ethan ran a hand through his dark hair.

I scrunched up my nose. It had been silly of me to think I'd be able to keep anything from Ethan. "Milton was completely innocent, a bit eccentric, but harmless." I sighed. "The necklace is the only thing we've stumbled across that seems like it could help me. You keep telling me to let it go, but I just can't."

Ethan stared out across the front yard. "I know you're frustrated, but the Glain Neidr could be anywhere, with anyone." He turned to look at me, and slid a hand up the curve of my neck to cup my face in his palm. "I love you, and I don't want you to inadvertently put yourself in danger trying to track it down. Please, can you drop it, for me?" His green eyes were clouded with worry.

Neither of us threw around the word *love* a great deal, so I knew just how serious this was to him. "Okay, I'll drop it." I pressed into the warmth of his hand on my cheek. "You know you're fighting dirty though, right?" I pulled back and arched an eyebrow.

"I'll do whatever I have to, to keep you safe." He leaned in and lightly brushed his lips across mine.

After a second he let me go and turned again towards the yard. "We're getting closer. We are." Ethan's tone was distant. Was he trying to convince himself?

Simon and Ethan had figured out all but a handful of my drawings, but there was still no discernable pattern. And they didn't seem to know where to go from here for answers.

"Let's go inside." I got to my feet. I just wanted to put the matter behind us for the time being.

Ethan followed me into the house. Even though he didn't seem to be mad at me, I still felt as though an invisible barrier was beginning to form between us. And I really, really didn't like the feeling.

Two

I wove my way through the crowded halls of East Halton High, headed for the school's library. The lunch bell had just rung and I planned to use the break time to research my paper on western civilization. I had just grabbed for the entry door when I heard someone calling my name.

My friend Ryan sprinted towards me. "Hanns, wait up." He sidled up next to me, out of breath from rushing, and leaned against the gray brick wall, taking a second to compose himself.

"What's up?" I released my grip on the library door.

"I wanted to ask you a favor." Ryan straightened up and repositioned his backpack.

"Okay."

"So you know how Trish and I have been dating for a while now, right? Well the thing is, it's sort of hard to get a romantic atmosphere going when we're touring around in my mom's minivan. I've kind of noticed that you get a ride from Ethan most of the time now. I mean, I'm not saying anything about that. If you say you're just friends, you're just friends." Ryan held up both hands in a *whatever* gesture.

"Ryan, just ask me."

"Could I borrow your car to take Trish on a date?" Ryan scrunched up his face.

"Oh." I blinked. I didn't love the idea of him borrowing my car, but if he was careful I couldn't really see why not. There was one thing I needed him to clarify, though. "When you say 'romantic atmosphere,' what exactly do you mean?" I crossed my arms, trying not to mentally picture Ryan and Trish getting amorous in the backseat of my poor little Toyota.

Ryan's eyes went wide. "What? No, nothing like that, I promise. I just need something that doesn't have sliding doors and a DVD player hanging from the ceiling."

I narrowed my eyes. "You're sure?"

"I promise. We won't do anything that would make you have to sanitize the interior of your car."

I grimaced. "Fine, you can borrow it, just stop talking about that. When do you want it?"

"Well, I was sort of hoping maybe I could grab it tonight and use it tomorrow."

Ryan scuffed his shoe across the tiled floor.

My eyebrows rose. "Tonight?"

"Yeah, I was going to ask you earlier, but I kept forgetting. It's just that, since there's no school tomorrow, I was sort of hoping to take Trish to Six Flags for the day. We don't have any Saturdays off together for the next month." Ryan shifted his weight back and forth, his tone practically a whimper.

I couldn't say no. "All right. I have to work tonight, but you can swing by my house and grab it right after school. Ethan gave me a ride today, so just come to my locker at the end of the day and we'll head over together."

"Thanks Hanns, you are so great. Come into the store anytime and I'll hook you up with free rentals."

I smiled. "I appreciate that Ryan, but it's not necessary. Just be careful with the car."

"I will." He nodded solemnly and stepped back so I could go into the library.

I found the books I was looking for and settled in at a table near the back of the dimly-lit room.

Ethan had gone off with Simon to submit their weekly report to The Three, the leaders of the Hleo, but he'd promised he would be back in time to pick me up from school. I drummed my fingers on the table. How was it going? I imagined fairly uneventfully. There hadn't been much progress made with my drawings, but, conversely, there hadn't been any threats since Paige and Uri, two dangerous members of the Bana, had attacked us on our way back from Veridan over a month ago.

I worked in the library through my last period. When the bell rang, I gathered my books and headed off to my locker. Ryan was already waiting for me, as was Ethan. "Hello, boys." I spun the combination and opened my locker to grab my weekend homework.

"I hear Ryan's borrowing your car." Ethan propped an elbow against the locker next to mine.

I shrugged. "Yeah, I haven't been using it lately, so why not?"

"Hannah's good like that." Ryan gave me an encouraging smile. He was obviously trying to talk me up to Ethan, but I wanted to stop him before the conversation could take an awkward turn. "Thanks Ry, let's get going." I shut my locker.

Ethan drove the three of us to my house and I handed off the keys to Ryan. He climbed in and slowly backed my car out of the driveway, I guess to prove how careful he would be. I gave him a wave, and he honked as he drove off.

* * *

Carmen, my boss, was buzzing around near the back of The Patch as I walked into the store where I worked. Ethan had just dropped me off, and she was arranging a new display of shorts. There weren't any customers at the moment, but she looked happy and I had a feeling I knew why. "Hi Carmen; getting ready for summer?" I set my bag behind the counter and joined her.

"Did you check the temperature today? Seventy-two degrees. You know what that means? Summer is on its way; I can feel it." Carmen practically sang the words while she pulled another stack of multi-colored plaid shorts out of a cardboard box on the floor and added them to the display table.

"Yeah, I heard people are renting the cottages near Kristen's parents' starting this weekend right up until summer." I grinned. This was the sort of information that would fuel Carmen's enthusiasm.

"That's what I like to hear." Carmen rubbed her hands together.

I got to work, helping her switch out some of the heavier clothes for lighter summer pieces. As we worked, we took turns manning the cash register and watching the change rooms.

My mind drifted to Ryan, and his idea of using the day off during the week to go on a date. I had forgotten that it was a teacher workday, and it gave me an idea. A week had gone by since I'd met with Milton about the Glain Neidr, and, as promised, I hadn't done anything to continue my search for the necklace. Still, I wanted to prove to Ethan that he could trust me, and to make sure we were truly okay. A romantic date somewhere we'd never been together might be just the right thing to get us back on track. And I had the perfect idea of where we could go. I couldn't wait to get home and start planning.

The evening went by fairly quickly. There were enough customers in and out of the store to keep changing stock from getting boring, and before I knew it, it was seven o'clock and time to close up.

I helped get the store back in order while Carmen counted the receipts and balanced the totals for the day. When we were done, I walked to the parking lot. Ethan had gone to see Simon while I was working, but he was back and parked in the same spot he had dropped me off.

"Hey." I got in the Jeep and pulled on my seatbelt.

"How was your evening?" Ethan started up the vehicle and pulled onto the road.

"It was fine, busy enough that time went fast. Carmen is happy because business is picking up now that the weather is warmer. How was your evening?"

Ethan rolled his eyes. "Simon was installing new software."

"So really thrilling?" I teased.

Ethan grinned.

We made small talk until he turned the Jeep into my driveway. I was torn between having him come in for a bit, or letting him go so I could get everything ready for the next day. I decided I'd better let him go. "If you're free, I have a surprise planned for our day off from school tomorrow." I gripped the handle of the door, ready to push it open.

"I'm free." Ethan narrowed his eyes. "What kind of surprise?"

"Come by around ten and you'll find out."

I started to climb out, but he put a hand on my wrist to stop me and leaned across the gearshift to bring his lips to mine. "Until morning then," he murmured as he slowly pulled away.

My lips were still tingling as I treaded inside to get the stuff ready for our date. Maybe I'd been imagining the distance between us lately, and everything was going to be all right after all.

Three

I stared at the items on the kitchen table, trying to figure out the best way to get everything into the old, double-lidded picnic basket I'd found. Sandwiches, cheese, grapes, sodas, and a blanket for us to sit on were strewn across the table. I'd made and wrapped all the food last night, but waited until this morning to pack the basket.

I'd gotten up early, straightened my auburn hair and pulled it back in a side ponytail, adding a headband for good measure before slipping into a powder-blue button-up dress with a soft floral pattern that I'd been told really accentuated my turquoise eyes. I wanted to look good.

There was a knock at the front door just as I was closing the basket's lid. "Hello?" Ethan's voice filtered down the hallway. He appeared in the entry of the kitchen and my heart skipped a beat. He looked amazing in a pair of well-worn dark jeans and long-sleeve olive Henley shirt.

"Hi. I just finished packing so we can head out."

"Great. So you're still not going to tell me where we're going?" He propped a shoulder against the kitchen wall and watched me work.

"Nope." I shook my head playfully. I started to breeze by him, swinging the basket loosely, but he caught me around the waist and lifted me off the floor. "Hey, no peeking," I protested, holding the basket out to the side in an attempt to keep him from getting near the picnic stuff.

His grin was mischievous as he pulled me close and brought his lips to mine in a lighthearted kiss. I felt his free arm reaching for the basket, and I pulled away in mock indignation. "Excuse me. I believe I said no peeking." I rested my hand on my hip and glared at him until he laughed, then shook my head and made my way around the kitchen table towards the back door.

"Just curious, that's all." Ethan followed me out the French doors onto our back deck. It was still early April, but the weather was beautiful and warm, perfect for a picnic.

"You'll have to be patient." I walked down the stairs and crossed the backyard to where our freshly cut grass met the forest surrounding the back of our property. We headed into the woods, but only walked a few hundred feet or so before we encountered an old wooden rail fence.

Ethan held out a steadying hand. I gripped it and climbed over the warped wooden railings, skillfully keeping the picnic basket out of his reach. We crunched our way across the fallen leaves and twigs of the overgrown forest until the trees thinned out and we stood at the bottom of the neighboring farmer's field. The weedy pasture grass tickled my ankles as we walked to a small, kidney-shaped pond, not far from the forest's edge. A huge old weeping willow stood by the shore of the pond, its graceful branches hanging down over the water, dipping low enough in some spots to skim the surface. Resting amongst the reeds at the water's edge sat a dilapidated wooden dock.

"We used to come here as kids. My mom would bring my friends and me out here on hot summer days, when we wanted to do something different than the beach. We would spend hours swimming and having picnics under this old tree." I put a hand on the massive trunk of the willow, the bark rough against my palm.

"I didn't even realize there was a spot like this so close to your property." Ethan scanned the horizon of the rolling field.

"Yeah, Mr. Smithson, the farmer who owns this field, would let us come whenever we wanted, but I haven't been here in years." A wave of regret washed over me. It'd been over five years since I'd spent any time at this peaceful spot, and even though it was still too cold to go for a swim, it was sad to see that time had taken its toll on the dock.

I pulled a red-checked blanket from the basket and we spread it out over the grass, in the shade of the willow. The branches surrounded us on all sides, creating our very own privacy curtain from the outside world. As we settled onto the blanket, I opened the basket and pulled out the food.

"There was a swimming hole like this close to our farm. Mary and I used to swim there all the time." Ethan grabbed a handful of grapes and popped one into his mouth.

"Really?" I unscrewed the cap off one of the drinks and took a swig, hoping he would share more about his sister and the time before he became a Hleo.

"Yeah. Mary was supposed to wear this crazy swimming dress thing. Women were expected to be covered up in every situation back then. My mother would make sure she had it on before she left the house, but whenever it was just the two of us she would always strip down to her knickers." Ethan chuckled.

"I can't even imagine trying to swim in a dress." I looked down at my outfit. It was a light cotton material, but I would never want to try to maneuver through water in it.

"It never slowed her down. There was a tree there too, similar to this one, although not nearly as big." Ethan gazed up at the lofty branches of the willow. "We had a rope tied onto one of the branches, and the neighbor kids, Mary, and I would all see who could make the biggest splash."

I laughed. "We did that too. You can still see a bit of the rope up there." I pointed to a frayed bit of twine that was tangled in amongst the branches. "I loved jumping off of there. One day a bunch of us decided we would all try to hang onto the rope at the same time. It ended up snapping off. The remains have been up there ever since."

Ethan smiled and took a bite of sandwich.

It was funny to think that, even though we had grown up over a century apart, our childhoods weren't that different. The exploits and imagination of children seemed to be timeless in a lot of ways.

We laughed and joked while we ate, eventually falling into a comfortable silence. The breeze whispered through the limbs of the willow, and danced across the top of the pond, causing small ripples to form. I was completely happy as I leaned into Ethan, resting against his shoulder. I tilted my head back to meet his eye. The golden flecks shone brightly and I brought my lips up to his. He cupped my face gently in his hands, and I turned into him while still kissing, so I could wrap my arms around his waist. With growing urgency, Ethan's lips pressed harder against mine. I curled my fingers around the soft material of his shirt. I barely realized I'd been lowering myself back, until I was lying down on the checked blanket.

Ethan lingered half over me and half beside me on the blanket. He pulled his lips away from mine for a second. Our eyes locked and a shiver of longing tingled down my spine. My arms had been around his waist, but now I slid my hands up over the strong muscles in his back and shoulders until they tangled into the strands of his silky dark hair. I tightened my grip, and pulled his face back to mine. His fingers swept a stray tendril of hair off my face and traced from my earlobe down my neck, then lightly grazed the front of my dress. The top button slipped open. Ethan's lips followed a similar trail, moving slowly from my mouth to the curve of my neck and down to my collarbone.

My breath came out in a pleasure-filled gasp. "Ethan," I whispered.

He pulled back, his eyes searching mine.

Is he thinking the same thing I am? "I'm ready for this. I wasn't before, but I know it's what I want now." My voice was quiet but confident, and I kept my eyes locked with his.

Ethan stared at me for a second, and then rolled away with a groan. He balled his hands into fists and covered his eyes with them as he lay down beside me. "Hannah, we need to talk about you and I being together in that way."

He sat up, resting his arms across his knees. I quickly scrambled into a sitting position, re-buttoning and smoothing down my dress. *Well, this isn't what I expected to happen.* I swallowed hard, desperate for him to explain.

"It's what I started to tell you that night at Veridan, but after Kai pulled me away I put it off and now—" Ethan was interrupted by the buzz of my phone vibrating across the blanket.

"Not now." I exhaled and hit the ignore button. It immediately rang again, and I sighed as I picked it up. *Katie.* "Hey Kate, what's up?" I greeted my best friend as evenly as I could. I kept my eyes on Ethan, my mind racing. What had he been about to share?

"Hannah." Katie's voice sounded strange.

"What is it?" I frowned and sat up straighter.

"Luke just got off the phone with Ryan's mom. Ryan was in a car accident this morning." Katie's voice hitched, and my heart jumped into my throat. She was clearly trying to keep it together, but struggling to do so. "He's in critical condition at the hospital. They'd just taken him into surgery before she called Luke."

A ringing pulsed in my ears, and my head spun. "Is he going to be …?" Breathing was getting difficult. I kept my eyes on Ethan. He slipped his hand onto my shoulder and gently rubbed it.

"They don't know. He's in surgery because of internal bleeding." Katie's voice cracked, and she drew in a shaky breath.

"What happened?" My voice was getting more panicked with every question.

"They aren't really sure, but it looks like Ryan blew through a stop sign and got t-boned on the driver side," Katie explained. A wave of sickness washed over me as I pictured Ryan getting hit while driving my car.

"What about Trish?" I suddenly remembered Ryan's date.

"She's going to be okay, I guess. Her injuries weren't as serious."

"We'll be at the hospital as soon as we can. Ethan's with me and we'll head over right now." I started gathering up the scraps of food, throwing them back in the picnic basket while Ethan helped me.

"We're already on our way to be with Mrs. Deluca, we'll see you there." Katie hung up.

"Ryan was in an accident in your car?" Ethan had clearly filled in the gaps, which was good, because all I could do was nod. "It's going to be okay." Ethan put a steadying hand on mine as I fiddled with the latch on the lid of the picnic basket.

I swallowed hard. "I hope so."

Four

The drive over to the hospital was a quiet one as I silently prayed that Ryan would be okay. Déjà vu washed over me as we pulled into the hospital parking lot, and I thought of when Ethan and I had rushed here because of my dad.

We made our way through the hospital corridors until we reached the surgical department. Katie and her boyfriend Luke were sitting with Mrs. Deluca in a row of gray vinyl chairs, in a drab little waiting room. Our friends, Heather, Kristen, and Mark were there too, and they all stood as we approached.

Mrs. Deluca pulled me into a comforting hug.

"Have you heard anything?" I asked as we all settled into the seats again.

"He's still in surgery; we're just waiting for the doctor." Mrs. Deluca pushed stray wisps of dark hair off her face, her voice barely a whisper. My heart ached for her. She was a single mother, and Ryan was her only child. If the tragic occurred and she lost him, she would be absolutely destroyed.

"It'll be okay," Katie said, just so someone did, but I glanced down at the floor. None of us could be certain that was true.

The silence felt deafening as the minutes ticked by. Surrounded by year-old magazines, a television providing more noise than entertainment, and other concerned relatives waiting for word about their loved ones, we all stared off, lost in our own thoughts.

It had been just after one o'clock when Ethan and I arrived at the hospital and it was well after four when a doctor wearing surgery scrubs appeared. I held my breath as he pulled Mrs. Deluca aside to speak in private. Slowly I exhaled when I overheard him use the words, 'stable condition,' 'removed his spleen,' and 'stopped the bleeding.' It sounded like Ryan, although severely banged up, was going to recover. Everyone else's posture relaxed as well.

Mrs. Deluca and the doctor headed off down the hall together towards Ryan's room. She was gone about fifteen minutes. When she returned, her eyes were rimmed with red, but she had a relieved smile on her face. "Hannah, he's asking to speak to you."

My eyebrows shot up. "Okay, sure." I scrambled out of my seat. *Why would he want to speak to me first?* I was sure he would have wanted to see Luke, his best friend.

I followed Mrs. Deluca out into the hall and she pointed to a door about halfway down. Slowly I walked into the dimly-lit hospital room. Ryan was lying in the bed with monitors and other machines hooked up to him, while an IV bag on a pole next to his bed dripped some sort of meds down into him.

I inched my way to the foot of his bed, staring at the swollen and bruised face of my friend. His eyes were black, a large bandage ran around the top of his head, and a thin breathing tube ran across his face under his nose.

"Hey," I whispered, softly touching the fuzzy blue hospital blanket that covered his lower half. His eyes were closed. If he'd fallen asleep, I didn't want to disturb him, but he slowly opened them and gave me a small smile.

"Hey." His voice was hoarse.

"I thought I told you to be careful," I chastised gently, trying to think of something to lighten the mood while I eyed the bandages around his midsection and left shoulder.

"I was never a very good listener." He laughed, but then grimaced. How much pain was he in? "Hannah, about your car, there's something you should—"

I waved a dismissive hand. "Ryan, you don't need to worry about that even a little bit right now."

"No, Hannah, I need you to know something. There was something wrong with your car. I did blow through the stop sign, like you probably heard, but when I was approaching the intersection I was stomping on the brakes as hard as I could. The car just kept going." Ryan paused every few words; clearly speaking required a lot of effort from him.

I didn't want to make it worse, but I felt blindsided. "Are you saying something was wrong with my brakes?" The words came out slowly, my mind reeling. Could his accident somehow be my fault?

"Yeah, but don't look at me like that. I didn't tell you to make you feel bad. I just needed you to know that I was being really careful. I couldn't stand it if you thought I'd just carelessly driven through a stop sign."

"Ryan, I'm so sorry." I took a deep breath, my stomach churning.

"It's done, don't worry. I'm just glad it didn't happen when you were driving it; you might have gotten really hurt."

Ryan's considerate words only made me feel worse. The room was spinning and I shot a look at the door. *I need to get out of here.* "Just get better soon, okay?" I gave his hand a light squeeze, and scrambled back out to the hallway.

As soon as I was on the other side of the door, I pressed my back against the cool brick wall. *Breathe, just breathe.* The lemon-scented-disinfectant smell of the hospital caused a wave of sickness to wash over me. I swallowed hard, trying to fight it back. How could the brakes not work in my car? I'd never had any mechanical troubles in the past, and somehow I couldn't make myself believe that it was purely an accident now.

I stumbled to the waiting room in a daze, trying to figure out how this could have possibly happened. My eyes locked with Ethan's when I walked in, and a concerned frown immediately wrinkled his forehead.

"How is he?" Luke asked. I turned my gaze to Ryan's best friend. Worry was written all over his face.

"He doesn't look very pretty, but he'll live." I gave my friends a reassuring smile. "I think it's okay for you to go see him." I motioned down the hall.

Katie and Luke turned to Mrs. Deluca for approval and she nodded. They hopped up out of their seats. As they were passing by, I grasped Katie's arm to stop her. "I really don't like hospitals, too many bad memories. Now that we know Ryan's going to be all right I'm going to take off, but let him know I'll come back tomorrow to see him, okay?"

Katie patted my hand. "Sure. I'll call you later."

After she and Luke disappeared down the hall, Ethan and I said good-bye to Heather, Kristen, Mark, and Mrs. Deluca. Then we made our way back out to the hospital parking lot.

Ethan paused by the front of his Jeep. "What is it?" His green eyes searched mine.

"Ryan told me the reason he got into the accident was because the brakes didn't work on my car." I stared at the ground; the words hard to say out loud.

I glanced up. Ethan's brow was furrowed. "He's sure?"

"He said he was pressing the brake to the floor and nothing happened."

Ethan's jaw tightened as he moved to pull the passenger door open for me, but he remained silent.

I chewed on my lip while we drove. "What if it's happening again? Someone important in my life is lying in a hospital bed because of me?" I wrung my hands together, not even trying to remain calm as my dad's trip to the hospital after being kidnapped by Uri, a member of the Bana, played fresh in my mind. That had only been a matter of months ago; his arm was just freshly out of a cast.

"We can't know anything until I'm able to examine your car," Ethan said, but from the dark look in his eyes I could tell he was pretty sure that foul play was involved.

I nodded. There was a chance, even a small one, that this was purely an accident and I was being paranoid. I wouldn't relax until we'd confirmed it either way, though.

"We'll swing by and grab Simon. I'll drop you off then the two of us will go take a look at the wreckage to figure out what happened." Ethan slid his hands back and forth on the steering wheel.

"Just the two of you?"

"It will draw less attention, and I'd feel better if you were safe at home in case it wasn't just an accident."

"Fine." I slumped against the back of my seat. Ethan and Simon could go and inspect all they wanted. Paranoid or not, something deep inside me told me exactly what the two of them would find.

Someone had deliberately sabotaged my car.

Five

I tapped the backseat of Ethan's Jeep in frustration. We had just picked up Simon, and he and Ethan were trying to figure out what our next step should be as we drove to my house. It was annoying enough to keep hitting dead ends when trying to figure out my drawing ability, and to continually be concerned about my own wellbeing, but to think that someone else in my life had been seriously injured because of me was impossible to accept.

My gaze shifted from Ethan to Simon. The two of them were planning the best way to inspect my wrecked automobile. Ethan kept running a hand through his hair and over his face, and Simon spoke with an unusual lack of wit. Clearly they were bothered.

"Is it always this difficult?" I clenched and unclenched my fists.

"Oh love, you needn't feel bad." Simon twisted to look at me in the backseat, giving me a sympathetic smile. The words he hadn't said spoke far louder than the ones he had.

"Do *protecteds'* friends and family usually end up in the line of fire?" I pulled my headband off and shook out my hair.

"Hannah," Ethan began, but he didn't seem to know how to finish.

"If we could just get rid of Alexander, then Bana members would stop coming after you. He is one person that needs to be wiped off the face of this earth," Simon offered flippantly.

I frowned, recalling movies I'd seen with evil organizations in them. "How would that help? Isn't there always another bad guy waiting in the wings to sweep in and take the leader's place?"

Ethan and Simon exchanged a knowing glance. I raised an eyebrow and waited.

Simon tapped the end of his nose and then pointed at me. "Alexander is a bit of an exception to that particular rule."

"What does that mean?" I leaned forward.

"A very long time ago, Isaac decided that he would like an heir. He'd been running the Bana for several hundred years and believed that there could be no one more trustworthy to share leadership with, no better ally for his mission of world domination than his own son. And so Eric was born, a perfect mirror of his father, trained to see the world the way Isaac did, as a place to be ravaged and controlled for his own desires. But in teaching Eric to be like him, Isaac failed to anticipate what would happen when his son grew up to desire ultimate power and control, just like his father. Eric came to the realization pretty early on that the only way to gain everything his father had was to take his father out of the equation, so he came up with an elaborate scheme that ultimately ended with him taking his own father's life."

"How Shakespearian of him," I commented wryly.

"Yes, well, as it turned out, something astounding happened when Isaac was killed. All of the Bana Isaac had created, the ones he'd branded with his version of the serum, were immediately struck down dead. It's ancient history now, but suffice to say, it rocked the world of both the Bana and the Hleo. It took Eric generations to rebuild his empire to what it had once been. As he worked to create a new replacement army, he very skillfully tried to recruit members of the Hleo so there would be an even balance between pure and synthetic Bana. I'm guessing he figured if something were ever to happen to him, at least his legacy would continue through the Hleo he'd turned." Simon rested back in the passenger seat.

"That's incredible, so where does Alexander fit in?" I blinked and shifted my gaze to Ethan, who had just turned onto my street.

Ethan met my eyes in the rearview mirror. "Eventually Eric wanted what Isaac had, an offspring he could share his ideals with, and thus Alexander was spawned back in the mid-1700s. Eric lasted almost two hundred years before Alexander decided it was his turn to take over. Eric knew it was coming, and had put a few safeguards in place to keep it from happening, but the change in leadership was inevitable. Alexander had the advantage of knowing that killing his father would result in the loss of numbers to his Bana flock, and so he'd begun creating his own Bana."

Simon turned his attention to Ethan. "I always wondered if Eric knew right from the beginning that there was something fishy about Alexander's insisting on doing this, or whether he simply believed his son was trying to follow his example."

"Eric was pretty paranoid; I imagine he wasn't comfortable with the idea." Ethan pulled into my driveway and threw the Jeep in park.

My forehead was creased in a deep frown as I tried to get my mind around this very strange revelation. "So Alexander started making his own Bana, with his own serum, so that when he killed his father he would still have an army?"

"Yeah. I think at first Eric must have thought he was safe because the bulk of synthetic Bana had been created by him, but I'm guessing he must have started getting really worried around the turn of the century when the numbers began to shift in Alexander's favor." Simon sounded almost amused by the shortsightedness of the Bana's previous leader.

"So, how in the world does that work? I mean how does killing one person make others die?"

"The branding serum for the Hleo and Bana has a small amount of blood in it. The Three's blood is in the Hleo serum, and Alexander's in the Bana's. There's some sort of complex telepathic nature to the chemical mixture the Bana serum is made with that makes it different than the Hleo's serum. I don't think even they fully understand how it works." Ethan tapped the top of the gearshift. "One thing's for sure though, because the synthetic Bana realize their lives are directly linked to their leader, they guard him more fiercely than any other person on earth."

"I guess they would," I observed flatly. The three of us fell into silence again. I stared at my porch, hesitant to get out of the vehicle. I thought about Simon's original suggestion that if we could kill Alexander we would be safe.

"We should get going if we want to investigate your car before it starts getting picked apart by the police and insurance people. There's a good chance it's already at an impound lot, which will be a bit of a challenge to deal with. We'll come back as soon as we know something more." Ethan climbed out of the Jeep and pulled his seat forward so I could exit as well.

"Sounds good." I took a step onto the grass so Ethan would feel free to go, but he slipped his arms around my waist and pulled me in close to him. His lips softly brushed my forehead.

"Please be careful," I whispered, and his hands tightened on my back.

"You too." He pulled back and cupped my face in his hands. He kept his eyes locked with mine for a moment. *He looks so worried.* Before I could voice the thought, he jumped back in the Jeep and was gone.

I took a slow breath, and headed inside. I needed to find something to do, or I'd drive myself crazy waiting for Ethan to come back. *Dad.* I was not looking forward to telling him what had happened to my car, but it was better not to put it off.

I approached the open door to his office. He sat behind his desk with a stack in front of him, likely papers that needed grading. As a history professor at Hartford University, his semester was close to wrapping up. I hesitated in the doorway, not wanting to interrupt, but he glanced up and beckoned me forward.

"How was your day?" Dad sat back and crossed his arms as I plunked down in the chair across from him. I stared at him for a second, then slumped forward, propping my elbows on his desk and dropping my face into my hands.

"Hannah, what's wrong?" Dad jumped up and came around to my side of the desk.

I sat up straight and filled Dad in on Ryan's accident and the odd circumstances surrounding it.

He listened quietly, waiting for the whole story before responding. "We should wait for all the details before you jump to conclusions. Ethan's done an admirable job of keeping threats away from you; it seems unlikely that he would miss someone sabotaging your car." Dad leaned against the edge of his desk. He slid his glasses off and wiped them on the hem of his sweater, before returning them to his face and straightening up. "I'm very sorry Ryan got hurt, but incredibly glad it wasn't you. I'll contact the insurance people about the car. In the end, a car can always be replaced, a person can't, and that's what we should be grateful for." He squeezed my shoulder a lightly.

"Thanks Dad. You're right, I'm so glad Ryan is going to be okay. I just need to know what happened, either way." I gave him a small smile, relieved that he was handling the destruction of my vehicle so well. And he did have a point; Ethan didn't let a lot of things by him. But Dad didn't know exactly how much danger I'd been in either. We hadn't told him about our second run in with Paige and Uri on our way back from Veridan, and he never had been given all the details about Adam's attempt on my life. Could his opinion be completely counted on if he didn't have all the facts?

Dad rested a hand on the pile of papers. "I can put off this grading for a little while if you'd like. Wait for word from Ethan with you. We could have a cup of tea."

"That's okay. I have a ton of homework I really should be working on. Hopefully that will keep me distracted. But I'll come find you once I know more." I stood and tucked the chair back against his desk.

"Okay, well, I'm here if you change your mind." He treaded back around to his side and sat down.

"Thanks Dad." I left him to his work and headed upstairs. Even though most of the students at East Halton had already gotten their acceptance letters to colleges and universities, the teachers were still piling on the homework, and I had two papers due the following week. I stretched out on my bed and worked on my western civilization assignment until the sun set.

Gazing out my window into the darkness, I bit my lip. My mind was divided between two separate yet equally frustrating dilemmas. The first was that, more than likely, someone was coming after me again, and Ryan had gotten hurt because of it. I didn't know how I'd ever make it up to Ryan if it turned out his accident had been meant for me. We'd had over a month of peace and, as unlikely as it was, I'd begun to hope the Bana were done with me. Now we would have to resume high alert. I hated being on high alert.

The other thought I couldn't keep from bouncing around my brain was what Ethan could have been about to share when we were interrupted at the pond. *What is preventing us from sleeping together?* I needed to know, but at the same time wasn't sure I wanted to hear what he had to say.

Since returning from Veridan, where Ethan and I had gotten the closest we had ever been intimately, things had returned to our

G-rated physical interactions. Ethan had been right that night; I wasn't ready to sleep with him then, but now ... Out at the pond, Ethan had made it seem we were on the same page about having sex, and then suddenly it appeared as if we weren't. I hoped he would return soon, tell me that Ryan's accident had simply been that, an unfortunate accident, and then we'd be able to talk. In spite of my trepidation, I needed him to explain what his groaning hesitation had been all about.

The buzz of the phone on my bed pulled me away from my obsessing. I grabbed it and answered without checking to make sure it was Ethan. "Hey, have you found anything?"

"I'm sorry, I … I don't know … is this Hannah Reed?" A surprised male voice stammered on the other end of the line.

"Who is this?" I frowned in confusion. Who else besides Ethan would be calling me at nine-thirty at night?

"This is Milton Cambry. I'm sorry to disturb you at this late hour, but I've had quite a breakthrough in my search for the necklace, and I was so excited I had to share it with someone."

My eyebrows shot up. "That's okay. I told you to let me know if you found anything, you don't need to apologize for the time. I should be the one to apologize for my greeting. I thought you were someone else."

My stomach flip-flopped. I was breaking my promise to Ethan. My plan had been to brush Milton off if he contacted me again, but he sounded so excited. If it did turn out that Ryan had nearly been killed because of me, then I needed to do something to make the attacks stop. The Glain Neidr might be just the thing.

"That's no problem," Milton assured agreeably.

"So, what have you found?" I leaned back against my pillow.

"Well, I'm not really … I mean the thing is … I don't really trust open phone lines," Milton rambled.

I narrowed my eyes. *Why would he call if he isn't going to share what he's discovered?* "So …"

"I was wondering if you wanted to meet to discuss what I've found. I think you'll be very interested. It's a mysterious twist to be sure."

"Now?" I checked my watch.

"Oh no, I would never ask you to meet this late in the evening. I was wondering about tomorrow morning perhaps?"

I bit my lip; if I waited until then, Ethan would be back and I'd either have to find a way to convince him to go to the meeting with me or try to sneak away again. Neither option seemed likely to work.

"Tomorrow's no good for me, but I am free right now, and you have me very curious. I'm game to meet if you are." I held my breath. There was silence on the other end of the line.

"Well, if you're sure it's not too late," Milton responded, hesitation thick in his voice.

"It's not. Where would you like to meet?" I hoped he wouldn't expect me to drive all the way to Hartford again.

"Do you know Connie's Coffee?" Milton asked. "It's about halfway between here and East Halton, exit eleven off of highway two."

"I know it. I'll be there as soon as I can." I jumped off my bed. If I made this a fairly quick trip, maybe I'd get back before Ethan even knew I was gone.

"See you soon then," Milton said and hung up.

I ran down the stairs and was almost out the door when the reality that I didn't have a car hit me, stopping me in my tracks.

I quickly detoured back to the study. "Hey Dad, I just remembered I need to run an errand for school, do you think I could borrow your car?"

"I suppose so, but it's getting late. Are you sure you need to go tonight?" Dad shot me a quizzical look.

"It's for tomorrow or I would leave it." My stomach lurched as I lied to my father. "I shouldn't be gone too long, if Ethan comes back while I'm out, and I have my cell phone if you need me."

"I suppose it's all right." Dad didn't sound too sure. "The keys are on the front hall table."

"Thanks. I'll be back soon." I went and grabbed his keys out of the ceramic bowl he usually set them in and headed outside.

Please let this pay off. I pulled Dad's car out of the driveway, praying that Milton would have answers for me and that going off to meet him all alone, late at night, wasn't a huge mistake.

Six

It took me less than half an hour to get to Connie's Coffee. I breathed a sigh of relief as I pulled into a parking spot. The coffee shop was well lit, and a handful of patrons were inside, as well as three workers milling around behind the counter. I probably had nothing to worry about with Milton, he seemed innocent enough, but I still knew to be careful. And if Ryan's car accident hadn't been an accident, that meant a new threat was in the area that I needed to be on the lookout for.

As I entered the restaurant, I scanned the seating area. Milton had stationed himself at a corner table, away from the other people in the eatery. He had a cup of coffee and a bear claw pastry on the table in front of him, so I bought a coffee before joining him.

"Good evening, Miss Reed." Milton stood when I approached.

"Good evening, and thanks for meeting with me." I settled in across from him, and took a sip of coffee.

"I should be the one to thank you. I enjoy having someone to share my findings with, and I'm especially eager to share what I've stumbled across this time." Milton was bouncing in his seat, like a kid in a candy store.

"I'm all ears." I leaned in.

Milton glanced around the restaurant, as though the elderly couple by the counter, or the group of guys I recognized from school goofing around near the exit, were somehow a threat to him. "I believe you'll find you need to be all eyes." Milton reached into the tote bag protectively tucked away on his lap. I frowned, watching him carefully set an old, beat-up leather journal on the table.

"What is it?" I kept my eyes on the maple-colored, fraying leather. The book was well worn, and I guessed at least a hundred years old from the way it was hand-bound.

"A friend of mine, a fellow historian who is also a Glain Neidr enthusiast, contacted me last week with some incredible news. He was able to get his hands on one of the most interesting relics I've come across in a very long time. It appears to be some sort of manuscript containing blue prints, diagrams, and other instructions for an old secret organization." Milton lowered his voice, but I could still catch the excitement sparking in it.

"What?" My mouth dropped open at the mention of a secret organization.

"I know; it's astounding. I found myself quite giddy when I first got a chance to pore over its pages." Milton's eyes were even wider than normal through his thick glasses.

"And what does the journal say?" I held my breath.

Milton's face fell. "Unfortunately, I haven't been able to discover very much yet. You see, the text is written in an ancient language that neither my colleague nor I recognize. It is similar to some Old English Runic alphabets, Gaelic, and perhaps a hint of Latin, but the symbols aren't exactly the same as any of those. That's actually the reason my friend came to me with the journal in the first place. I have more experience with dead languages than he does. It's taken some time to try to decipher the words written on the pages of the journal, and much to our chagrin, as we began deciphering the alphabet and the words, it became clear that the journal itself was written in code."

I gestured to the old book. "So to figure out what is in this journal, you need to figure out how to read a dead language and then decipher the code the author used when he wrote it?"

"Yes, that's exactly it. We've been very slow to make any real progress, but I think we've figured out the lines written on the first page, the words that explain what this journal is." Milton placed a gentle hand on the book, his excitement mounting again.

"And ...?" I hunched my shoulders, wishing he'd just fill me in instead of pausing dramatically. He looked around again, grabbed a pair of surgical gloves from his bag and slid them on, then carefully pulled the front cover back to reveal the strange symbols he'd been talking about.

I didn't know a lot about old languages, although I'd thumbed through some of my Dad's books over the years finding the different symbols visually interesting, and from what little I could remember these characters did remind me of Old English or Gaelic, as Milton had suggested. He turned the book so I could see the page.

"You see these symbols here." Milton pointed to a row of forked lines, dots, crescents, and triangles with squiggles, running across the middle of the first page. "It took a while, but I think we've deciphered them correctly, and if we have then it says, 'These are the words of the one who pulls the strings of destiny, contained on these pages is the wisdom to rule over all.'" Milton's stubby finger hovered delicately above the symbols as he spoke, as if he was scared to touch the brittle pages of the journal, even with gloves on.

The same lightheaded feeling I'd experienced when I spoke to Ryan crept over me, as though my mind was receiving information too hard to process. "Pulls the strings of destiny." I repeated the words back slowly, knowing immediately that this journal was somehow connected to the Hleo, although I was completely baffled by exactly whose it was, or how it had ever made it out into the open.

"Amazing, isn't it?" Milton was practically salivating.

"How does the Glain Neidr fit in with this book?"

"We still need to figure that part out, but take a look at this." Milton carefully flipped through the fragile pages. They were full of writings and drawings and images that did appear to be archaic blueprints, and there were other diagrams and symbols written out like formulas, or lists. When he turned to the page he was looking for, I gasped. Whoever had written this book had drawn a picture of the Glain Neidr. I would recognize its perfect circle, threaded through with a gold chain, anywhere, even in a crude, hand-drawn sketch. I reached for the image, but stopped short of touching the old brown paper. I was desperate to understand what I was staring at, but all that was drawn under the stone were more strange symbols still needing to be deciphered.

"I think the necklace is still in this society's possession. If we can find the society, we can find the Glain Neidr." Milton took a triumphant bite of his pastry.

I stared at the drawing. A secret society had the Glain Neidr, a secret society that played a part with destiny. He didn't know it, but what Milton was telling me was that the Hleo had the necklace, and that meant Ethan was hesitant to go after it because he didn't want me to get my hands on the necklace. But why?

"I guess you're getting really close then. I mean, as soon as you can decipher the rest of the text, you should be able to figure out who this secret organization is and how to track them down." I picked up my coffee cup, but set it down again without drinking.

"I know what you're thinking, that this looks and sounds crazy—"

"I've heard crazier things." I waved my hand to ward off his doubt.

I was about to ask Milton if he knew the name of the secret society, when the distinct sensation that I was being watched came over me. I straightened in my chair, and tried to survey my surroundings casually. No one in the coffee shop was specifically looking in my direction, but the feeling wouldn't go away. I glanced over my shoulder; Ethan was watching me from outside. His Jeep was parked next to my dad's car, and he was leaning against the front grill, staring at Milton and me with his arms crossed. The blood drained from my face; I'd been caught. It would only be a matter of minutes before I would have to face the music.

"This is all so incredible, but unfortunately I have to get going." I shifted in my seat.

Milton's expression changed from one of excitement to suspicion. "It is incredible," he echoed slowly, his eyes, so wide before, now guarded behind his spectacles. I'd made a mistake. I'd been in too much of a hurry to go; I could feel it. He shut the journal and covered it with his hand protectively.

"I'm really sorry." I inched my hand closer to his, but didn't touch him. "I want to talk about this more and to look at more pages, really I do; you have no idea. It's just that my dad's sort of strict, and I didn't actually tell him where I was going, only that I was running an errand." I motioned to the clock on the wall. "It's later than I thought and he'll be expecting me back any minute now. I don't want to get in trouble."

Milton checked the clock as well and his face relaxed. "I suppose it is getting quite late."

"I really appreciate you showing me this journal, and please, if you're able to figure out anything else in it, especially regarding the Glain Neidr, I'd really love to know." I stood, but gave him an appreciative smile.

"I promise to keep you in the loop." Milton nodded and I exhaled in relief that I hadn't scared him off.

We said goodnight and I slowly walked towards the door on the side of the restaurant my car was parked, while he strolled off in the opposite direction. I thought of Milton's discovery about the Glain Neidr. The meeting had been interesting and definitely worth the risk, but as I pushed through the exit, avoiding Ethan's gaze, I was pretty sure he wasn't going to agree.

Seven

I held up my hands as I crossed the dimly-lit parking lot. "Look—"

"Are you crazy? Do you know how dangerous what you're doing is?" Ethan's usual calm demeanor was gone. He drove his fingers through his dark hair in frustration.

I shrugged. "He's harmless."

"How do you know that, Hannah?" Ethan's green eyes flashed fire. "How do you know he isn't a member of the Bana, stringing you along, trying to lure you into a trap?"

"I just do." I squared my jaw defiantly. The truth was, I didn't know for sure, but Milton definitely didn't look like a member of the Bana.

Ethan threw his hands up in the air. "You told me you were going to stay away from all of this, that you were going to drop it. Then you sneak off in the middle of the night to meet up with some stranger at a random coffee shop along the highway after an attempt is made on your life. Of all the—"

"That was before Ryan got hurt. Tell me Ethan, right now, what happened with my car?" I stared him down.

He hesitated, dropping his chin and squeezing his eyes shut. "The brake lines on your car were cut in a way that would look like mechanical failure, and the sensors tampered with so there would be no warning that the car was slowly leaking brake fluid."

Even though deep down I'd known he was going to tell me something along those lines, it still felt as though I'd been punched. I wrapped my arms around myself, trying to stop my stomach from lurching.

"Hannah." Ethan reached for me, but I backed away. I didn't want to hear that I wasn't responsible for this, or that there was no way I could have known, because the truth was Ryan had almost died because of me and the stupid people who wanted me dead.

"Don't say it." I shook my head and turned from him to stare at the restaurant.

"This isn't your fault." Ethan slid a gentle hand onto my shoulder.

I bristled and whirled back around to meet his gaze. "How can you say that? Of course this is my fault, it's always my fault. Every time a person ends up directly in the line of fire and suffers because of me and my stupid visions, it's my fault. We don't even know if the Bana want to kidnap me or kill me, and I'm sick of it, Ethan. Can't you see how sick of it I am?" I waved my arms wildly. The group of guys from school had exited the coffee shop and were looking over at our heated exchange with curious stares. I ignored them. "I'm walking around like some sort of sideshow at a carnival and I don't know how to fix it. I need something to change."

"I get it, I do, but what you're doing isn't safe." Ethan's voice was soothing as he held out his arms to me.

I crossed mine. "Milton isn't Bana. He's an eccentric little man who has devoted himself to finding the Glain Neidr." I studied his face closely. *This is your chance Ethan; come clean and admit you know the Hleo have the Glain Neidr.*

Ethan dropped his arms to his sides, his fists clenching. "You're right, Hannah, Milton Cambry's not Bana, but the people who are into these mystical artifacts are fanatical, they'll stop at nothing to get their hands on one, even if that means hurting someone in the process." Ethan's shoulders had tensed. I knew the sign; his composure was wavering.

"Just stop with all this dangerous talk, I know the stone is with the Hleo." I leveled a steely glare at him, hurt that he kept lying to me.

Ethan's jaw dropped. "What are you talking about?"

"You don't have to keep it from me anymore. Milton told me. He told me that the necklace is with a secret organization that controls destiny. All this time you just kept saying you didn't know where it was, or that it was too dangerous to go after. How exactly are the Hleo dangerous, Ethan?" I leaned right into his personal space, not at all concerned that my voice was coming out in a full on yell. *Let people overhear me, I don't care anymore.*

"It's not with the Hleo, it's with the Bana," Ethan shot back, his voice as forceful as mine.

"The Bana." I blinked and took a step back. I don't know why, but the Bana had never entered my thoughts as Milton had been talking. Now, belatedly, I realized that made perfect sense.

"Yes, the Bana, the other organization that plays with destiny." Ethan glanced around, then lowered his voice. "And it's not with just any Bana member. It's with Alexander. He wears it as a source of power so he can see into the future the way Gabriel does. Not only that, but there's a duplicate, a fake that the Bana have fabricated. That way, if someone does attempt to steal the stone, chances are fifty-fifty that they aren't even grabbing the real one. Whichever necklace isn't around his neck is kept in one of the many secret Bana storage facilities around the globe." Ethan's jaw was tight. "That journal your friend Milton has stumbled across, I can't be sure, but it sounds like it's Eric's personal journal. And I mean Eric, father of Alexander, destroyed by Alexander without afterthought so that he could take over the Bana. He created the journal as a sort of insurance policy, figuring his son couldn't get rid of him if it was floating around and contained all the secrets of the Bana's organization. I was under the impression Alexander had made sure it was destroyed, but I guess it got away from him somehow. If this odd little gentleman has been able to get his hands on it, all I can say is, if Alexander knew of its existence, Milton would be in a lot of danger."

"Is that what Kai told you at Veridan? That the Glain Neidr was with the Bana?" I shifted my weight from one foot to the other.

Ethan pressed his fingers to the bridge of his nose, as though trying to stave off a headache. "Yes." The word came out in a sigh.

"Why didn't you just tell me?" My forehead creased. "Maybe I would've been more understanding if you'd explained that to me right from the beginning." A lump formed in my throat at his lack of trust in me. I swallowed it away.

"I'm not used to sharing sensitive information, especially with my protecteds." Ethan lifted his shoulders lightly.

I drew in a sharp breath. "I'm more than that." Calling me a protected felt like a slap in the face. I strode over to my dad's car, jabbing at the unlock button on the remote.

Ethan caught up to me and grasped my elbow to stop me. "I know. I'm sorry." He turned me to face him. "Alexander's ruthless, and he has every synthetic Bana protecting him as though it were their lives at stake, because it is. He guards the Glain Neidr with all the fervor he guards himself with, so whether it is with him or in storage, we'd be going up against the full arsenal of the Bana to get it. I was hoping that I'd be able to figure out another solution. I know you want answers, but I have to keep you safe." Ethan's eyes searched mine.

He wanted me to cave, and there was a big part of me that wanted to sag against his chest, feel the strong muscles in the arms that surrounded me, and forget this terrible fight, but the anger and hurt won out. "Well, we haven't figured anything else out. Maybe it would be hard, but I know you could get past Alexander and his army, I just know it. I need to believe the Glain Neidr will work, Ethan, it's the only shred of hope I have that my life will go back to the way it was before all of this. It's become too much; I need things to be normal again. To go back to the way it was before I found out about the Hleo and Bana." The words tumbled out, clearly cutting through him. His eyes were dark with pain, but I couldn't stop myself, not after everything that had happened.

Ethan stumbled back a step, as though I'd pushed him.

"I need a night to myself, okay?" I climbed into Dad's car before he could say anything more, and drove away, refusing to look back and see him standing alone in the empty parking lot.

How could Ethan have shut me out like that about the Glain Neidr's location? How could we be a real couple if we kept things from each other? I gripped the steering wheel tightly with both hands. That was the one question in my life I did know the answer to.

We couldn't.

Eight

My alarm beeped. A new day was beginning, but I kept the covers securely over my head. After about a minute, I couldn't ignore the sound anymore. Yanking back the blankets, I slammed my hand down on the button, plunging the room into silence again. It seemed darker than normal, and I flipped over in the bed to glance out my window. A thick fog had settled in. I sat up, hugged my knees to my chest, and stared into the smoky mist enveloping the newly-budding leaves on the trees in my backyard. My fight with Ethan played over in my head. I grabbed my phone off the night table to check for missed messages. There were none. I bit my lip, and tried to accept that Ethan was simply abiding by my wishes and giving me the space I'd asked him for.

I frowned. *Why would I even set my alarm on a Saturday morning?* Then I remembered; I'd picked up an extra shift at The Patch.

I groaned and dragged myself out of bed. The fog must mean that it was colder outside than it had been for the past week, so I threw on a light sweater and jeans before heading downstairs to get coffee.

Dad was gone for the weekend on a course. His girlfriend, my art teacher, Rose Woods, had gone with him, planning to meet up with an old college friend to do some shopping. Thankfully they had taken her car, so I had the use of his. I kept an eye out for Ethan's Jeep on my way to work, but he appeared to be keeping his distance. His absence caused an uneasy feeling to run up my spine, but I tried to shake it off as I pulled Dad's car into the parking lot behind The Patch.

I needed to clear the air. I needed Ethan to know that when I'd mentioned things going back to normal I hadn't meant him. The thought of not having Ethan in my life made breathing difficult. I wouldn't be able to relax until I was sure he knew that.

Carmen seemed to sense that I wasn't in the greatest frame of mind. She asked me at least three times if everything was okay. I brushed her off. I didn't want to get into it with her, especially since I couldn't really explain why Ethan and I had been arguing. She let me do clean-up duty while she manned the cash. I kept my phone in my pocket in case Ethan tried to get a hold of me, pulling it out every twenty minutes or so to make sure I hadn't missed a text.

About half an hour before my shift ended, my phone vibrated and I snatched it out of my jeans. It was Katie. She and Luke were heading over to the hospital to keep Ryan's mom company. She invited me to join them. I probably should have, and a wave of guilt washed over me, but I declined. Until I talked to Ethan, I wouldn't be able to focus on anything else. He and I could go over to the hospital later. I told her to pass on my best wishes and to text if they needed me.

My shifted ended at one, and I jumped in Dad's car and drove over to Ethan's house. I couldn't keep this silence going between us any longer. Ethan's driveway was empty. His Jeep and Simon's VW were nowhere to be seen. *Where could they be?* I pulled in and jumped out to ring the bell, just in case. If Ethan was watching from a distance, hopefully my action would bring him out of hiding. I stood on the little front deck of their bungalow and waited. I was just turning around to walk back to my car when the door opened.

I whirled back around, expecting to see Ethan or Simon, but instead a dark-haired woman in a long-sleeved black shirt and army cargo pants stood in the doorway with her arms crossed. A protective instinct kicked in and I quickly took a step back.

"Hannah?" She cocked her head to the side as she took me in. Her hair was in a loose French braid and it swayed with the motion.

"Um, yes." I swallowed.

"Come on in." She stepped back into the house, holding the door open so I could join her. I hesitated. *Who is this woman?* When she beckoned me inside, I caved, curiosity winning out over my apprehension.

I glanced around the small living room. It looked the same as ever, with Ethan and Simon's low-budget furniture set up on one side of the room, and a small dining room table on the other. Papers and file folders were spread out across the table.

"I'm sorry, but should I know you?" I held my grip on the doorknob, on the off chance that I was in danger and might need to make a hasty escape.

"My name is Lucy. I'm your new Hleo," she stated matter-of-factly. She walked over to the table and rifled through the folders.

"What?" I blinked a couple of times. *What is she talking about?*

"I am your new Hleo," she repeated slowly. She didn't even bother to look up from the papers she was holding to address me directly.

"Where's Ethan?" I clenched my fists, a funny feeling creeping over me.

"He's gone, as is his little helper Simon." Lucy closed one file and opened another.

"He's gone," I whispered. The air escaped from my lungs, but no more would go in. I couldn't breathe. The words didn't make any sense. Ethan would never just leave. He was my protector, my defender, the person who mattered most to me.

"Yes, and now I'm here." Her tone was overly professional, and her gaze, when she finally directed it at me, was condescending. Did she think I wasn't capable of understanding what she was saying?

"Did he leave a note or some other good-bye at least?"

Lucy narrowed her eyes. "That would be against protocol."

"But, but …" It was all I could get out. How could he just be gone, as though he had never existed? Why wouldn't he try to at least say good-bye and explain all this to me himself?

"Look Hannah, Ethan broke the most important rule the Hleo live by when he got involved in this little thing the two of you had going on." Lucy waved a dismissive hand in front of her. "If he didn't have such an excellent service record, I'm sure he would have been permanently removed from duty. I'm not really sure why he wasn't." She scrunched up her nose. I didn't like the way she'd said 'permanently removed.' *What could that mean?*

"So, where is he now?" I kicked the edge of the rug in the living room with the toe of my shoe.

"Hannah." Her tone answered the question.

"He can't just be gone." I shook my head as my voice went up a notch. I sounded like a whiny child, but I couldn't help it. This had happened with absolutely no warning. Hysteria rose inside me as I desperately tried to get a grip on the situation.

"Well, he is." She shrugged. "Now, I've been going over the file Ethan had on you, and I think you were making some progress figuring out the scope of your ability, but we need to push harder if we're going to find any real answers." Lucy turned back to the file. I watched her skim through a few pages, and my feet began shuffling back towards the door.

This was all wrong, it had to be. Maybe if I went out and came back in it would be different, Ethan would be here, and I would be able to breathe again.

"What are you doing?" She glanced up at me with a perplexed frown.

"I have to go," I muttered as I twisted the doorknob.

"We need to work." She motioned to the papers on the table. She seemed baffled about why I would be so upset.

"I can't." I turned and bolted outside. I jumped in the car and closed the door, resting my head on the steering wheel and swallowing back sobs. I would not break down and cry in Ethan's driveway. I needed to get home, away from that terrible woman, before I allowed myself to do that.

My hand was on the key in the ignition, about to turn it, when someone tapped on the driver's side window. Lucy stared down at me. She took a deep breath, as though she was working to be patient, but struggling to do so.

"Please, just leave me alone," I whimpered through the glass. I turned my gaze back to the steering wheel.

"Open the window, Hannah." From my peripheral view, I could tell she'd crossed her arms. I waited ten more seconds, then reluctantly obeyed.

She was silent for a moment and I looked up to see the slightest softening in her icy-blue eyes. "I understand that this is a shock to you, but the rules are in place for a reason. It's probably going to be difficult for you to accept, but it's the way it has to be to keep you safe." She crouched down and rested her arms on the window ledge of the door. "Now, I really need you to be at your best so we can work together. I want you to take some time to process this. Then we can move on and get back to business. Do you think you can do that?" she asked. Apparently that was as heartfelt as she was going to get.

"Fine," I said through gritted teeth. I just wanted her to let me leave so I could go home.

"Fine." She nodded and stepped back onto the lawn. "I'll give you the rest of the weekend to yourself and then we can start up again," she added.

I closed the car window and pulled out of the driveway, pretending I hadn't heard her. Pressing down on the accelerator, I sped off in the direction of my house. I drove on autopilot, my mind reeling. My world had just been turned upside down. Lucy might as well have been speaking a different language for how much sense she had made. No, that wasn't quite true. I understood the words, but my brain wouldn't accept that Ethan was gone. How could he have left with no warning? Surely, even if it was against the rules, he would have found some way to find me, to explain to me what was going on. He wouldn't simply disappear.

The car's tires kicked up gravel and dirt as I pulled onto the shoulder and threw the car into park. I would fight this. This was my life; if the Hleo society thought I would simply accept someone I loved being ripped away from me, they were sorely mistaken.

I dug my cell phone out of my jacket pocket, checking for messages or texts. There weren't any. I punched in Ethan's number. It rang twice before an automated voice informed me that the number had been disconnected. I knew I'd heard correctly, but I tried again. When the automated voice came on again, I hit the end call button. Knowing the result wasn't likely to be any different, I scrolled down to Simon's number, dialed, and let the same automated voice tell me that the number had been cut off. I stabbed at the end call button with my finger, then sat in the driver's seat and bit my thumbnail. What else I could do? What part of Ethan's life might Lucy, or whichever of the Hleo was doing this to me, not have gotten to yet?

An idea began to form in my mind, and I pulled back out into traffic before the thought had fully materialized. I spun the car around in a u-turn and headed for East Halton High. Maybe Ethan would have tried to leave me something in his locker, some sort of sign that he wasn't just abandoning me.

Ms. Woods had mentioned a local artists' workshop in the gym that weekend. I checked the time on the dashboard clock and said a silent prayer that it was still going on and the school would be accessible.

The school's parking lot had a handful of cars in it as I pulled in and jogged across the lot to the entrance closest to the gym. A big sandwich board sign was propped up outside the door, letting people know the artists' workshop was inside and people could register in the art room. I sighed with relief and hurried to Ethan's locker.

After glancing around to make sure no one was watching, I spun the combination to Ethan's lock. I took a deep breath and slid the door open. The locker was empty. There wasn't a single item in it; if I didn't know better, I'd think it had been unassigned all year. I stared into the metal cubicle for a second before slamming the door shut in frustration. A stocky, middle-aged woman wearing a painter's smock walked by and jumped at the sound of the locker clanging, almost dropping the canvas bag full of painting supplies she was holding.

I muttered an apology and breezed by her, heading back outside. My mind raced as I plunked myself down in the driver's seat of my dad's car. *Now what?* I was racking my brain for something or someone that could give me a clue to Ethan's whereabouts, when Travis popped into my head. Was it possible that the Hleo, whose house Ethan had taken me to after I'd almost drowned fleeing from Paige, would be able to tell me where Ethan was? It was a long shot, but he was only an hour away. If he couldn't reveal Ethan's location, maybe he could at least tell me how I could get a hold of him, a special way of contacting him or something. If I could just get a message to Ethan that I was *not* okay with his leaving and I needed to talk to him as soon as possible, I was confident everything could be worked out.

For the entire hour it took me to drive to Travis's house I wrestled with turning around and telling myself to accept this for what it was, the ultimate brush-off, and praying that Travis would be able to help me.

The fog had lifted earlier and it had turned into a clear, blue-sky spring day. The trees of the surrounding forest zipped by and I checked the speedometer. I was well over the speed limit and I lifted my foot off the gas a little. I was desperate for answers, but getting into a speed-induced car accident wouldn't be very helpful.

My gaze kept darting from the road to the rearview mirror, watching for any sign of this Lucy person driving behind me. She was, after all, my new protector, I supposed, but the coast appeared to be clear.

It was late afternoon by the time I drove down Travis's street. I hadn't been in the greatest of mental states the last time I'd been here, so it took me a little while to find his house. I parked across the street and climbed out of the vehicle. As I approached the bungalow, my last shred of hope began to fade; a little girl was playing in the front yard.

A redheaded woman, who appeared to be in her mid-thirties, opened the front door and stepped out onto the porch. "Hi there. What can I do for you?" she asked with a friendly southern drawl.

I stopped at the bottom of the porch stairs. "I'm sorry to disturb you, but I was wondering if you might be able to help me. I'm looking for a friend of mine; his name is Travis. I was under the impression he lived at this address."

"You must be talking about the old owner. We just moved in about a month ago," the woman said, her face beaming with pride.

"Oh, that's nice. It's a lovely house. I don't suppose you would have any sort of forwarding information." I wriggled my nose, already knowing that she wouldn't.

"I'm sorry sweetie; we actually bought the house from the bank. I don't even know the old owner's name." The woman shook her head. She glanced over at the little girl, watching her as she pushed a Barbie around in a hot pink convertible.

I nodded. "I see." I swallowed hard, trying not to appear crushed by the discouraging news. Of course it made sense that the Hleo would use discreet measures for getting rid of property. I wondered if Travis's leaving had anything to do with Ethan and me, or whether it had just been bad timing.

"Thank you for your time." I stepped back down onto the driveway again.

"Sorry we couldn't help you," the woman replied apologetically as I walked away.

"That's okay." I shrugged and forced a fake smile.

I was about half way home before I started trembling too hard to drive. I pulled over at a forested rest stop to compose myself. My thoughts jabbed at me, hurting worse than any sort of physical pain. It was over. What else could I do? What other conclusion could I come to? Ethan had vanished and I was left with this woman I was almost positive didn't like me. I was alone. I sat in the car shaking, trying to catch my breath, but unable to. The edges of my vision blurred, and, the will to fight gone, I rested my head on the steering wheel and gave in to the darkness.

Nine

It felt like hours, but only a few minutes passed before I jolted awake. I only knew that because the clock on the dashboard showed four minutes later than it had the last time I remembered looking at it. I glanced around. There were no other cars at the rest stop, and thick forest surrounded the parking lot and small travel plaza on three sides. Even though cars continually zoomed passed on the highway, I felt incredibly isolated.

Numbness washed over me as I accepted the utter defeat of my attempts to track down Ethan. All I wanted to do was crawl under the covers and never see the light of another day. I didn't care what the future held if it was a future without him.

When I finally got home I did go right to my room, pulled the sheets back on the bed, and climbed in, still in my clothes. The world could continue on, leaving me behind with my misery, and the terrible thought that the last words I'd spoken to Ethan were a plea to be free from the Hleo.

My cell phone rang a few times, and then the house phone. I checked the call display to see Katie's name on both, and rolled over in bed, ignoring her. After the third buzz of a text I checked my phone. Katie was home from the hospital and was asking if I wanted to hang out. I texted that I had a headache so she would leave me alone, and then tossed my phone onto my night table. At some point in the night I fell into a dark, despairing sleep.

I would have stayed hidden in my blanket fortress with my head buried under my pillow indefinitely, but I woke up when I heard the front door open.

Lucy had said she would leave me alone for the rest of the weekend, and Dad was on his course. I bolted upright in my bed. In my stupor after returning from Travis's I had stupidly neglected to lock the door; now anybody could be down there. My self-preservation instincts kicked in and I scanned my room, searching for something I could use to defend myself.

Footsteps treaded on the stairs, moving closer to my room. I silently pulled the covers back, and tried to think of the best place to hide. My heart thumped hard in my chest. A knock sounded on my door and I frowned. Would an intruder knock? Or an assassin? Before I could move, the door opened and Dad poked his head in my doorway.

"Dad?" I furrowed my brow and blinked to make sure he was really standing there. "I thought you were gone until Sunday night."

"Hannah, it is Sunday night." Dad walked into my room, a worried expression on his face.

"Oh, I guess I lost track of time." I rubbed my temples with my fingers, feeling dazed.

"Are you all right?" Dad came over and sat on the edge of the bed beside me.

"I'm okay." I wasn't sure what to say to him. I needed to explain what had happened; he would eventually find out that Ethan had left. I was sure it would be better to just tell him and be done with it, but I wasn't positive I could say the words out loud.

"Hannah?" Dad searched my face.

I took a breath, carefully reining in my emotions before trying to speak. I couldn't cry in front of Dad. He hadn't known Ethan and I were dating. "Um, so Ethan and Simon have been replaced. I guess they thought that a woman Hleo might be better at helping me figure out my drawing ability." I stared at my hands clasped tightly in my lap, trying to keep my tone casual.

"Really? That seems rash."

"I don't really understand. I just know it's done." I pressed my lips together. The aching pit in my stomach caused a wave of nausea to wash over me.

"Well, that's a shame. They were incredibly talented. I always felt better when they were around." Dad took off his glasses to wipe them with the hem of his shirt. "And I always thought that you and Ethan made an attractive couple," he added.

My eyes went wide. "You knew?"

"I've known for quite some time. It was actually Rose who let me in on the secret. She was talking to me one day about what a cute couple the two of you made. I thought that was odd since you weren't dating, and tried to explain this fact to Rose. She very plainly told me that she knew when two people were in love, and the way the two of you looked at each other, she knew. It came as quite a shock to me, but when I observed more closely, I picked up on what she had seen." Dad slipped his glasses back on and studied me, his smile sympathetic.

"Oh Dad." I bit my lip, not really knowing how to explain.

"I didn't like it, but I did understand the deception, Hannah. I know that Ethan was breaking the rules to be with you." Dad rested a hand on my shoulder.

"It was more than that." I wrinkled my nose. "We weren't exactly sure how you would take the news."

"I have to admit, it was hard to accept at first. I almost confronted you several times, but once I had a chance to digest the idea, and I could see what a gentleman Ethan is, I found it oddly comforting to know that you were dating a 140 year old who knew how to handle himself in a knife fight."

In spite of everything, I laughed.

Dad squeezed my shoulder. "I find it incredibly hard to believe that he would ever just leave you. Anyone who spent any amount of time around the two of you knew that Ethan cared deeply for you. I know things seem bleak at the moment, sweetheart, but I wouldn't count Ethan out just yet."

I nodded. "Thanks Dad. I hope you're right." I wanted to believe what he was saying, but was struggling. Ethan had only been gone a couple of days and I felt like part of me was dying. Even if he did have a plan, how long would I have to wait to hear from him? What if months went by without word from him?

"The new Hleo, Lucy, I don't think she likes me very much. She seems very severe." I glanced up to the ceiling and sighed.

"Maybe she just needs to warm up to you. As long as she keeps you safe, that is the main thing, I suppose." Dad stood up but stopped at the foot of my bed.

"I guess that's true. How was your weekend?" I wanted to move on to a new topic. My brain needed a rest from Hleo stuff for even a few minutes.

"It was nice, very interesting. They had an archeologist from Peru giving some new insights into the construction of Machu Picchu. And Rose enjoyed catching up with her friend Melissa. I'm just sorry I wasn't here to offer some support through the difficult transition."

I shook my head. "That's okay. I'm glad you both had a nice time." I didn't want him to feel bad, there was no reason for us to both be in misery.

"Can I get you anything, something to eat, a cup of tea perhaps?"

"No, that's okay. I'm just going to stay here for a while longer." I ran a hand over my covers. I couldn't even remember the last time I'd eaten anything, but I didn't feel hungry. I didn't feel anything at the moment.

"If you're sure. I'll be downstairs if you change your mind." He moved to the doorway.

"Thanks." I gave him a half-hearted smile.

After he left, I changed into my pajamas and brushed my hair and teeth. A dragging heaviness slowed every action, but I didn't want to sleep in my clothes for another night. I climbed into bed and pulled the covers up over my head again, hoping that Dad was right and that very soon things would begin to make sense again.

Ten

My messed-up emotional state had taken its toll on me and I'd forgotten to set my alarm. It was almost eleven by the time I woke up. Forgetting for a moment what had occurred over the last few days, I sat up quickly, but within seconds the memories came flooding back and I sank down against my pillows. I hated the thought of beginning yet another day without Ethan.

I had curled up in a ball under the covers, trying to muster the energy to drag myself out of bed, when the grinding sound of a power tool running downstairs pierced the silence. I pushed back the blankets and lowered my feet gingerly to the bedroom floor. Dad would have left hours ago for school, and once again fear rose in my chest at the possibility of dealing with an unknown threat.

Now that Ethan was gone, I was going to have to get used to looking out for myself. I didn't like Lucy, and I definitely didn't trust her with my life.

I tiptoed to the stairs and carefully made my way down, pressing my back to the wall and clutching an umbrella—the closest thing I could find in my room resembling a weapon— tightly in my hands. I reached the bottom and peered down the hallway. A deep frown wrinkled my forehead when I saw what was making the noise. Lucy. She stood on a kitchen chair attaching something to the wall near the back door. A security camera? Seriously? She'd tucked it into the corner between the wall and the cabinets so it had a clear vantage point out into the backyard.

"I would have thought that, being able to protect you out in the open, Ethan would have taken advantage of using extra security measures we usually have to go without. I don't know what he was thinking." Lucy twisted a screwdriver, not even turning to address me directly as she fiddled with the camera.

"Who gave you permission to do that?" I scowled at her back. *How dare she criticize Ethan's methods?* I tossed the umbrella down on the kitchen table and crossed my arms, watching her work.

"I'm trying to protect you. I don't need *permission* to do my job," Lucy replied flatly.

"Isn't that a bit of overkill?" I pointed to the little black recording device.

"There are many different blind spots in this home; it would be incredibly easy for someone to sneak up and launch a surprise attack. The cameras will cut down the Bana's advantage. It's just one of the things I can't believe was overlooked." Lucy connected a wire to the equipment. Angry heat rose to my cheeks as she again put a little dig in towards Ethan.

"Cameras? How many have you installed?" I blinked. *How long has she been at this?*

"Five altogether. The front entrance, the back yard, the front yard by the garage, one near the roof line facing the front yard and down the street, and this one right here." Lucy tapped the gadget gently. Her voice dripped with pride.

I stared at the camera with disdain, biting the inside of my cheek to keep quiet. *What did she mean by other security measures? Is she planning to do something else in my home?* What gave her the right to come in here without asking and start making changes, anyway? I stalked over to the coffeemaker and made myself a cup of coffee. I thought about emptying the remainder into the sink, but forced myself to leave it in the pot so Lucy could help herself if she wanted some.

"I assume by your lack of activity the past two days that you've decided to accept the inevitable and are done traipsing all over in search of some clue that will lead you to Ethan?" Lucy dropped her arms to her sides and turned to look at me.

My mouth gaped open. So she had been following me. My fingers tightened around my mug. Of course she had; I should have known.

"How you knew the location of a fellow operative in the area is beyond me, but clearly Ethan threw all caution to the wind a long time ago." Lucy went back to tightening a screw on the base of the camera, while my glare at her deepened.

I was about to spit out that he'd been forced to take me to Travis's to save my life, and shouldn't she have read that in one of Ethan's reports on me, since all I had seen her do was read reports, but I bit my tongue. I wasn't actually sure if Ethan had let The Three know about our near drowning a few months ago. After their suggestion that I come stay with them, I knew he'd been somewhat selective with what he shared in an effort to keep them from pushing the idea.

I set my coffee mug down hard on the island in the kitchen. "I'm done."

"And will you be venturing out of the house today, or are you planning to continue your role as a recluse?" Lucy asked.

I clenched my jaw. The condescension in her voice was almost unbearable. "I forgot to set my alarm." I spat the words out through gritted teeth.

Lucy shrugged. "It really makes no difference to me. If you stay in we can start on the focusing exercises I wanted to try with you."

I fought the groan trying to escape my lips at the thought of spending extended periods of time with this woman. At the moment, figuring out my drawing ability was the last thing I wanted to think about.

"Can you just give me one more day? We can begin with all of that tomorrow." I ran my hand across my forehead, hoping Lucy had enough compassion to grant my request.

She stepped down off the wooden kitchen chair and turned to face me, narrowing her eyes as though trying to evaluate me. "Fine, one more day of lament, but then we really need to get to work. Ethan had only begun scratching the surface with you. I suppose he enjoyed playing house, and wanted to prolong the experience." Lucy rolled her eyes and walked out of the kitchen.

I stared at the empty doorway. I couldn't decide if her flippant comments left me more shocked or angry. Why did she have so much hostility towards Ethan, and towards me? I'd only just met her. She had no valid reason to be so rude to me. I picked up my mug and took a long sip of coffee, hesitant to leave the kitchen. If that was how Lucy was going to treat me from here on out, I needed to figure out my ability right away. The sooner I did, the sooner she and the Hleo would be out of my life for good.

Eleven

I couldn't be bothered going to school for the afternoon. Katie had sent me another barrage of texts, wanting to know if I was okay and where I was. I gave her a quick brush off, insisting that I still had a headache and hoping that would be enough for her to leave me alone. I had a shower, worked on homework for a little while, and ended up in the living room mindlessly flipping through afternoon television.

    Lucy was around. She alternated between typing away on a tablet similar to Simon's, and poring over files that she'd spread out across the dining room table. I had just finished watching the final reveal on a home renovation show when she poked her head into the living room. "I need to run back over to the bungalow and grab a few things. I assume you're going to stay put while I'm gone."

    "I'll be here." I kept my eyes on the television screen.

    Twenty minutes later, the front door opened. I stared ahead blankly, not moving, figuring it was Lucy, but then I heard Katie. "Hey, so you're okay, right? I assume headache is code for busy with Ethan, but I thought I'd better check to see if you need soup or something. I know I said I'd keep you guys under wraps, but seriously, both of you playing hooky on the same day is really starting to look suspicious. I think you've missed more school this year than I can remember you missing our entire lives. Is he still here? His Jeep wasn't outside." Katie strode into the living room and plopped down beside me.

    Hearing Ethan's name felt like a punch in the stomach, and I gripped the pillow on the couch tightly. "No, Ethan's not here."

One look at me and a frown wrinkled Katie's forehead. "Hey, what's wrong?"

"He's gone, Kate." I took a slow breath as the ache in my chest deepened.

Katie scrunched up her face. "Like on a trip?"

"No." I shook my head. "He, that is, his parents, switched jobs suddenly and he had to go with them."

"What?" Katie grasped hold of my arms. Her gaze burned into me as though she suspected I was tricking her. "That is impossible, Hannah. How could he move in three days? He was here on Friday." She cocked her head to the side.

"I guess they had it planned, but didn't tell him until it was time to go on Saturday." I swallowed hard, wondering how exactly Ethan's departure had gone.

"But…" She sat for a second, looking stunned. Then her face brightened. "So he moved, that's not the greatest news in the world, but you guys will find a way to make it work. We can drive over to see him on weekends and stuff." She jostled me with her elbow, speaking in that cheer-up-Hannah voice I knew and loved; it wasn't going to work this time.

"He moved to Scotland." I threw out the first country on the other side of an ocean that I could think of. I needed Katie to see how bleak the situation was. For all I knew he *could* be in Scotland, or Australia, or Thailand. All that I knew for sure was that he wasn't here.

"Scotland." She sank back against the couch, her face falling again. "Well, we've got passports, so we could fly over there. Summer holidays are coming; it's not the easiest, but I mean …" She was losing steam.

"We ended it," I whispered, hoping I could get through explaining how final Ethan's departure was before tears started spilling over.

"But how could the two of you just end it?"

"I don't know." I wiped stray tears away, not wanting to cry, but hurting too much not to.

"Oh Hanns." Katie pulled me into a tight hug. We sat on the couch for a long time, until I didn't have any tears left. When I pulled back, she wiped a strand of hair back from my cheek. "Are you sure it's over? I mean, I have never seen two people more into each other than you two. I love Luke, don't get me wrong, but it's not exactly epic like what I see between you and Ethan." Katie's expression was so compassionate I had to work to force the large lump that was forming in my throat away again.

"It's over; we decided the easiest thing would be no contact so hopefully we will get over each other faster." I played with the sleeves of my sweater; physically aching at the thought of never looking into Ethan's green eyes, hearing his caring voice, or feeling his strong arms around me again.

"Okay well, I'm here. We're going to get through this together, beginning with a night of wallowing. I'll go get some ice cream and cookie dough at the store. Is there anything else I should add to the list? Pizza's a must, but what about a little Chinese, to mix it up?" She was already off the couch and heading for the front door.

"Whatever you want." My lips curled up in as big a smile as I could muster, which wasn't very big. I wanted Katie to believe her efforts would pay off, but a night of junk wasn't going to do anything to heal this hurt. Ethan had been ripped away from me for disobeying orders; nothing could make me feel better.

"Oh, hey, I almost forgot." Katie ambled back over to me, rummaging through her purse. "I have no idea how, but a letter for you from the Essex School of Arts was delivered to my house. It arrived today. Weird, huh?" Katie handed me the envelope.

I turned the ivory-colored paper over in my hand. There was a stamp on the envelope, but no post markings. *Strange. I've never heard of that school.*

"It's in Massachusetts. You aren't thinking of ditching our Stanford dream, are you?" Katie's tone was teasing, but her face held vague apprehension.

I opened my mouth to assure Katie that I would never do that, when a thought froze me. Essex was the name of Ethan's hometown, the place where his parents and sister were buried. My heart jammed in my chest. This letter was from him; I just knew it.

"No, nothing like that, Kate. I got on their mailing list when I went to an art show they put on in Hartford last year. I was staying with you at the time so I wrote down your address." I tripped over what I was saying, trying to get an explanation out as fast as I could. If she felt secure in our future plans, maybe she would leave to go get food. I wanted to rip the letter open badly, but I couldn't in front of Katie. "You know what, I would love a big bag of barbeque chips to go along with everything else."

"I'm on it." She saluted and then she was gone and I was alone with my mysterious letter.

I put a finger to the flap to tear the top of the letter open and my breath caught in my throat. The return address was 43 Simon Rd, Essex, MA, from Dean of Students, Mary Marsden. Ethan's partner's name, as well as the name of his sister, or at least what her name would have been if she'd ended up marrying her fiancé, Stanley Marsden, instead of tragically being murdered.

I slowly ripped the envelope, keeping it intact as much as possible. Then, with my hand shaking, I pulled the letter out. It was one page in Ethan's handwriting:

Dear Hannah,

I am so sorry I left you the way I did. I know that this is all very sudden for you, and it was my greatest fear that we would end up separated, and I could not be the one protecting you. Please don't lose heart. I need you to know that I love you, and have known you were the one for me from the moment we met. The time we have spent together has changed me, and I am a better person for having you in my life. The circumstances being what they are, I cannot be with you right now, but rest assured that one day soon we will find our way back to each other. I remain forever yours,

Ethan

I read it over and over again. I held it up and breathed it in, longing for even a hint of his scent. I traced the letters with my fingers, and then read it again. It was hope on a piece of paper.

I wished it said more, that it explained what had happened, where he'd gone, and what the plan was for us to be together again, but as I reread the letter I began to get the impression that there was some sort of hidden message in it. The vagueness and wording of his statements seemed like they were spelling out something more, but I had no idea what.

Katie had been gone for almost forty-five minutes when the front door opened. I quickly stuffed the page back into the envelope and shoved it under the couch cushion. Whether it was Katie or Lucy, I couldn't let them see Ethan's letter. I didn't want to try to explain to Katie, and Lucy would likely confiscate and destroy the letter, then proceed to get Ethan in trouble for *breaking protocol.*

Thankfully, it was Katie, loaded down with bags of food. She ended up putting on a movie and staying all evening, and I was glad for the company. Dad was busy at the university, and didn't come home until after ten.

Lucy never did return. Not that I could see, anyway, although I did suspect she was close by. Or maybe watching me on one of her many security cameras set up to *protect* me. I drew in a sharp breath. Was it possible the real reason behind all the new surveillance was to keep an eye on me without my knowledge? The thought infuriated me.

Several times throughout the evening, my fingers slipped between the couch cushions and touched the tip of Ethan's letter. He hadn't abandoned me. He had reached out to let me know he was working on the situation. This letter was a lifeline.

Now I just had to figure out how it was going to get Ethan back to me.

Twelve

It had been almost a week since Ethan's disappearance. His letter stayed close by me, and I studied it whenever I had an opportunity, still not sure if it meant more than it seemed to.

Katie had been doing her best to keep me distracted, and at the moment we were on our way over to the hospital. Ryan was getting out, so Katie, Luke, and I were heading over to cheer him on, and help his mom. Katie was driving her mom's car since the 1963 Lincoln Continental convertible Luke had been fixing up for the past two years still wasn't road worthy, and my car, which had been completely totaled in the accident, hadn't been replaced yet.

"What do you think?" Katie glanced at me from the rearview mirror. I sat up straighter, my gaze darting from her to Luke. I hadn't been paying attention. I'd been staring out the passenger window watching the trees and houses go by, once again lost in thoughts of where Ethan could be, and what he could be doing. I couldn't help it; anytime I had a free moment to think, those were the thoughts that consumed me.

My friends were all sympathetic. Most of them had figured out Ethan and I had had some sort of romantic relationship going on, and felt bad for me that he was gone. Lucy, on the other hand, was clearly growing more impatient with me every day, especially since I hadn't had a flash since her arrival. I didn't know if this was happening on purpose or not, if, on some unconscious level, I didn't have any desire to cooperate with her. I'd tried to explain to her that I had no control over the frequency of my visions, but she still seemed annoyed. She hadn't actually said so, but I was pretty sure that was because she was looking forward to poking and prodding at my brain to figure out how my mind worked.

"I'm sorry Kate, what were you saying?" I leaned forward in the backseat. She and Luke exchanged a look. I wrinkled my nose, wondering if they were getting tired of my sorrow-fueled absentmindedness.

"I asked what you think of getting Ryan some welcome-home balloons, or a stuffed monkey or something from the gift shop."

I shrugged. "Oh, um, well Ryan probably has a lot of stuff to bring home already, and I'm pretty sure he doesn't care about that sort of thing."

Luke burst out laughing. "Told you." He poked Katie in the arm. Apparently I had sided with him unwittingly.

"I just thought it would be nice, but whatever," Katie grumbled, staring straight ahead through the front windshield.

"Sorry Kate." I put a hand on her shoulder, but I couldn't help and smile a little. Luke almost never won their disagreements, and it was fun to watch him gloat.

We pulled into the hospital parking lot and made our way up to Ryan's room. Mrs. Deluca was already there, bustling around packing up clothes, gathering up the flower vases and cards, and scolding Ryan whenever he tried to move. He was sitting on the edge of the hospital bed, looking better than he had in days, and I sighed with relief. I'd been over to see him a handful of times since the accident, and every time he had been lying in the hospital bed, injured and broken. Although the skin around his eyes was still purple, and his left shoulder was bandaged and in a sling, I was glad to see he looked more like his old self.

Ryan's mom, humming happily, fastened a suitcase shut. She'd been sleeping at the hospital most nights, worried about her only son's recovery, and I could only imagine the relief she must be feeling that he'd finally gotten the all clear to go home.

"You're looking pretty good." I sank down on the bed beside Ryan and rested a tentative hand on his good shoulder.

"Thanks, Hanns." He gave me a lopsided grin.

Katie rolled the food tray a little closer to him so she could plunk down in the chair beside the bed. "Yeah, now you just look like a raccoon, instead of roadkill."

"Funny." Ryan threw a packet of crackers off of his breakfast tray at her.

Luke intercepted the missile and ripped the package open. "So how has the food been? As bad as they always say it is in movies?" Luke shook the cracker contents into his mouth and eyed the uneaten blueberry muffin from Ryan's breakfast.

"It's all yours, man." Ryan waved his hand in a 'go ahead' motion and Luke snatched it up. "It actually hasn't been too bad."

"No, but you're too skinny." Mrs. Deluca set the suitcase down by the door. "Once you're home I'm going to make all your favorite dishes and get you nice and healthy again."

"Thanks, Mom." Ryan rolled his eyes.

"I think I have everything pretty much ready to go. If you could all grab something, I'll be right back." Mrs. Deluca was gone out of the room before we could respond. I picked up the two vases of flowers closest to me, while Katie clutched a balloon bouquet and Ryan's pillow off the bed. Luke picked up the oversized duffel bag. When Mrs. Deluca gave an order, there was no choice but to obey.

She returned moments later with a wheelchair. "Okay, I've signed you out so we're good to go. You just have a seat here and we'll be on our way." She pushed the chair up beside Ryan.

"Mom, I don't need that. I'm fine." Ryan slowly got off the bed, shaking his head.

"You're still recovering from surgery, so you'll do as you're told, or I'll really give you some injuries." Mrs. Deluca put a hand on her hip and stared him down. His shoulders slumped and he reluctantly sank into the chair.

"That's a good boy." She patted his healthy shoulder and he groaned. "Here, Hannah, I'll take the flowers. Why don't you push Ryan?" Mrs. Deluca held out her hands.

"Okay." I passed off the vases to her, and we ambled down the hospital hallway.

After a short ride in the elevator, we went through the lobby and out the front doors. Mrs. Deluca gripped my arm to stop me and I halted Ryan's chair under the front entrance overhang. "You wait here. Katie, Luke, you come help me load up the van, then I'll bring it around. I'll be right back."

"Mom, I'm perfectly …" Ryan opened his mouth to protest, but Mrs. Deluca, Katie, and Luke were already headed in the direction of Mrs. Deluca's minivan. "… Fine." He threw his good arm into the air.

"You really do look better." I observed while we waited for the vehicle. Guilt over what had happened washed over me for the umpteenth time. If only there was some way I could go back in time and keep him from ever using my car.

"Thanks. I hear chicks dig scars; I wonder if they'll go for a splenectomy scar." Ryan grinned and patted his side gingerly.

"Maybe if you spend huge amounts of time at the beach with your shirt off." I laughed. It felt good to laugh. Ryan could always make me smile, and I appreciated his willingness to put the whole terrible situation behind him and joke about it.

Ryan twisted to gaze up at me from the wheelchair. "Hey, I heard about Ethan. I'm really sorry." His eyes were sympathetic and his tone serious. "I sort of figured you guys must be dating, I think we all did. I mean, that guy followed you around like no one I've ever seen, and I've followed a girl or two in the past. He was hooked for sure, so it must be really tough."

"It is." The familiar lump formed in the back of my throat at the mention of Ethan's name and I swallowed hard. Ryan had caught me off guard. Usually I mentally prepared myself for discussions of any kind regarding Ethan. I hadn't brought up his leaving to Ryan since I was trying to keep the focus on him rather than my love life, so I hadn't expected him to say anything.

"Let me know if there's anything I can do to help." He shifted in his wheelchair uncomfortably.

"Thanks, Ryan."

There was nothing he could do, nothing anyone could, but I appreciated how much my friends were trying.

Ryan's mom pulled up to the curb in her beat-up minivan before we could say anything more, while Katie and Luke followed behind in Katie's mom's sedan. Luke jumped out to give Ryan a supportive hand, helping him get settled in the front seat of the van before he and I climbed back into Katie's car and we followed Mrs. Deluca over to their house.

Ryan's mom had set up the living room like a little hospital room, pulling out the sofa bed and arranging a side table with all the stuff he would need to be comfortable. She insisted that he lie down while we visited. He tried to argue that he could walk up a flight of stairs to get to his room, but she wouldn't hear of it, citing that the doctor had said he needed to take it easy.

A twinge of missing my mom ran through me as I watched the two of them. Dad really did try, but motherly nurturing wasn't something that came instinctually to him, so it had been a long time since I'd had someone remind me to take a sweater, or check my forehead for a fever, or ask if I needed a glass of water.

After a half an hour Mrs. Deluca began making comments that Ryan really needed his rest, a not-so-subtle hint that it was time for his friends to go home. We all said good-bye, and headed back out to Katie's car.

"It's still pretty early; do you guys want to get some pizza or something?" Katie pulled out of Ryan's driveway and started towards the center of town.

"I'm not that hungry. I should probably get home. I still have some algebra waiting there for me," I replied. Ethan's letter was in my sock drawer, and all I wanted at the moment was to go home and hold in my hands, to read his words and stare at his handwriting so I could feel a small connection to him. Ryan's mention of Ethan had created a longing in me and his letter was the only thing that could help even for just a little while.

Katie and Luke dropped me off and I ran upstairs and rifled through my drawer until my fingers closed around the envelope. I flopped down on my bed, pulled the now well-worn letter out of the envelope, and traced Ethan's words with my finger.

I was almost done reading when footsteps sounded just outside my room. I jammed the letter under my pillow, just before Lucy appeared in the doorway. "Your friend seems to be improving at a nice rate." She leaned against the doorframe.

I narrowed my eyes. In the week that she'd been around, Lucy had annoyed my father with her brazenness at coming in and out of our house, warned me of all the things I needed to stop doing if I wanted to adequately protect myself, and badmouthed Ethan's lack of attentiveness in his guardianship of me. She had never tried to engage me in any sort of pleasant conversation. Why would she make such a comment now?

I nodded warily. "Yeah, Ryan's doing much better." I fought back my irritation at her sudden appearance, and the fact that she was keeping me from the one thing that made me feel the slightest bit better.

"You should be able to put your mind at ease about him now and stop concerning yourself with guilt over his accident. It's just one more distraction that keeps us from getting on with our work." Lucy rapped on the doorframe's wood.

I actually bit my tongue. Of course that was why she was mentioning Ryan; she thought my mind was too clouded with worry about his wellbeing to have an image flash.

"Right." I turned to stare out my window, hoping she would get the hint and leave.

"Have there been any images yet?" Lucy asked. I could feel her eyes on me, probably trying to read my body language to see if I would lie to her.

I sighed. "No, nothing yet. I promise you'll be the first to know if there are." I was tired of repeating myself, and this had to be the fourth or fifth time she had asked me about my flashes in the last few days.

"I think we need to take a different approach then. Until you do have a flash, obviously I won't be able to try to analyze it, but there are other things we can be working on. Ethan was hesitating with you. I don't know what his problem was, but he was holding back." My mouth dropped open as she took a step into my room. How could she even suggest such a thing?

I locked my gaze with hers, and squared my shoulders as I prepared for an argument. "All we've been working on for the past several months, from the moment Ethan recognized his sister in one of my drawings, is figuring out my ability. We've catalogued, analyzed, archived, and broken each image down until I can't stand drawing anymore. How could you possibly see that as hesitating?" I crossed my arms. Constantly having to defend Ethan was infuriating me.

"That's all well and good, but your drawings are only half of the puzzle. It's not just about figuring out your drawings, and the patterns of how they occur and why, it's also about your mind. Did Ethan ever go through any sort of mental focusing techniques with you?"

"Yes, he did. Nothing he tried worked." I recalled nights, early in the winter, of doing breathing and memory exercises. Nights before Simon had arrived and it had truly been just Ethan and me in the house. We had always started with the most serious of intentions, but through the different breathing and visualizing exercises we would be drawn into each other and he would kiss me lightly. Inevitably, those work sessions had dissolved into nights of goofing around and making out. The pleasantness of that time only made the pain of his absence more acute and I shoved the memory away.

"Fine, but did he check your brain waves during your visions to see what's happening? Do any sort of medical testing on you at all? I'll bet the answer is no, right? He wasn't in a hurry to figure this mystery out, because had a good thing going here with you. He probably worried you'd get mad at him if he poked and prodded at you too much." Lucy paced back and forth, banging the side of one hand against the palm of the other for emphasis. I stiffened at her mention of poking at me and trying to read my brain waves. Images of electrodes stuck to the sides of my head with wires running out of them came to mind. I didn't know what I would do if that was something she had in store for me.

"You want to hook me up to machines and read my brain waves?" I pulled my pillow to my chest and hugged it tightly.

"Whatever gets the job done. For now, we'll do some focus exercises and go from there," Lucy said. "I want us to go through a series of visualization and image-deprivation techniques, using your old sketches. And we're also going to start self-defense training. I can't believe Ethan didn't at least try to teach you some basic moves."

"Self-defense training? I don't really think I need that, and besides, with work and school and everything, I doubt I'll have time–"

"It won't take up any more of your time than your analysis work with Ethan did. You can come over to the bungalow after school on the days you don't work. It's spacious and your friends won't stumble in on us there. I'll teach you some simple maneuvers. That way, if I'm ever too far to reach you in a threatening situation, at least you won't be completely helpless." She stood with her posture straight as a board as she laid out her plan.

I gritted my teeth. *How dare she call me helpless and judge my open-door policy with Katie.* Lucy had already reminded me on multiple occasions that I needed to lock the door behind me when I entered my house.

She had stayed away the day Katie had—as Lucy put it—*barged in* to check on me, because we hadn't created a plausible explanation about who Lucy was and why she was in my life. We'd decided that, if and when she did meet my friends, we would tell them she was one of my mom's distant cousins, staying in the area for a job contract.

"Fine, whatever you want." I didn't even try to hide the sullen tone in my voice.

"Great, we'll start tomorrow then. I'll be downstairs working in the dining room if you need me for any reason." She gave me a self-satisfied smile and turned on her heel.

I waited a few minutes to make sure she'd reached the ground floor before I jumped off the bed and swung my bedroom door shut. I wanted a physical barrier between us. The more I got to know Lucy, the more I disliked her. Her prickly, efficient nature made Ethan's disappearance even harder to bear.

I carefully pulled his letter out from under my pillow, worried she would reappear at any moment, and reluctantly slipped it back into the envelope. With Lucy in the house, I couldn't take the chance she would discover it, and I hid it back in the bottom of my sock drawer.

Once the letter was securely away and I was lying down on my bed again, I thought about Lucy's words. Maybe Ethan had been dragging his feet about figuring out my ability. It had never felt like that to me, but in a way it made sense. It also explained why he'd been so against trying to go after the Glain Neidr, dangerous or not. But if he had been delaying the process, why? The only conclusion I could come up with was that he must have been trying to prolong our time together. My chest clenched. If that was the case, it meant that ultimately he had always known that he would eventually leave me.

Ethan had written that he would find a way back to me, but maybe the pain I'd been experiencing in the last week was inescapable. I had been his assignment after all; there was always going to be some point at which his mission with me would be over. What did I think was going to happen when that time came? He'd never once come right out and said that he was going to quit being a

Hleo for me. I had no idea how that would even work, with him being ageless. Allowing himself to be reassigned must mean that he still wanted to be a Hleo, or else wouldn't he have walked away the moment they told him he'd been caught? And if that was true, what was the point in hoping for his return? I stared up at my ceiling as these thoughts overwhelmed me and filled me with despair.

After a few minutes, I rolled over and punched my pillow in frustration, hating the way I felt. I needed to get control; I needed to take matters into my own hands. I didn't have a lot of faith in Lucy's *mental exercises*. The only thing I could think of to make all of this go away was to get my hands on the Glain Neidr. If the mystical necklace really could give me power over my visions, then I might be able to use it to figure out what my all-important decision was to be, make it, and be free from the Hleo.

The picture Ethan had painted of the dangers inherent in attempting to retrieve the necklace was grim, but that didn't mean it was impossible. Maybe Milton's journal would have some sort of clue. I rolled off my bed and sat down at my desk, firing off an email to him. I thanked him again for including me in his discovery and asked if he'd made any progress. It wasn't a huge step towards getting my life back, but at least it was a start.

Thirteen

"Okay, I want you to close your eyes, and think about the image that should come next." Lucy hovered over me, speaking in her drill-sergeant manner. I was sitting at the dining room table of her bungalow while she held up a series of my old drawings in front of me in the order they had supposedly happened. The idea being, if I could get my mind to see these images in a chronological sequence, then it would naturally fall on the image that should come next in the series.

She would show me six or seven drawings and then keep the successive picture hidden, hoping I would be able to see that image in my head and share it with her accurately without actually looking at it. I didn't seem to be able to get across to her, no matter how many times I reiterated it, that once the images were on paper they were gone from my mind. It didn't matter if I stared at one particular image for extended periods of time, or whether I watched them rapidly going by in a successive line, as I was currently doing, they wouldn't rematerialize in my mind's eye.

"Honestly, nothing's coming." I kept my eyes closed so I wouldn't have to see the blatant irritation on her face.

It was closing in on a month since Ethan's departure. Lucy had begun to push hard, trying to get somewhere with her analysis of my ability. I still hadn't flashed. It was the longest I had gone since Ethan had come into my life back in the fall. I knew it was driving her crazy since I wasn't giving her much to work with besides the old data that Ethan, Simon, and I had already gone over, but I had no control over the way my head worked. We simply had to wait.

She didn't say a word, but her long, slow exhalation of breath spoke volumes. I opened my eyes.

In the last three weeks, Lucy had taken me through breathing exercises, memory tests, and psychological analysis exams. She'd even tried hypnosis, which I'd been completely uncomfortable with. I had a feeling my anxiety over letting her into my sub-conscious had kept it from being at all effective.

"Okay, let's take a break from this and move on to self-defense tactics." Lucy strode across the room to the training area.

"Great." Sarcasm dripped from my voice, but I followed her over to her exercise circle.

We divided our time together between her mental exercises and lessons in self-defense. She'd dispensed with the couch and chair that had once sat in Ethan and Simon's little living room, and replaced it with a round mat used as a sort of wrestling ring. She would put me in pins and holds that I would then have to try to get myself out of. While I might have enjoyed the lessons if Ethan had been the one administering them, I hated every second of being in such close contact with Lucy.

I stood on my usual side of the mat, rolling my shoulders to loosen up. Lucy walked over to the wooden stand she had leaning up against the wall of her living room. It was covered in different sorts of weapons, from bo staffs to nunchucks. As of yet, she'd only been trying to teach me hand-to-hand defense skills such as how to get out of a chokehold, or flip someone over my shoulder who had grabbed me from behind, but today she grabbed two bo staffs and sauntered into the middle of the circle.

She held one of the long bamboo sticks out to me. "I would think, with all the threats you and Ethan have faced, you'd be more grateful to be getting some education on how to protect yourself." She sounded mystified as to why I wasn't gung ho to spend my afternoon getting tossed around like a rag doll.

I grabbed the stick from her, but kept my mouth shut. She never went easy on me, telling me that learning the right way meant making sure I knew how ineffectual the techniques could be if carried out incorrectly. I suspected it was just her excuse to push me around.

"I suppose you've been content to play damsel in distress up until now though, huh?" She did a few quick stretches.

My blood pumped harder, pounding in my ears. "What am I supposed to I do with this?" I spat out through gritted teeth. My knuckles were white as they gripped the stick.

"You won't always have a weapon handy, but most of the time there will be some sort of object that you can grab and improvise with. I'm going to teach you some techniques that you'll be able to utilize with any sort of long stick, a broom handle perhaps, or even an umbrella." Lucy flicked her wrist and twisted the staff in a few successive circles with the expertise of someone who clearly knew what she was doing.

"Fine." I stepped onto the mat.

She launched into the correct way to hold the staff, how to use someone's weight against them if they grabbed onto it, ways to swing the stick from the neck of an attacker down to sweep the legs out from under them. We practiced for almost an hour at these maneuvers before moving on to what to do if I came up against someone who also had some sort of long stick-type weapon.

We clashed and banged the sticks against each other in different ways until eventually she would always manage to hook hers under my legs and bring me tumbling to the ground where I inevitably landed on my rear end.

I glared up at her from where I lay sprawled out on the mat. "You know you don't have to trip me every single time." My backside was aching. I was sick of getting taken down.

"The point is for you to figure out how to keep it from happening," Lucy tapped the floor with her stick, waiting for me to stand up again.

"Maybe I don't care if I figure it out." I dragged myself to my feet.

"Of course you don't. You've had someone holding your hand and making sure you never have to be able to do anything for yourself," Lucy sneered.

I cried out, swinging the stick at her in rage. She blocked my attack with ease, and we clashed again. "You think Ethan was doing anything for you by not teaching you how to protect yourself, keeping you from experiencing the realities of what being part of the Hleo world is all about?" Lucy ducked under the stick I swung at her. She spun around as her stick connected with mine. "No matter what happens, from here on out you know about us. You will always be a liability. Even if you have your moment and you're allowed to go back to life before you knew about the Hleo, it will never be the same. There will always be the possibility that a member of the Bana will hunt you down and try to pump you for information about the society. I'm just trying to keep you from being completely defenseless when that time comes, so hopefully you won't give up too many secrets." Lucy blocked me, but I swung at her again and again, trying to break through her defenses and connect with her body.

"That's all you care about, isn't it, the Hleo society? You couldn't care less what happens to me." I brought the stick down low, trying to get to her knees, but she blocked the shot as though she was in my head and knew what I would try before I did.

"I'm protecting you because it's my job to protect you. If your last protector had been doing his job, he would have realized just how important it was to keep you from learning the truth. It's the basic principle we live by; don't let protecteds find out who we are or who they are." Lucy rolled her eyes, and I swung as hard as I could, desperately wanting to take her down a peg. My stick was about to connect with her shoulder and I felt victory coming, when she sprung to the side, sticking her staff between my ankles and twisting, so that once again I lost my balance and ended up in a heap on the floor.

"What's your problem?" I shouted up at her. I'd listened to her berate Ethan for almost a month now, and I couldn't take it anymore.

"My problem is that one of the pillars of the Hleo society committed an act of aliege." Lucy's eyes were blazing as she stood over me, clutching her stick.

"Aliege?" I furrowed my brow.

"It's our equivalent to treason. Ethan, considered one of the best, the most trustworthy and loyal to the cause, unfaltering in any situation, allowed himself to get caught up by the charms of a schoolgirl, who, as far as I can see, has little more to offer than any other person any of us has ever protected." She banged the end of her stick against the ground, shocking me with her honesty. I'd expected her to brush me off, not engage me in this fight. Her words were like a slap in the face.

"Why don't you like me?" I stayed on the ground, feeling wounded.

"It's not that I don't like *you*, exactly. I don't like this situation. The rules were broken. Ethan chose to ignore the most sacred rule concerning how we act towards protecteds, and you're the one he chose to do it with, but instead of justice being carried out, he gets to continue active duty, and I get to come here and babysit you. All of this because The Three have a special fondness for your mother, even though, from what I've seen, you're nothing like her, except maybe in your propensity to create trouble."

My eyes widened. "You knew my mother?"

"She was tough, and she knew the advantage of having the upper hand on an opponent." Before she could say more, her phone buzzed on the dining room table.

She strode past me and picked it up. "It's Veridan; I'm going to take it in the other room." Lucy crossed over to the bedroom and shut the door before I could say anything.

As I sat in the middle of her combat circle, listening to her muffled voice, the anger and frustration of the last month boiled over. I didn't want to do Lucy's mental exercises, and I didn't want her to be the one teaching me how to defend myself in a fight. I didn't want this woman who hated everything about me to be my only line of protection, and I didn't want to keep staring at Ethan's cryptic words on a page as my only connection to him. I wanted to scream, to punch things, or to run away and never think about destiny or my stupid ability again.

Before I knew what was happening, I was up off the floor and racing to the exit. I'd never even been in Ethan's backyard, but within a matter of seconds I had slipped quietly out the door, bounded down the deck stairs, and crossed the small yard, slipping into the woods that Ethan's neighborhood backed onto.

Blindly, I pushed my way through the thick brush and trees that were now lush and green after a recent wave of warm weather. The canopy overtop was full, offering shade from the sun. I'd been walking for a few minutes in no particular direction when I came across a path and followed it, if only to keep myself from getting lost.

As I walked, Lucy's words played over in my mind. Somehow I'd never considered that knowing about the Hleo could be a dangerous thing for me for the rest of my life. Up until now, Ethan had always been part of that equation, but what would happen when the day came that I had my destiny moment and the Hleo protection duty was pulled back, and declared unnecessary? Would I be able to defend myself on my own if the Bana came knocking, wanting answers about Hleo business? I needed to find Ethan.

Every facet of my life was at the mercy of the mysterious, faceless Metadas, and I was tired of trying to do what the force controlling this world wanted. Why should I care what it wanted when all I had gotten in return for my efforts was almost being murdered every once in a while, and the heartache of the one person I had ever been in love with being ripped away from me?

I reached a crossroads in the path and was standing, unsure of where to go, when my frustration overwhelmed me. "What do you want from me?" I threw my arms up and yelled at the treetops. "Why would you bring him into my life just to pull him away again? It would have been easier if I'd never met him. It's like a cruel joke, what you're doing. Pick someone else's brain to throw images into, because I am done. You hear me? I'm done." I shouted the words as firmly as I could, trying to convince whoever might be listening—and maybe myself—that I had any sort of control over the situation.

A noise like the sound of a small animal darting into brush came from behind me. I whirled around to stare in that direction, but I couldn't see anything. "Is that all I get from the great and powerful master of the universe? Silence? Because I have to say, I expected more. I mean if you're going to screw with my life so completely, then I want some sort of sign that you even exist. I want some sort of explanation about how I am supposed to function without Ethan, because it is proving to be impossible for me. He was the only thing that made this past and future vision thing remotely bearable, and now that he's gone, I just feel lost." I pressed my palms against my eyes for a moment before dropping them my sides and clenching my fists. "Do you really honestly care who I date? Aren't there more important things to worry about in this world than my love life?" If anyone *could* hear me, they would think I was a complete lunatic, but I didn't care.

The wind wove its way through the trees, causing the leaves to shudder on the branches a little, but that was it, no big earth-shattering sign to let me know The Metadas was real and that it had heard me. The anger slowly drained, until all that was left inside me was the familiar numbness I had been cloaked in since Ethan's departure. I stared at the ground, accepting what I'd already known deep down; I was being ruled by something that didn't care about me, or see me as anything more than a pawn.

I shook my head. "Of course," I whispered.

I stood for a minute, trying to swallow down the pain of being completely alone before glancing around to make sure I actually was alone.

When I saw no one, I sighed; I'd better head back to Lucy's house. She wouldn't be pleased with me for taking off on her. Three steps back on the path my foot caught on a raised root. I stumbled forward, throwing my hands out in front of me to brace myself as I smashed onto the ground. My mouth opened to cry out in frustration that, after all I'd been through, I was still clumsy and hurting myself, when something caught my eye. Hanging only a foot or so from my face, tangled tightly around the thin twigs of a bush, was a strip of material. I carefully reached for it and pulled it free. It was a long strip of light, gauzy cotton. Even though it was weathered and dirty from being exposed to the elements for a long time, I knew right away that I was holding a piece of Ethan's sister's dress. The dress he had given me to wear at the Masks Gala.

I bit my lip. It was possible that I had stumbled onto the path Adam had dragged me down the night of the gala, and happened to fall right at the perfect spot to see the piece of fabric by coincidence. *Possible, but not likely.* I had asked for a sign from the Metadas. It seemed that this was it. But what could it mean? I ran the material through my fingers, my mind going back to the moment Ethan had given me the dress, and the way he had looked at me the first time he'd seen me in it. The fear I'd felt the last time I'd been in these woods, and the relief in Ethan's eyes when it was all over and he'd dealt with Adam at the library. All those moments shared, creating bonds between us that I couldn't just sever and forget had been forged.

As I slowly trekked back out of the woods, I kept the little scrap of material tightly clutched in my hand. A sense of calm washed over me. If the Metadas didn't want Ethan and me to be together, then why would it give me a sign in the form of something personal of Ethan's? Could this be confirmation that our story was not finished, that I would be able to figure out some way to find him?

I managed to retrace my steps back to Ethan's house with a smile on my face and a newfound patience. I could deal with Lucy if it was only going to be temporary. I took a deep breath when I saw her standing on her back deck, her phone in her hand. Her glare deepened when I remerged from the woods. She would have something to say about the danger of me disappearing on her, but I could take it. She could hate me, and think that I was all that was wrong in her precious world. I could take whatever she had to throw at me, as long as I had concrete hope that someday I would see Ethan again.

Fourteen

I'd pretty much given up on the idea that Milton was going to email me back. It had been weeks since I'd contacted him and he still hadn't responded. I was sure it was because of my hasty departure the night we'd met. He was still the only real lead I had on the Glain Neidr, and the only hope I had of figuring out my ability on my own. Lucy had ramped up her mental exercises and physical training. I couldn't be sure, but I had a feeling it was a punishment for taking off on her. Either way, I was anxious to send her packing.

Monday evening, a week after I had found the material in the woods, I was sitting at the desk in my bedroom trying to finish up some reading for chemistry. The muscles in my neck were tense from sitting in one position too long, and I rubbed at them, trying to loosen them up. I dropped my hand when my computer chimed, notifying me of an incoming email. Milton's name was on the sender line and I clicked it open and scanned the words. A frown spread across my face.

```
Dear Hannah,
I appreciate your continued interest
in my work, but I find that it is
proving to be more difficult than I
had hoped. I have taken on a heavier
workload at my store, and so have had
to set aside my research for the time
being. I will contact you if I am
able to start up my efforts again,
and discover anything worth sharing.
Sincerely,
Milton Cambry
```

I narrowed my eyes, reading the message over twice. He was brushing me off. He had practically been bouncing in his seat at the coffee shop over the journal and the secrets it contained. I found it hard to believe he would simply *set it aside for the time being.* After a minute, I closed my laptop and flopped down on the bed, resting my chin in my hand.

If Milton was trying to shut me out of his search for the Glain Neidr, that made things difficult. The key to the necklace's whereabouts was in that journal, I was sure of it. But how could I learn anything if Milton wasn't in a sharing mood anymore? I drummed my fingers on my bedspread. I didn't have enough information on the Glain Neidr to look on my own. My little bits of research were nothing compared to what Milton knew. I needed him.

I straightened up on the bed and took a deep breath. I would just have to convince Milton to let me back in on his investigation. But after that 'don't call me, I'll call you' email, the only thing I could think of to change his mind about me would be a face-to-face meeting. I would have to show up at his shop and try to talk to him. I bit my thumbnail. How would I ever get over to Hartford without Lucy finding out?

I spent the rest of the night devising a plan to distract Lucy long enough for me to slip away for a few hours unnoticed. I couldn't leave my house because she was constantly keeping watch on those cameras she'd installed. I would either have to skip out on school, or leave from Katie's or one of my other friend's houses. I decided on school. Lucy never entered East Halton High; she was too worried one of my friends would see her, so she elected to stay in the parking lot, or at a property near the school, watching over me by tapping into the school's security system. East Halton High had a total of four security cameras, really only capturing activity throughout the halls of the school. Lucy had complained many times about the school's lax security, but I was glad. The camera's limited range would work to my advantage.

With my plan in place for the next day, I slipped under the covers. Now I just had to hope that Milton would be willing to talk to me.

* * *

I stared at the clock on the art room wall. I had been in class twelve minutes, and needed to get going if I was going to get back without Lucy noticing. I had everything in place. I would tell Ms. Woods that I needed supplies in Hartford. She had an incredibly relaxed attendance policy and would let people sign themselves out of class if they had a good reason, even allowing them to slip out of the old fire exit door in the back of the art room. Katie had given me a ride to school, then I had asked Kristen if I could borrow her car for a dentist appointment, promising to return it before the end of the day. I'd told Lucy I was planning on staying in the art room during what would usually be my western civilization class, trying to catch up on some work, so she wouldn't expect to see me moving through the hallways between classes. All that was left was getting from the art room to Kristen's car—which I'd made sure was parked nowhere near Lucy—without getting caught on any of the cameras. I was really starting to master the art of deception.

I slowly got up from my desk and walked over to Ms. Woods. She was helping another student with a stippling technique on canvas. I waited until she had stepped back from the work and noticed me. "Yes Hannah, is there something you need?" Her eyes glanced at the backpack slung over my shoulder, and then back to my face.

"Actually, I picked up these amazing watercolor pencils in Hartford a few months ago that work better than any other kind I've ever used. My set is almost gone, but I need them to finish the piece I'm working on right now. I was hoping you might let me sign myself out so I can go pick up another set." I tried to maintain eye contact and keep my tone casual.

She nodded. "Sure, why not?"

"Great, thanks." I started towards her office where the sign-out sheet was, but she put a hand on my arm to stop me.

"Do you have a way to get there?"

Ms. Woods knew I didn't have a car at the moment and I appreciated the concern. "I'm good. My friend is letting me borrow her car."

"Okay then. Be sure to drive safe." She smiled and let me go.

"I will." I signed myself out and walked to the back of the art room, stopping by the fire exit door. I took a few long, slow breaths, psyching myself up for the next part of my plan.

Lucy had two different spots she liked to park in while I was at school. From one, in the school lot, she had a direct view of the art room's fire escape door, but from the other, the driveway of an abandoned property near the football field, she didn't. She'd been stationed in the school's parking lot for the last few days. I knew she liked to change it up every couple of days or so, but ultimately I only had a fifty-fifty chance that she wouldn't see me exiting the school.

I slid the door open, just wide enough to squeeze through. Once outside, I hunched down and strode to the back of the school, staying close to the wall. A chain link fence ran the perimeter of the back of the school, with a narrow passageway between it and the school's brick wall. Besides the occasional student trying to sneak a quick smoke, the space didn't see a lot of action. I'd only used it one other time, but it was the only way to get to the front of the school building without going by Lucy. I crept my way around until I saw Kristen's Volvo just where she had said she parked it, in the much smaller front parking lot. Most students didn't even bother trying for a spot there because they always went to the same people, Kristen being one of them. I glanced around for any sign of Lucy; so far so good. I ducked down at the corner of the school, using a decorative hedge for cover. Kristen's car was about one hundred feet from me, all I had to do was get to it and get out of the parking lot unnoticed and I would be home free.

I took a breath, stayed low, and ran towards her driver's side door, praying that I wouldn't trip over my own feet. Within thirty seconds or so I had the door open, the engine running, and I was backing out of the parking space, ready to go confront Milton in Hartford.

I made good time getting to Hartford, driving faster than I probably should have, but I had a very tight deadline. As it stood, I would only have about fifteen minutes to talk to Milton before I had to turn around again, if I wanted to get back to the school before the end of the day.

The street Milton's store was on was pretty busy and I had to settle for a parking space about six stores down from his. I hopped out of Kristen's car, making sure to lock the doors, and strode down the sidewalk. As I got closer to Milton's storefront my nerves kicked into high gear. The windows had been boarded up with planks of wood. The front door had a big spray-painted sign hanging on it, *closed*. I peered through the gaps in the boards, and gasped. It had been overstocked and messy the first time I was here, but now Milton's store was destroyed. Tables were overturned, the glass cabinets had been knocked over, and broken glass was lying everywhere. I swallowed hard, anxious to know if Milton had been the victim of a petty robbery or something more sinister. The lock on the door looked like it had been pried loose, and I twisted the knob. It was still locked, but as I leaned on the door I could feel that it wouldn't take a lot of effort to push my way in. Breaking into Milton's store wasn't ideal, but I had to know what was going on, and if he was okay.

I glanced around. There wasn't anybody on the street nearby, but I didn't want to take the chance that someone was watching from inside one of the stores who might call the police, so I pulled my house key from my bag and pretended to insert it into the lock. I took a deep breath and pushed my shoulder against the door as hard as it would go. It took two strong shoves, but the door swung open, leaving the lock hanging from the doorframe.

I stood in the doorway surveying the damage, and there was a lot of damage. Books had been ripped apart, china had been smashed to bits, and the bigger pieces of furniture had been destroyed. After pushing the door shut behind me, I stepped farther into the dark space, not sure if I should call out for Milton so that if he did happen to be there I wouldn't scare him, or if I should stay quiet for my own safety.

Staying silent seemed more prudent, and I slowly maneuvered my way to the back of the store where Milton's office was, trying not to disturb anything on my way. The door to the office was shut. I took a deep breath, worried about what could be waiting for me on the other side, then turned the knob and let the door swing open. The office was in the same torn-apart shambles the sales floor had been. Drawers were pulled out and a few were lying upside down on the floor. The table had been overturned and papers were scattered everywhere. I skimmed one lying near my foot. Milton's research on the Glain Neidr. His newspaper clippings, his photocopies, all the articles he'd amassed on the stone were now strewn about his little kitchen office area.

    The strangest thing, however, was Milton's computer. A laptop sat on the counter by the sink, plugged in and turned on. I walked over to it, and my breath caught in my throat. The email he had sent me was displayed on the screen. I backed away, an ominous premonition spreading over me.

    I tried to keep my breathing even as I strode towards the front of the store and exited out onto the street, pulling the door shut behind me as best I could. Hugging my arms around my waist, I scanned every direction for any sign of someone watching me while I made my way back to Kristen's car. Once I was safely inside with the doors locked, and on the highway headed for East Halton, I exhaled a deep, shaky breath.

    There was no way the damage done to Milton's store was due to a robbery. The computer and other valuables I'd noticed among the wreckage would have been long gone. Whoever had broken in had clearly been searching for something, and I had a strong feeling that something was the journal Milton had stumbled onto. What about the email though? I pursed my lips. Had Milton written the email before he'd been attacked? Or had he been forced to write it by whoever had wrecked his store? An even scarier thought came to mind: what if Milton hadn't written that email at all? I wondered where he was, and if he was okay. A shiver ran up my spine; no matter how it had gone down, ultimately someone out there, likely a member of the Bana, knew that I was on the hunt for the Glain Neidr necklace.

    As I approached East Halton, I glanced in the rearview mirror. As far as I could tell, the coast was clear, but I didn't completely trust my ability to identify if a car was following me or not.

    I had to find Ethan. It was the only option I had left. Lucy was no help. I wasn't completely convinced she would put herself out to keep me safe at all costs. And now Milton was … well I didn't really want to think about what had become of Milton Cambry.

    I got back to East Halton High, parked, and went on with my day as though nothing had happened. After school, Katie dropped me off at The Patch for a shift. I manned the cash register distractedly, wanting to feel relieved that it seemed I had pulled off my escape from Lucy, but instead feeling terrified for my safety. I needed to figure out a way to find Ethan. I had a feeling my life was in very real, and very imminent, danger, and he was the only one who could help me.

Fifteen

Three days after I had gone to Milton's store, I woke up to the sound of a bird chirping loudly near my window. The bright red numbers on the clock beside my bed caught my eye and I groaned; I didn't have to wake up for another hour. I rolled over and tried to force myself back to sleep, but I couldn't, not today. From the way the light was flooding into my room I could tell that it was going to be a sunny day, a perfect sort of weather day, but I just couldn't make myself enjoy it.

May twelfth, officially a month since Ethan's mysterious departure, and my birthday. I sighed as I stared at the wall, the covers pulled up around my neck in a warm, comforting cocoon. Usually I liked my birthday; I didn't need a huge fuss from my friends and family, but being in May the weather usually warmed up enough to do something fun outdoors, and Katie loved being able to come up with creative ways to celebrate, which always proved to be memory-making. But this year was different. I'd been excited at the thought of spending my birthday with Ethan, celebrating turning a year older and drawing a year closer to his recurring age of twenty-one. It would have been our first birthday celebration together. I'd found out after the fact that his official birthday was September twenty-seventh, not that he thought much about it anymore.

Now my birthday was just another day without him; another day with little more than a letter that might contain a secret message, a strip of material acting as a sign of my possible future with Ethan, and the fear that the Bana were closing in on me.

Mentally preparing for the day, I hauled myself out of bed, shut my alarm off with over ten minutes left before it would beep, and trudged to the shower.

My cell was buzzing on my dresser when I walked back into the bedroom twenty minutes later, freshly clean and wrapped in a towel. For a split second I was filled with hope that Ethan had found a way to contact me, but it was Katie. I sighed, then reminded myself that her early morning call could only be to wish me a happy birthday, and grabbed the phone.

"Happy Birthday, chica," Katie greeted happily before I could even say hello.

I couldn't help but smile. "Thank you, Katie."

"Just wanted to be the first one to wish you every happiness on this, the day of your birth," Katie continued dramatically.

I rolled my eyes. "Thanks, Kate. I'll see you at school, okay?"

"I'm looking forward to it," she replied in a singsong, mischievous tone.

I narrowed my eyes as I hung up. What could she have planned? After slipping my phone into my pocket, I headed downstairs for a quick bite to eat before going to school.

When I arrived at East Halton High, my friends were already standing by my locker. Something was up. "Good morning, everyone." I reached for my lock, but kept my eyes on them.

"Morning," they replied, more or less in unison. I laughed and shook my head.

I spun the combination on my lock while my friends all kept their eyes on me. As soon as I had the door unlocked, it flew open and a bunch of helium balloons pushed their way out into the hallway. Behind the balloons was some sort of confetti cannon that shot a spray of colorful little circles right into my face and hair. Everyone burst out laughing.

"And I wondered why you were all staring and grinning at me." I scrunched up my face and dusted bits of confetti out of my hair and off my shoulders. Other students shuffled past, some extending birthday wishes to me as they went.

"Polka dots suit you." Heather helped me brush the hard-to-reach pieces of paper off my back.

"Thanks." I shook my hair, trying to get the last bits of confetti out of it.

"I figured your last birthday as a high school student needed a memorable beginning, and everyone agreed." Katie tugged the balloons down from the ceiling by their strings and tied them to my locker door.

"Plus we got to shoot stuff at you." Ryan motioned to the now-empty cannon.

"Always appreciated," I replied wryly. Once I'd cleaned myself off, I noticed a sparkly homemade box decorated with construction paper, sequins, and glitter glue sitting in the bottom of my locker. A group picture had been pasted to the top. My stomach lurched at the sight of Ethan standing beside me in the shot, smiling and looking like he belonged amongst my group of friends. My fingers grazed over the unfamiliar image gently as I forced away the emotions, shoving them down before they could overtake me. I repressed a smile and spun around to face Luke and Ryan.

"Guys, you shouldn't have. I'm touched that you would go to so much effort for me." I pressed a hand to my chest dramatically and held up the little decorative box for the girls to see.

"Ha, I thought you knew I'm more of a feather man with my arts and crafts projects." Ryan sniffed, and I burst out laughing.

"So who is *actually* responsible for this?" I swiveled from Kristen and Heather on one side of me to Katie, standing by her locker on the other.

"It was a collaborative effort. Kristen took the picture the night we all went to that terrible Mexican restaurant. You remember, right?" Katie pointed to the photograph. "I put together the box and Heather is responsible for its contents."

"Well, it's nice, very sparkly." I started to lift the lid to find out what was inside, but Katie brought a hand down swiftly over mine to stop me and snatched the box away.

"Wait, you can't open it yet." Katie held the box away from me and wagged her finger in my face. "There's a surprise inside that's meant for after school, you'll just have to be patient."

"That's not fair; why wouldn't you just give it to me after school then?" I crossed my arms, pretending to protest since I knew it would delight my friends for me to act a little outraged at having to wait.

"That's the fun part. You can be thinking and wondering all day about what could be inside." Kristen wriggled her eyebrows.

I nodded, resigned to playing along. "All right, I'll leave it for now, but this is going to be hard."

Katie stuck the box back into my locker, giving me a warning look not to touch it. It wouldn't be hard to wait though. I would never let my friends know, but the only thing that box could contain that would excite me was a letter with the location of Ethan, and a way to get to him. I highly doubted they had been able to pull that off.

School went by quickly. I was able to finish a painting for art class. I'd decided that a sketch of one of my flashes from a few years earlier, of a couple sitting on the end of a dock gazing out over a lake at sunset, would be easy to copy and make a decent painting.

With all the Hleo stuff I'd been dealing with, I had let my art class work slip, and now I was left with four big pieces to complete by the end of the term, which was only a little more than a month away. I knew I could do it, but it wouldn't be my best work.

When I got to my locker at the end of the day, Katie was the only one standing there. A point I found a little odd since I knew everyone was waiting for me to open the picture box.

"Where is everybody?" I gently picked up the box and handed it to Katie to hold while I got my backpack ready to take home.

"Oh, we're going to meet up with them a little later," Katie replied cryptically.

"All right," I said warily as Katie handed me back the box. "So it's okay for me to open this now?" I slipped a finger under the lid, ready to flip it.

"Go for it." She leaned in close so she would be able to see whatever was inside too. I carefully pushed the lid open to reveal a white porcelain figure skate lying on a square of pink silk that had been carefully tucked in around the little object.

"Okay." I tried to sound enthusiastic about the gift, when really I was just confused.

"I wasn't sure if you would get it, but think back to your previous birthdays, does this stand out as significant for any of them?"

I stared at the little skate hard. After a minute or so, I remembered that we had gone skating at the town arena for my eighth birthday. It had been a cold spring, and the town had decided to extend the life of the ice rink until the middle of May.

"My eighth birthday?" I shrugged, still not sure if I was on the right track.

"Yeah, so you do remember, excellent. Okay, I'll explain. This is the first clue for your mega-amazing birthday treasure hunt. Using the different clues we've come up with, we are going to make our way around East Halton, visiting different locations your birthdays have taken place over the years until we arrive at your big treasure, the location of tonight's festivities." Katie clapped her hands together. She clearly thought this was the greatest idea ever.

I grinned. After all my work with Lucy, I could really use a night of normal fun, and revisiting old birthday spots sounded like the perfect distraction. "If this clue is about my eighth birthday, then I guess we're headed to the arena?"

Katie linked her arm through mine. "To the arena." She charged down the now-empty school hallway.

We hurried to Katie's car, leaving my new replacement Mazda hatchback parked in the school lot. We zipped across town in the direction of the old dome building that housed the town's ice rink in winter, and various concerts, craft shows, and other events the rest of the year. The parking lot was empty when we arrived, and we made our way to the entrance. I wasn't sure if the building would even be unlocked, but Katie confidently grabbed the handle and yanked it open. We walked into the gray and green concrete entryway, past the walls of trophy cases displaying awards and pictures of the town's different sports teams, towards the space that usually held the rink. It was gone for the season, but as soon as we pulled the doors open to the expansive arena area I could see that someone was standing in the middle of the cement floor, right where center ice would be. He was in the shadows, but when we got closer I could make out Luke's blond mop of hair.

"Hey." I waved as we made our way over to him in the echoing space.

"How'd you do? Did you know right away what the skate was about?" He gave me an encouraging smile.

"I needed a little help from Katie," I admitted.

"Well, I'm sure you'll get this one right away." Luke brought a small box out from behind his back. I took it from him and gingerly pulled the lid off, revealing the figure of a small brown horse.

"A horse." I wrinkled my nose and racked my brain. The only birthday that came to mind involving horses was my eleventh. East Halton had held a spring fair to raise money to beautify the main street, and it had happened to fall on the weekend of my birthday. My parents had taken me and my friends to the fair instead of the traditional party at my house. There had been a ride with ponies, four little horses connected in an X configuration that walked in a circle for a few spins. It was the only time I could remember ever being on a horse.

"The spring fair with the pony ride when I was eleven?" I raised an eyebrow.

"You got it." Katie clapped her hands together gleefully.

"So I guess we're off to the fairgrounds?" I glanced from Luke to Katie. They both nodded and we headed back out of the arena again.

"By the way, how did you guys get in here?" I asked when we reached the foyer area.

"My cousin refs hockey here in the winter, and he lent me his key." Luke held up a brass key ring.

I nodded. "Nice."

From the arena, Katie took me to the fairgrounds and all over East Halton collecting little trinkets and my friends along the way. Each one had been stationed at a different location where one of my previous birthdays had been held.

By the time we arrived back at my house—what I assumed was the final stop—I'd collected a skate, a horse, a shopping bag from the birthday I'd spent at The Patch, a toy golf club from Pirate Pete's mini golf course, chopsticks from Chen's Family Restaurant, as well as a ton of take-out food, a mermaid cake that was impressively similar to the one my mom had made me when I was seven, and a little stuffed clown. Each item led me to my next stop, stirring up great old memories at the same time. The clown, my last clue, represented my tenth birthday. My mom had hired a clown to come perform the usual party tricks, but he'd been terrible. He told horrible jokes, couldn't do balloon animals, and eventually just stood around in my backyard looking bored until my dad told him to leave.

Ms. Wood's car was parked in the driveway when we pulled in. She and Dad were sitting at the kitchen table as my friends and I made our way inside, and they got up to join us in the front hallway.

"It didn't take you too long to get this far," Dad commented as we piled into the living room.

"I think I've done pretty well." I tilted my chin up proudly.

"You have. I believe one more clue ought to do it." Dad glanced over at Ms. Woods, who headed into his study. She emerged after a few seconds, holding a little box covered in vintage-looking wrapping paper.

"It's so nice I almost don't want to open it and wreck the paper." I held the box delicately in my hands.

"Don't worry about that." Ms. Woods waved her hand dismissively. "I got it at the dollar store in town, it only looks old."

"Okay, here goes." I ripped open the last of the clues on my birthday treasure hunt and pulled out a little handmade glass ornament of a sand castle. My breath caught at the sight of it. My mother had owned one just like it. It had been hers as a child, and I'd accidentally knocked it off the ledge in her bedroom when I was about nine, shattering it into a million pieces. Even though Mom had assured me it was okay, and that accidents happen, I'd always felt terrible about destroying a personal treasure from her childhood.

"Where did you get this?" I looked from Dad to Katie in amazement, trying to figure out who was responsible for such a meaningful gift.

"I remember you always admired your mother's when you were a child, and after that unfortunate accident with it, I had always wanted to be able to replace it for her. Rose and I were in an antique store in Boston last month when I had that research seminar and I saw it there." Dad grinned knowingly, obviously remembering the memories attached to the little item as well as I did.

"Your dad showed me the sand castle and that's how this whole thing started. I thought it would be fun to give you a bunch of trinket gifts and reminisce a little." Katie nudged my arm with her elbow.

"Thanks so much for all of this, it's been really fun. I feel a little old after thinking about all my different birthdays, but it was still very fun." I laughed and put the castle carefully back in the box before setting it on the coffee table.

"We're not exactly done yet. This is still a clue, so where do you think we're headed?" Kristen lifted a hand in the air.

My eyes widened. "The beach!"

"She got it," Ryan joked, as though it would've been difficult for me to figure out.

I thanked Dad again for the little sand castle, and left the other items sitting with it on the coffee table. Then my friends and I headed off to the beach for the official festivities.

We drove to The Sutcliffe Inn. Ryan's mom worked there, and she had given him access to their private beach area for the evening. It was a private cove with one hundred feet of sandy waterfront, beautifully manicured and set away from the public beaches. Rows of plush lounge chairs sat near the back boundary of the beach, just at the bottom of a wide set of stone stairs that curved through the embankment down to the shore. A large bonfire pit was situated off to the far side, with a fire already burning brightly. Blankets, a cooler, and other party necessities, including speakers, had been piled on the lounger closest to the fire, and my friends headed straight over to the gear. Heather and Kristen grabbed the blankets and got the Chinese food we'd picked up during our scavenger hunt ready to dish out, while the guys poked at the fire, throwing a few more logs on top of it.

After we'd dug into the food and the mermaid cake, we all relaxed and hung around enjoying the warm May evening.

A low wall of stacked rocks and boulders created a jetty that blocked the private beach from the public on the west side, and I climbed up and settled down, crossed-legged, on a flat rock. The sun had almost set, the last of the pink and orange hues fading as the deep blue of evening sky enveloped them. My friends danced and joked around in the glow of the bonfire light, and a smile crossed my lips. They had gone to so much work just to give me a great birthday.

Ryan clambered up the rocks, moving slowly because of his lingering injuries, and plunked down beside me.

"So what do you think Hanns, how'd we do?" Ryan shoved his good shoulder against mine playfully.

"Be careful, you don't want to hurt yourself any more than you already have," I warned in a motherly tone.

"I'm fine, don't be silly. But really, are you having fun?" He tone became serious.

I turned to stare at him. "Of course! This is probably the best birthday I've ever had."

"So it worked, then?"

I frowned. Katie was standing near the fire pit, but she clearly heard him. Her head whipped around and she glared at Ryan, then stalked over and started climbing up the rocks towards us.

"What worked?" My eyebrows furrowed together.

"You were so busy you forgot all about him." Ryan leaned close, his eyes wide. Immediately I understood what he meant.

"Why are you such a dolt? How can she forget about him if you bring him up?" Katie's blonde curls gyrated wildly while she raged at Ryan.

"Oh, right," Ryan muttered; his gaze dropped to his feet.

I patted his arm. "That's okay; it did work, for a little while at least."

"Shove off, loser." Katie knelt behind him and pushed on his good shoulder, forcing him to move.

"Ouch." He whimpered, probably hoping for sympathy, but Katie continued to glare at him. Ryan stood and hobbled back over to Luke and Mark, who were trying to balance on a pile of rocks they'd stacked together.

Katie flopped down into the space where Ryan had just been. "I can't believe he did that, after all my hard work."

"Hey, it's okay; the attempt is definitely appreciated. This has been an amazing birthday." I draped my arm around Katie's shoulders.

Katie sighed. "Yeah."

We both stared out over the water for a bit. The lake was calm and the large full moon reflected in a perfect circle off the waves, giving a luminescent glow to everything for miles.

"I had this great plan, though." Katie's face fell. "I wanted you to go through the whole treasure hunt and then I thought we could end up here and the ultimate treasure would be Ethan standing on the beach holding a rose and waiting for you. It was supposed to be all romantic and everything, but I couldn't make it happen. I'm sorry, Hanns."

My stomach kicked with disappointment that Katie hadn't been able to bring Ethan back, even though I already knew that would have been impossible.

"I mean, it's like he's disappeared off the face of this earth. I couldn't find him on Facebook or Instagram; I even did a general Google search for him and nothing. I guess you guys really took it seriously when you said no contact." Katie picked up a pebble and flung it into the water.

I knew she didn't mean anything by it, but her observation that Ethan seemed to have disappeared off the earth rang too true, and the ache in my stomach grew stronger. "It's the way it has to be."

Heather and Kristen sank down beside us, laughing and giggling. Apparently the guys had tried to talk them into going skinny-dipping, but they had refused, and joined us on the big rock to make sure their point was made.

We stayed at the beach until the bonfire died down and all that was left were a few smoldering embers. As we gathered our stuff up and headed back to our vehicles, I thanked all my friends repeatedly for the great evening.

When I got back home, Ms. Woods and Dad were sitting in the living room watching some old black-and-white movie. I recognized the leading man as a classic actor from the 1950s, but couldn't remember his name off the top of my head.

"So, how was your night?" Ms. Woods sat up straighter on the couch as I joined them. She'd been leaning on Dad's shoulder affectionately, but placed a polite gap between the two of them in my presence.

"It was really fun. I can't believe how much work Katie and everyone went to." I balanced on the edge of the armchair. I really did have a great collection of people in my life.

"You deserve it; you're a pretty terrific person." Ms. Woods rested a hand on my knee.

"Thanks, Ms. Woods."

"I wholeheartedly agree." Dad smiled.

I rolled my eyes. "Thanks, Dad."

"I guess it's getting late. I should be going." Ms. Woods stood.

"I'll walk you out," Dad said.

We all sauntered towards the front door. My intention was to keep going and head on upstairs to my room, but Ms. Woods stopped me. "Oh Hannah, I think Katie must have sent me one of the treasure hunt items, but then forgot and asked me to do the sand castle with your dad instead. She mailed it in a letter to me, but when I opened the letter there was an envelope with your name on it, and something bulky inside. I didn't open it since I figured it was somehow related to your party, and technically addressed to you. I left it sitting on the table there." Ms. Woods pointed to the plain white envelope lying innocently on the hall table.

"Thanks Ms. Woods, I'll check it out, but I honestly don't know what more she could have included." I picked up the envelope and headed for the stairs, curious about what could be inside. As I walked, I turned the envelope over in my hand and a funny feeling came over me. For some reason, I didn't think it was from Katie; the address was typed, not her style, and it didn't make sense that she would mail something she could easily have passed off to Ms. Woods at school. I pulled the outer envelope apart so I could see the inner one, and stopped dead in my tracks on the stairs. My name was written on the plain white envelope in Ethan's handwriting.

I twisted around to look at Ms. Woods, wanting to grill her for more details, but I sensed that she and my dad were waiting for some privacy to say a proper good-night. "Uh, thanks Ms. Woods, see you later," I quickly mumbled and raced to my room. I flopped down on my bed and tore at the envelope, desperate to see what Ethan had sent me.

There was no letter, only a marble figure that looked like a large chess piece. It fell out of the envelope and landed on my bed. I scooped it up and examined it. It was a bronze-colored decorative column with a strange symbol I didn't recognize on the top of it, three flat five-point flowers connected to each other by one tip and enclosed in a thin metal circle. On each petal was a little engraving that sort of had the appearance of a star, except the tip that pointed to the center of the flower was slightly longer than the rest. The object had a round base, wide enough to sit on a flat surface, and the whole thing measured a little longer than my middle finger. The bottom of the base was made of gold-colored metal, with the same symbol etched into it, except for the addition of a fancy scroll letter H right in the middle where the flowers met. I frowned. *H for Hannah?* I bit my lip. Why would Ethan send me a stamp?

It was clear that Ethan was trying to send me some sort of secret message, but I had no idea what that message could be. I turned the marble piece over in my hand and my lips curled up in a smile. Even if I didn't know for sure what it was, or what it meant, ultimately Ethan had reached out to make sure I knew he was still thinking about me. I breathed a small sigh of relief as I went to bed clutching the little figure in my hand. It really had been a good birthday.

Sixteen

I climbed into the driver's seat of my new Mazda, making sure to stick Ethan's present in the cup holder so it was close by. I'd kept it near me from the moment I had received it. School had just ended for the day and I was on my way to work, ready for another busy shift at The Patch. The store's business was picking up again with locals eagerly looking to buy new summer pieces, and since Memorial Day weekend was right around the corner, the town already had a handful of tourists drifting through, gearing up for the summer season.

It had been just over a week since my birthday, and I still had no idea why Ethan would have sent me a stamp with my initial on it, or how it tied in with the letter he'd sent to Katie. I was trying not to get frustrated, but I wished Ethan hadn't been so cryptic with his clues. He had far too much faith in my deduction skills.

Carmen and I were busy most of the night, helping people try on things and restocking shelves. I manned the cash and had to stay nearby it most of the evening to handle the line. At seven there were still a handful of straggler shoppers that seemed in no hurry to be on their way. It was almost twenty after seven by the time Carmen was able to lock the door and begin balancing the register.

I tidied up while she did paperwork and then I came around and stood beside her, waiting patiently for her to finish. I'd stuck Ethan's little treasure in my bag and I fished it out to play with while I waited. I tried not to have it out in the open when I knew Lucy would be around, on the off chance the stamp had something to do with the Hleo, but she'd never graced the Patch with her presence.

She'd backed off a little after my birthday; we'd only trained one day since then, and she appeared to be reverting to a more covert surveillance strategy. I hadn't seen her around the house at all. Part of me wondered if it had to do with my lack of flashing. That she had come to believe her presence was hindering my ability.

"Are you thinking of making all your correspondence very official?" Carmen pointed at Ethan's gift.

"I'm sorry, what?" I set the little item on the counter.

"The wax stamp you're holding. It's a bit old-fashioned for my taste, but hey, if you're thinking of bringing out your inner renaissance chick, I say go for it." Carmen shrugged.

"Wax stamp?" I ran my thumb across the metal etching on the base.

"Yeah, centuries ago, important families would seal their mail by pressing their family symbol into wax to close the letter. I'm surprised, with your history-buff dad and all, you didn't know that." Carmen sounded pleased with herself.

I had wondered why the bottom wasn't rubbery, but a metal etching being pressed into soft wax made total sense. *How did I not realize that from the start?*

"So it's a family's letter stamp." I stared at it, frowning.

"I think so. I just figured you had it because it has the letter H on it, as in Hannah, but yes, it looks like it would be for a specific family." The record that was currently playing began to skip and Carmen rushed over to grab the needle on the turntable. "I hate when it does that." She lifted the vinyl LP and slid it back into its jacket before filing it away on the record wall. "Why do you have it if you didn't know what it was for?" Carmen contemplated me.

"A friend sent it to me as a joke. Thanks for helping me figure it out." I slipped the letter stamp back into my bag. *Why would Ethan send this to me?*

"No problem," Carmen replied.

I left the Patch shortly after. When I got home I made sure Lucy wasn't around and then headed off to Dad's study. Maybe he would be able to give me some insight into Ethan's mysterious gift. Thankfully he was sitting at his desk, a well-worn copy of *The Pilgrim's Progress* in his hands. When I entered the room, he glanced up.

104

"Hey Dad, I was wondering if you could help me with something." I sat down on the chair across from him and dug around in the bottom of my bag.

"And good evening to you too, Hannah."

"Sorry, good evening. Do you know what this is?" I set the wax stamp on the desk between us. I didn't want to taint Dad's observations with any preconceived ideas, but I hoped he'd confirm what Carmen had told me.

Dad placed a marker in his book before setting it down on the desk, and then he picked up the little object and examined it closely. "It appears to be an old-fashioned wax letter stamp. From the looks of it I would say it's a modern-day reproduction though. I'm guessing it's for a family with a surname beginning with H. Is there more you'd like to know about it?"

"And you're sure about that?" I leaned forward across the desk.

"Well, the H is a dead giveaway about the surname." Dad tapped the etching on the bottom of the stamp and grinned. I rolled my eyes.

"But besides that, this symbol on the top seems to be a modernized representation of a family crest. See these little flowers, these are called cinquefoils because of their five points, and the little stars inside of them are referred to as ermines. Both of these symbols are commonly used in the ancient art of heraldry." Dad ran a finger over each item.

"So, any clue which family's symbol this might be?" I held my breath.

"Oh Hannah, I have no idea. Both of these symbols were used on hundreds of family crests throughout the years in different variations." Dad shook his head and my shoulders slumped. I had known it was unlikely that the specific family's crest would be recognizable from just a few symbols, but with Dad's expertise in history, I had been hopeful.

He took in my reaction and his eyes narrowed. "Where did you get it?"

I bit my lip. Should I let him in on my secret? Dad had been pleasant to Lucy, but I knew he had no real fondness for her, so I wasn't worried he would spill the beans if I did tell him the truth. I glanced at the door of his office, listening to make sure she hadn't come in undetected, but for now we seemed to be on our own. I traced a finger along the wood grain on the top of Dad's desk. "Ethan sent it to me on my birthday. Actually, he sent it to Rose. She passed it on to me, thinking it was from Katie, remember? Anyway, right after he left, he sent me a note saying he was sorry for leaving and that he would figure out a way to come back. Then he sent me this without any sort of explanation. I'm trying to figure out how the two things go together and what Ethan is trying to tell me."

Dad's brows furrowed. He was quiet for a minute. What could he possibly think of my vanished ageless boyfriend sending me cryptic correspondence?

"Hannah, you know Ethan better than I do; is it possible he was simply sending you something with an H on it for Hannah, to let you know he's still working on his plan?"

I sighed. "I guess so, but for some reason it feels more significant than that." I picked up the letter stamp and ran my thumb over the flowers in the circle.

"Okay, what are your thoughts?" Dad clasped his hands in front of him on the desk.

"I don't know. What if this symbol is for the family surname of the protected Ethan has been assigned to now, and he wants me to figure out who he's protecting so maybe I can use the name to find him or something?" I stared at the little crest.

"That could be a possibility, but you aren't even sure Ethan is protecting someone new. And if he is, I know you don't want to hear this Hannah, but Ethan could be on the other side of the world. I really hope he wouldn't expect you to traipse across the globe in search of him. That doesn't seem overly prudent." Dad frowned with fatherly concern.

My desire to defend Ethan in every situation kicked in, but I bit my tongue. I couldn't see Dad appreciating me telling him that I would gladly go to the ends of the earth if it meant finding Ethan.

"I guess not. I'm sure I'm just reading into it too much. It's probably like you said, the H for Hannah thing, and Ethan just sent the best thing he could find as a birthday present."

I didn't believe what I was saying, though. I had no reason to be, but I was convinced I was right, that the family crest on the letter stamp was somehow connected to where Ethan was now.

"I think the best thing you can glean from this is that Ethan is still trying to make it work, just give him some more time." Dad reached across the desk and covered my hand with his.

"Yeah, you're right. Thanks for the information." I squeezed his hand and then stood to leave.

"Actually, while you're here, there's something I've been wanting to talk to you about." Dad cleared his throat.

"What's up?" I hoped he would make it quick. I wanted to start in on my search for the surname that belonged to this family crest.

He shifted in his seat. "I know this is last minute and I should have talked to you earlier, but I've been putting it off. Rose and I were thinking of going away tomorrow for the Memorial Day weekend, but I wasn't sure how you would feel about that after everything that's occurred with Ethan."

I shook my head. "Dad, I'm fine. Of course you can go away for the weekend." I offered him the most sincere smile I could muster.

"You're absolutely certain?" Dad ran a hand across his forehead.

"I promise. I'm sure Katie will be around, and I have lots of homework."

"Okay then. We'll be heading out fairly early tomorrow morning so I won't wake you, but I'll leave a note telling you where we'll be and how you can reach me."

"Sounds good. Have fun and don't worry about me." I slid the stamp back in my bag and left to go upstairs, energized to think that I may have a lead that would help me find Ethan.

Seventeen

I shut my bedroom door behind me and grabbed my laptop, ready to begin my investigation of all the H family crests that had cinquefoils and ermines in them. I had settled in on my bed, my fingers resting on the keys, ready to type my information into Google, when a pulsing throb began between my eyes. I pressed a hand to my forehead, about to try and rub away the pain, when I got a flash, a middle-aged couple sitting on an outside stone patio at a fancy restaurant. Fields of grape vines stretched behind them under a starry night sky.

No sooner had the image materialized than it whipped past my mind's eye and was replaced by another flash, a little girl in bright yellow rubber boots splashing in puddles on a country lane.

The pulsing sensation grew and another flash replaced the second one, a man sitting in the food court of a mall eating a plate of noodles, surrounded by busy shoppers.

I squeezed my eyes shut and gripped my bedding, willing the images to stop, but another flash popped into view, and then another and another. My breathing had sped up and lightheadedness pushed at the corners of my mind until I gasped and everything went dark.

"Hannah, Hannah can you hear me?" A man's voice rang in my ear, and someone tapped my cheeks gently.

I opened my eyes and my dad's very concerned face came into view. I winced as I looked around, my head still pounding. I was lying on the floor beside my bed. "What happened?"

"I was hoping you could tell me. I heard a thud and ran upstairs to find you unconscious on the floor." Dad placed a supportive hand behind my back and helped me up onto the bed.

I took a few slow breaths. Gradually my head cleared and the pain dissipated. "I don't know. I got a bunch of flashes all at once. It sort of overloaded my brain I guess, and I passed out." I pressed my fingertips to my temples.

Dad sank down beside me on the bedspread. "Has this ever happened before? I thought you only ever had one flash at a time."

I bit my lip and turned to stare at the full moon shining brightly through my bedroom window. "I do, or I did. I've never had more than one at a time. Ever." *What is going on with my brain?*

"Hmm. That's very strange. I wonder what it could mean." Dad rubbed my back soothingly. "Are you sure you're okay? That's the important thing."

I hesitated, doing a quick mental check to make sure that everything felt okay, but just as quickly as the feeling had come it was gone again. "I am, honestly. I feel completely normal again."

Dad studied me, as though to make sure I was being truthful.

"I promise, Dad. I'm fine. Maybe Lucy's concentration exercises are working."

"You think that's what it could be?"

"It's the only thing that I've been doing differently the last few weeks." I sighed. "I guess I better call her and inform her of this new development."

"Take a moment to breathe. You can always inform Lucy later. Make sure you're really all right before you try to figure this out."

"Thanks, Dad. I'm good. I'll call Lucy while you pack for your weekend with Ms. Woods." I reached for my phone, which was sitting beside my laptop on the bed.

"I don't think I should leave you alone."

"Dad." I cocked my head to the side. "Don't cancel your plans. This was a one-time weirdo thing, I'm sure of it." I waved a dismissive hand.

Dad's frown didn't lessen.

"Please." I locked eyes with him, doing my best to give him a convincing grin.

He sighed. "All right. But if you feel at all off, please yell." He stood and moved to the door.

I nodded. "I will."

He gave me one more once-over before backing out of my room and closing the door.

I waited for a moment, then I moved the laptop to my desk and flopped back on my bed. *Now what?* I had to tell Lucy, but what was she going to do with this new information?

I gripped my phone, resting the edge of it against my lips. Maybe before contacting Lucy I should try to see if I was able to bring the jumble of images back to the forefront of my mind. I settled my head against my pillows so that, if I passed out again, at least I would be comfortable, and closed my eyes. Taking a deep breath, I thought of the first image. Immediately the vineyard patio restaurant appeared in front of me. I concentrated on the woman's face and it sharpened into focus. It was lined with age, but still had a refined elegance. Her eyes were a piercing light blue, standing out even in the dark lighting of the scene. The man wore a casual suit and had gray, almost white, hair and a healthy-looking tan. The two of them were laughing and appeared to be toasting, holding up wine glasses to clink together. Their style of dress seemed fairly current, so it must have be an image close to present day.

I opened my eyes and stared at the ceiling for a few seconds, then closed my eyes again, took another breath, and thought of the little girl. The image of her, clad in her bright yellow boots, projected in my mind. This time I kept my eyes closed and thought of the man in the mall. The snapshot of the little girl faded to black and was replaced by the bustling mall scene. An image of a young woman jogging with her golden retriever on an early-morning subdivision street followed the man in the mall. Then came an elderly couple driving along a gravel road in a horse and buggy, similar to the kind Amish people used. Finally, I thought of the last vision, an older man standing on a commercial fishing boat holding up a large fish. He wasn't overly tall and the fish was almost the same size as him. A group of people, his crew, from the looks of it, stood in the background on the deck of the boat watching him with obvious interest. As I forced the details of the last image to fade from my mind, I opened my eyes again. My breathing had sped up a little, and there was a low pulsing between my eyes, but no pain.

Okay, that wasn't too bad. I sat up on the bed and stared at the moon. Lucy had made it very clear she wanted to know the absolute second I had a flash. I was exhausted, but I had a hunch she would somehow be able to tell I was lying if I put off telling her until tomorrow, and part of me hoped she would actually have an answer about why I had been bombarded with multiple flashes. I punched Lucy's number into my phone and waited.

"Is there something you need, Hannah?"

I rolled my eyes. *She can't even say hello?* "You wanted to know when I had a flash." I matched her deadpan tone.

"Yes, I did."

"Well, I just had six one right after the other."

"What?" The shock in her voice was unmistakable. "I'll be right in." She hung up before I could respond.

I glanced out my window, wondering where she was at the moment. Another thought struck me and I jumped up to hide Ethan's treasure under my pillow. I'd forgotten all about it, but Lucy finding the little letter stamp could be potentially devastating. I reached into my backpack and pulled out my most recent sketchbook. *There goes my evening.*

As promised, it was only about two minutes before Lucy let herself into the house, using the key she'd taken the liberty of getting herself cut, and tromped up to my room.

"Okay, walk me through what happened." She strode over to my window seat and perched on the edge of it.

I quickly recounted how the barrage of images had intruded my psyche while Lucy listened intently.

"Hmm, interesting." She ran a hand along her chin.

"That's all you've got? Interesting? No theories as to why this is happening?" I was being spiteful, but I couldn't help it.

"As of right now, Hannah, no, I don't have any theories. I think the best thing is to try to get these images onto paper and we'll go forward from there." Lucy's tone remained reserved, but she didn't seem offended.

We spent the next two hours working. Rather than letting me just draw the images the way Ethan had always done, Lucy kept stopping me and had me walk through what was going on in my mind when I drew each section. She would make me breathe deeply, ask me to make each image zoom in and out in my mind's eye, and then ask how exactly I was making it do that. She asked endless questions: did the clarity of each image fade as I got more of it on paper? Could I sharpen my focus on one particular area? Were there any clues that gave away the exact location of any of the images? Did I have any sense or understanding of who the people in the images were? How was my mind able to move from image to image? Could I tell which person in each image was the protected?

I answered as best I could, although I was pretty sure she wasn't satisfied with my responses. Her frown grew deeper and deeper as the evening progressed.

Completely hindering the speed at which I drew, she stuck a blood pressure cuff on me, checked my pulse, shone a flashlight in my eyes to watch for pupil dilation, and recorded all her findings in a little notebook. Thankfully she didn't pull out any sort of electrodes, but I had a feeling that if we didn't start figuring out why I was seeing protecteds that would be the next step. After an intensive night of drawing, I only managed to get two of the images fully sketched out.

"It's not as much as I would have liked to accomplish, but I think we can call it a night." Lucy held up both sketches in her hands and scrutinized my work, her head bobbing back and forth.

"Great." The sarcasm dripped from my voice. I couldn't help it. It was after eleven, and I'd never worked so hard on any two sketches. My body felt weighed down from physical and mental exhaustion.

Lucy ignored my tone. "I'll be back first thing tomorrow, and we can set to work on the rest, as well as follow up on these two."

"Fantastic." I shuffled from my desk to my bed and flopped down.

She took my drawings with her, and sauntered out of my room.

Once I heard the front door close and click locked again, I dug around under my pillow and pulled out Ethan's letter stamp. *Do I Google family crests or do I go to sleep?* I stifled a yawn. Begrudgingly, I put the stamp away again and slipped under the covers. I would deal with those flashes and whatever Lucy had planned for me in the morning, and get them completely out of the way, before turning my attention to the letter stamp and my quest to find Ethan.

Eighteen

Lucy arrived just after eight the next morning, ready to go with her next set of examinations.

I followed her into the dining room, where my drawings had ended up the night before. "So did you figure out who the couple was in the drawing? Which one is the protected? Anything about the little girl?"

Dad's note was sitting on the front hall table as we passed by. I picked it up to see that it outlined all the hotel details. I was not to hesitate to call if needed—those words were underlined—and I should expect him back Monday around noon. A jealous knot formed in the pit of my stomach. *He gets a romantic weekend getaway with Rose while I get interrogation time with Lucy.* I set the note down and shook my feelings off. It wasn't his fault that the timing of his growing bliss happened to coincide so poorly with my misery.

"I did discover that information, but it isn't pertinent for you to know. Don't worry, I added it to the analysis grid." Lucy picked up the drawing of the couple and studied it closely.

I knew asking her had been a long shot, and gritted my teeth to keep my mouth shut. I hated that she wouldn't give me the personal details about the drawings the way Ethan had. Learning about the people in my images was one of the few things I still enjoyed about my flashes.

I spent the whole morning working on the last four drawings, as well as going through her list of different focusing exercises, trying to make the original two drawings from the night before re-appear in my mind. Nothing she tried worked. With every failure

Lucy got more annoyed, while I grew more pleased. After all her criticism about Ethan's deficient methods, I couldn't help but be happy that hers weren't working any better.

I was working on the shading of the crew members from the fisherman image when something about one of them struck me as odd. I closed my eyes and concentrated hard on the image of them in my mind, focusing in on each of their faces. The first was a big burly man with a thick beard. The next guy was about my age, with long hair pulled into a ponytail, but it was the last person who drew my attention.

It was a woman, dressed in yellow overalls with copper-colored hair, looking over at the proud fisherman with wry disdain. It was Lou. *What is my biological mother's best friend and fellow Hleo doing on a fishing boat, of all places?* I couldn't quite stifle my gasp at the shock of seeing a Hleo that I knew in my image.

"What is it?" Lucy gripped my shoulder and I opened my eyes to stare at the sketch.

"I um … I thought I recognized this guy." I pointed to the teenager on the boat.

"Really? From around here? Or are you getting a sense that he is the protected in the image? Is a name coming to you at all?" Lucy straightened up.

"No, he just looks like a guy I go to school with, but it's not him." I shook my head.

Lucy exhaled, clearly running out of patience with my failure to give her what she wanted. "I think we should take a breather. I'm going to go grab some research materials from my house." Lucy pushed her chair away from the table and stood up.

"Fine by me." I gave her my best wide-eyed expression of innocence.

"Remember to lock the door behind me, and check out the window before opening the door if anyone comes while I'm gone." Lucy pulled her car keys from her pocket.

I glared at her. She loved treating me like a child, reminding me of obvious safety measures every chance she got. Those were things I had done my whole life, even before I found out I was a protected.

I twisted the lock and watched through the small window in the door as she walked down the porch steps and trotted over to her black Audi. I rolled my eyes. The minute she had pulled out of the driveway, I spun on my heel and headed back to the dining room.

Picking up my sketch of the fisherman, I studied Lou's image. The drawing wasn't quite complete so I could still visualize it. Suddenly I remembered something. Lou had given me her cell phone number when we met each other at Veridan. She might be my lifeline to Ethan, if I could find her contact information.

I raced up to my bedroom and threw open the closet door, digging through the piles of discarded clothes that had amassed there. After my ordeal with Uri and Paige, almost drowning at the mill, I'd tossed the jeans I'd been wearing that day into the back of my closet and not worn them since, but they were the same pair I'd had on when Lou had given me her phone number.

I managed to find them and fished through the pockets. When my fingers closed over a little scrap of paper, I pulled it out. My heart raced as I carefully unfolded the fragment. *Please let the numbers still be legible.* Although it was smudged, I was able to make out the number Lou had written down and I grabbed my phone and quickly punched the digits in before I could have second thoughts.

My legs were a little weak and I sank down on my window seat, listening to the sound of the phone ringing on the other end of the line. *Pick up. Pick up.* I was desperate to get a hold of Lou, but Lucy could come back at any time.

"Hello?"

Relief rushed over me at the sound of Lou's voice on the line. "Hi Lou, this is Hannah, Hannah Reed."

"Hannah? How did you …? Oh right." Lou sounded hesitant and anxiety crept up the back of my neck. *Would she help me?* "So … how are you?"

"I'm okay. I guess you've heard." I swallowed hard.

"Uh yeah, I've heard." Lou laughed, and I relaxed a little. "Everyone's heard, Hannah. Ethan Flynn breaking a rule in the Hleo world is a pretty big deal."

I rubbed my free hand over my knee. "Yes. Lucy has already made the magnitude of Ethan's indiscretion abundantly clear to me."

"They stuck you with Lucy Larsson?" Lou sounded genuinely surprised to learn who my new Hleo was. "That's rough."

"You're telling me. She's so awful, Lou. She hates me and I haven't done anything to her, not directly anyway."

"I can't say that surprises me. She was pretty upset when your mom left."

"Why? Why does she care so much about what Elizabeth did?" I recalled her words when we had been sparring at her bungalow.

"Did she not tell you?" Lou's voice was layered in bewilderment.

I straightened, pulling my legs up to sit cross-legged on my window seat. "Tell me what?"

"Lucy was Elizabeth's partner when Elizabeth deserted the Hleo."

"What?" My mouth dropped open. *Why wouldn't she have told me that very important detail?*

"Yeah. Lucy came to the Hleo about five years after Elizabeth, and she always sort of, I don't know, hero-worshipped your mom, I guess. Lucy thought Elizabeth could do no wrong. Elizabeth was the personality, like me and Ethan, and Lucy was the tech wiz. Elizabeth always fought to only work with the best, and I think Lucy felt super-honored when she got paired with your mom. They worked together for the better part of two decades."

"Two decades! She didn't utter a word about that." I shook my head.

"Well, she didn't handle it the greatest when your mom left. She was pretty bitter. I'm surprised The Three would assign her to watch you. Maybe they thought she had moved past her hurt feelings and would share things about your mom with you."

"Except she hasn't." My voice was flat.

"I gathered that."

"I can't believe this. She's been cold and distant and severe this whole time and I kept asking myself why. I guess now I know." I rested my head against the windowpane and stared out at the leaves rustling on the trees as a warm spring breeze stirred through them.

"Hannah, I'm sorry that it isn't working and I wish I could keep chatting, but I'm actually heading out at the moment." Lou sounded distracted, as though someone at her end was trying to get her attention.

Panic that my only line to Ethan was about to be cut coursed through me. "Lou, do you know where he is?"

"Oh, Hannah. You know I can't—"

"Please Lou." I chewed on my lip.

There was silence on the other end of the line for a moment. "Look, I'm at Treow, the Hleo's European headquarters here in France." She spoke in hushed tones. "I just finished up this really short assignment with a funny little gentleman in Scotland. Anyway, no one here has mentioned seeing Ethan, and I know they would, the Hleo love gossip, no matter what anyone tells you. So you can pretty much rule out that he's in Europe. He would have had to pass through Treow before heading out to his assignment. I'm coming back to Veridan. I'll do a little digging when I get back there and let you know if I find anything."

Hope swelled in me. "Thank you, Lou. You have no idea what that means to me."

"I'm not promising anything."

"I know, but I have faith in you." My smile beamed. "By the way, your protected, did he like to fish?" I wrinkled up my nose. *Might as well ask while I have her on the phone.*

"Wha ... why yes he did. How did you know that?"

"Just a guess. Scotland always makes me think of fishing for some reason." I bit my lip. *Please just accept that explanation.* Ethan had never admitted how he was getting the images of protecteds to any of the Hleo he spoke with, and although I was sure most assumed that it had something to do with me, until someone outright asked me about it, I was going to play dumb.

"You are one weird girl, Hannah Reed."

"Thanks, Lou." I was practically floating, I was so happy. *Finally, someone willing to help me find Ethan.* The doorbell rang. "Someone's here. I better go too."

"Okay. I'll call you when I can," Lou said and then she was gone.

I slipped my phone back into my pocket and caught a glimpse of myself in the mirror. Lucy had been gone quite a while. Had she forgotten her key? If so, there was no way I could act this jubilant around her. I swallowed back my smile and pasted on as serious an expression as I could manage before treading downstairs.

When I reached the door, I remembered Lucy's warning. Out of spite, I unlocked the door and yanked it open without checking to see who was on the other side. It wasn't Lucy. A guy with short blond hair stood on the porch with his back to me. I opened the door and he turned to face me. The blood drained from my face and cold fear ran through me as I locked eyes with Adam Chambers. Before I could scream, move, or react, he wrapped a hand around the back of my neck and pressed a cloth to my mouth. Without meaning to, I breathed in what I could only guess was chloroform and everything went dark.

Nineteen

What is that buzzing sound? I forced my eyes open. Everything was blurry, but gradually I was able to focus on the fact that I was in my father's study. The buzzing still echoed in my ears. The clock on the wall read twenty-two minutes after twelve, which meant I'd been out cold for about ten minutes. My head throbbed, bringing on waves of nausea, and I tried to pull my hand up to rub it, but my wrists and ankles had been zip-tied to the arms and legs of Dad's desk chair. My pulse raced. Adam was perched on the edge of my father's desk in front of me, nonchalantly eating an apple. He looked to have fully recovered from the last time I'd seen him, when he and Ethan fought each other at the Masks Gala. His hair was a little longer than it had been at the dance, but still styled perfectly, and he was dressed in jeans, a Henley T-shirt, and a casual suit jacket.

"Morning, gorgeous. You know, you really need to do some grocery shopping, there's barely anything to eat in your house." He slid off the desk, staring at the apple with disdain.

"Well, if I'd known company was coming, I would have baked a pie." I glared at him. I didn't want Adam to know I was scared, or terrified, more accurately. Ethan was gone, and my trust in Lucy's ability to protect me was scant. He could pretty much do whatever he wanted with me, but I didn't want him to know that.

Adam grinned and leaned in towards me. "Sorry about the incapacitation. I couldn't risk you screaming or trying to run. If you'd done something stupid I may have ended up hurting you, and the people I work for wouldn't be overly pleased if that happened."

My stomach lurched and I tilted my head back to put as much space between us as I could. My hands gripped the arms of Dad's chair tightly. "Ethan will be here soon." I shot him a steely gaze, hoping he wouldn't see through my lie.

Adam studied me and then scrunched up his face. "Hannah, Hannah, Hannah." He shook his head. "Come on. You know me better than to try that. I've been watching you for a while now, and it appears that Mr. White Knight has departed East Halton. What happened? Did you two have a lover's spat? I heard you made quite the couple." The mockery and condescension dripping from his voice made anger burn inside me. He had no right to comment on my relationship with Ethan.

"Well, there's a new Hleo and she's crazy severe. She will be here any second to take you down." I straightened in the chair, squaring my shoulders. I just hoped I sounded more confident in Lucy's abilities than I actually felt.

"Yeah, I've seen GI Jane guarding you. It's laughable how easy it was to take her out of the equation. I definitely expected more of a challenge." Adam walked around the room, casually thumbing through the books on Dad's shelf.

"What did you do?" My voice was barely a whisper as I fought to comprehend what he was saying.

Adam twisted around from the bookcase to stare at me, frowning at my reaction. "Hey, don't look at me like that, I didn't kill her." He sounded shocked that I would come to that conclusion, offended, even.

"Then what?"

"She's just tied up in an old cabin in the woods. I don't kill when I don't have to; it's not a game or hobby to me. I only off people for monetary gain. I'm not a monster." Adam tossed the apple core into the wastebasket by the door.

"My mistake. I guess since you were trying to kill me the last time I saw you, I got confused." I glanced down at Dad's ultra-organized desk, searching for some sort of sharp instrument. Not that I'd be able to grab it if there was. *How am I going to get myself out of this one?*

"Lucky for you my directive has changed. It turns out the higher-ups have found a purpose for you." Adam made a motion with his finger, as though tracing an outline around me.

"What do you mean?" I worked at keeping my breathing even, as fear threatened to take over. There was no way I wanted to end up anywhere near the people Adam worked for.

Adam held out a hand, palm up. "I don't usually ask for the particulars. I simply follow the orders with the biggest payout."

I wanted to cry. I had never been more alone than I was in this moment. The second he took me away from my house, my life would no longer be my own.

If Ethan were here, he never would have let Adam get anywhere near me. Unfortunately, he was gone, and I couldn't figure out where. *Wait a minute*; there was one person in this world who could track Ethan, one person who had made it his mission to stalk Ethan, to cause him as much pain and grief as he could, and that person was standing in my father's office.

I narrowed my eyes and studied Adam, trying to form a plan in my head. How would I get Adam to help me find Ethan? He would never do anything that didn't benefit him somehow. I bit my lip. He did have one weakness I could possibly exploit, his ego. I just hoped I wasn't overestimating how much he actually thought of himself.

"I'm flattered that they think so much of me, glad to help you make some good money." I stared down at my wrists, pretending to explore the possibility of escape. "You know, Lucy told me that Ethan has virtually disappeared."

"Really." I couldn't tell if Adam was interested or not so I pressed on. "Yeah, she said I didn't have a hope of ever finding him, that no one on earth did." I looked up to meet his gaze.

"And I should care about this why?" Adam walked back over to stand in front of me, and crossed his arms.

"I figured you would want to maintain your reputation as the one person he couldn't elude." I shrugged, a difficult action to pull off while tied to a chair.

"Hannah, do you really think I can't see that you're trying to play me?" His brown eyes crinkled in delight. My hope dwindled, but then he tapped a finger against his bottom lip. "However, you do pose a compelling proposition. I still owe Ethan, and I think he would be very interested to see who you've been keeping company with in his absence." A sly grin spread across his face.

I swallowed hard and tried not to let any excitement show. "What are you saying?"

"We've got a few days before they're expecting us back at headquarters. A little detour to visit Ethan to show him how miserably he failed you might be just the thing. And if I get the chance to return his kind gesture and bury him six feet underground, so be it. Being trapped gives a man a lot of time to think, and I imagine there would only be one thing on his mind after our visit." He looked me up and down smugly.

"Let's go, then." I didn't care what he thought he would be able to do to Ethan, because I had every confidence that if we found Ethan he would be able to get me out of this situation and maybe deal with Adam once and for all.

"Before I cut you free, I need some sort of assurance that you're going to be a good girl." Adam took a step closer to me.

"If you promise I'll get to see Ethan one more time, I'll behave myself and do whatever you want." I kept my eyes locked with his.

"Whatever I want, huh?" Adam raised an eyebrow, and I wished I'd chosen different words.

I squared my jaw. "As far as getting to Ethan is concerned."

"You'll only have one chance, Hannah." Adam stuck a foot up on my father's desk, and removed a switchblade sheathed to his ankle. "One chance. If you try any funny stuff and make this more work than it's worth, I will make you very sorry. I may not be able to kill you, but I can go after your father, or that curly-headed friend of yours." Adam moved in closer, the knife approaching my throat. My mouth went dry. He swung the blade down to cut through the zip-ties on my wrists, and laughed. "You should see your face, you look scared to death. Come on, gorgeous, where's the trust?"

"I guess I'll have to work on that." I rubbed my wrists while he cut my ankles free.

"So, did Commando Barbie give you any clues as to where lover-boy has gone?" Adam stuck his knife away again and walked around to sit in my father's swivel-back chair, propping his feet up on the desk. My fists clenched, but I managed not to comment on his blatant disrespect of the space. No sense battling with him already.

Should I tell Adam about Ethan's letter and wax stamp? Or let him figure it out on his own and keep those details to myself until we got closer to Ethan? I was hopeful that once we were on Ethan's trail I could figure out his location on my own, but if Adam came up with too many dead ends I was sure he would get bored, and that would be it; he'd abandon the search and I'd be in front of the leaders of the Bana within a few days.

"Lucy didn't tell me anything, it would be against *protocol*."

Adam studied me. "I take it you're not a fan?"

I mentally kicked myself for accidentally letting it slip how I really felt about Lucy. "She's efficient, or at least I thought she was until you showed up." I waved a hand at him. "Anyway, no, she didn't tell me anything, but I do have something that might be a clue to where Ethan has gone."

Adam straightened up, dropping his feet to the floor. He folded his hands together on the desk. "And what would that be?"

"I have to go get it. Is it okay if I go to my bedroom?" I stood, but waited for his approval before taking a step towards the exit.

Adam hoisted himself out of the chair. "Sure, I'm right behind you."

I rolled my eyes as we left Dad's study and headed up to my room so I could grab the letter. I dreaded the thought of Adam being in my bedroom. He was the last person I wanted in my personal space. I crossed over to my dresser and retrieved the letter from my sock drawer. When I turned to go back downstairs, Adam was walking around my room examining everything, the framed pictures on my desk, the posters on my wall, the view from my window seat; his fingers even grazed over the keyboard of my laptop.

"I've got it, we can go." I held up the letter and headed for the doorway.

"Just a second, I'm taking it all in, getting a better idea of who Hannah Reed is." Adam gave me a cheeky smile before following me downstairs.

Once we were back in the living room, I hesitantly handed over Ethan's letter. Adam read it and smirked. "This is really sweet."

I crossed my arms. "Think whatever you want about it, but maybe try looking past what's written. Ethan sent it to me a few days after he left. I think there's some sort of clue about where he is in it, but I haven't been able to figure out how to decipher it."

Adam read the letter again, this time seeming to study the words and phrases more closely. "I need a piece of paper and a pen." He flopped down on the couch.

I grabbed the requested items from my dad's study and handed them to him. He motioned to the armchair beside the couch. "You sit here while I work."

I obeyed, curiosity over whether he would be able to come up with a solution to Ethan's whereabouts winning out over my anger at being ordered around.

After half an hour, he'd written down many different combinations from the letter, then scribbled them all out again. Nothing seemed to be coming together, and I could tell he was getting frustrated. He tossed the letter down on the coffee table and stared into the cold fireplace. I ran my hands over my jeans, wiping away the sweat on my palms. If Ethan had made this mystery too hard and Adam decided it wasn't worth the effort I was in trouble.

"Did he give you anything else?"

I bit my lip. I didn't want to tell him about the letter stamp unless absolutely necessary. "He actually sent the letter to Katie's house addressed from this fake university, as far as I know it's the only—"

"Do you still have the envelope?"

"Yeah, it's upstairs, I'll go get it." I jumped out of the armchair.

Adam swung his gaze from the fireplace to me. "Do I need to remind you not to do anything stupid?"

"I'll be right back, Scout's honor." I held up a three-finger salute, then ran and grabbed the envelope. I pulled out the letter stamp as well. *Should I tell Adam about this?* I turned it over in my hand, willing it to make sense so I wouldn't need to mention it. It was a family's symbol, but whose family? I shoved it in the pocket of my pants and headed downstairs. For now I was going to keep it to myself. I would give Adam the envelope, and if he was still out of ideas then I would show him the stamp.

I ran back downstairs before he could get suspicious; I needed him to believe he could trust me. I handed him the envelope, and after about two seconds of looking at the plain white cover, a smug smile spread across his lips. "I know where we need to go."

"Where?" Hope surged through me. Was I actually going to see Ethan again?

"Uh, uh, uh, Hannah, I don't think so. You don't get to learn where we're headed or I'll have to deal with you trying to escape the whole time." Adam wagged a finger at me.

"Fine. But at least give me a hint of how far we're going, so I can grab my passport if I need to."

"I would bring ID, but it's not going to be a very long visit, so pack light." Adam folded up the letter and slipped it into his pocket.

"All right, so let's get going then." I was glad I happened to be wearing corduroys and a button-up sweater over a tank top and t-shirt. If Adam wanted me to pack light, I already had on layers, perfect for traveling.

I grabbed my shoulder bag from the hook in the front hallway. It had my wallet, a little money, my cell phone, and some other random things in it. I took a deep breath and glanced around my house. If things didn't go the way I hoped when and if we tracked down Ethan, this could be the last time I saw my house. *Don't think like that, have a little faith in Ethan.* He'd be able to save me, wouldn't he?

We were just about to leave when there was a knock on the front door. Adam stood in the doorway between the living room and front hallway and looked over at me. He put his finger to his lips, his eyes flashing a warning. Was he hoping the person on the other side of the front entrance would believe no one was home? Before I could move a muscle, the door opened and there stood Katie. My heart leapt into my throat as Adam's threat of hurting my curly-headed friend played over in my mind.

"Hey, whose car's in the driveway? Luke and Ryan would have a coronary if they saw it. I know it's a Camaro, but do you know what year?" Katie stepped into the front foyer and swung the door shut behind her.

I opened my mouth to speak, but Adam strode over to stand beside me, likely to keep me from giving Katie any sort of secret signals.

"Oh." Her blue eyes narrowed as she glanced from me to Adam.

"It's a '69, Katie. Glad you like it." Adam flashed his best charismatic smile. I worked to keep my expression blank while he tried to charm my friend.

Katie's smile seemed forced. "Adam, good to see you again." Reservation was thick in her voice. I knew she was dying to know what was going on. "Hanns, I'm guessing you forgot we were going to hang out today?"

She glanced over at the living room, as though she was expecting the three of us to make our way there. I stayed frozen in the hallway. Adam couldn't hurt me, but I had no idea what he would do to Katie to force me to cooperate with him. She was so important to me and fear for her safety was making it hard for me to breathe normally. I had to get her as far away from Adam as she could. "Yeah, I'm sorry Kate, but I did. Adam and I sort of have plans." I forced myself to give Adam a warm smile. He took a step closer to me so that we were almost touching, returning my smile. It took all my self-control not to recoil from him, but I couldn't tip off Katie that something was wrong.

"That's fine. We can get together tomorrow." Katie didn't sound too sure, but she reached for the handle of the door.

"Actually, I'll probably still be gone tomorrow." I bit my lip.

Katie whirled back around. Her eyes looked like they were going to pop out of her head. "Okay, I'll get out of your hair, but, um, Hannah, could I ask you a quick question … about schoolwork?"

"I'll be in here if you need me." Adam sauntered back into the living room. He shot me a warning look when Katie's head was turned.

Katie grabbed my elbow and tugged me closer to her. "Why didn't you tell me that you've started something up with Adam? I thought he was a sleaze to you at the Masks Gala."

I watched Adam from the corner of my eye. He had his phone out and was standing by the fireplace mantel with his eyes on the screen, as though he wasn't paying attention to our conversation. I knew better.

"It only just happened. I ran into him and we talked. He apologized and asked for another chance." I shifted my weight from one foot to the other.

Her forehead was furrowed in a concerned frown. "Look Hanns, I get it. You're hurting about Ethan leaving but, I mean, you guys never even … well, you know. And he's only been gone a little over a month. Do you really think a *sleepover* with a guy you barely know, who may or may not be trustworthy, is a good idea?"

I cringed inwardly at her mentioning my lack of experience with Ethan in earshot of Adam. The corners of his mouth twitched as though he was repressing a smile, although his gaze never left his phone.

"There's this art exhibit in Boston that I really want to check out, and Adam knows the artist so he's invited me. We're going to crash there because of the length of the drive." I shrugged, trying to play off what I was doing as completely innocent, while I lied to my best friend.

Katie clasped her hands together. "I could come with you. I'm sure Mom and Dad wouldn't care, and that way you wouldn't be alone."

"No!" It came out too loud, and I winced. Adam glanced up. "I … it's just that … the car is only a two-seater."

Katie's face fell. I'd definitely hurt her. "Okay, but I still think you need—"

"Katie, I know what I'm doing." I put a hand on her shoulder.

"Hanns." Katie took a deep breath. She looked bewildered, and how could I blame her? Going on sketchy road trips with strangers was not in my nature.

She opened her mouth to speak, but Adam walked back out of the living room and joined us again. "I hate to rush you guys, but we should get going. Sam's expecting us, and you know how artists can be." He flashed Katie another charming smile, but I suspected he had reached the end of his patience in pacifying her.

"Of course. I'll let you go." Katie nodded and moved towards the door again.

"I'll call you later, okay?" I hoped I would be able to keep that promise. Pulling her into a hug, I whispered in her ear, "Thank you for your concern. I love you." I fought to keep the quiver out of my voice. I could feel Adam's eyes on me, assessing what was happening, making sure no secret message was being shared, but I didn't care. *If this is the last time I ever see Katie I need her to know how much she means to me.* Katie whispered that of course she loved me too, and told me to be careful. Then she and her wild curls were gone, as quickly as they'd come.

"See? I told you I wasn't a monster. I let you say good-bye to your friend." Adam watched Katie pull out of my driveway from the front entrance window before opening the door and walking out onto the porch.

I didn't bother responding. Pain shot through my chest as I ambled down the porch stairs. What would I do if Adam failed to find Ethan and was able to deliver me into the hands of the Bana? *Please let this plan work.*

Katie had been right about the classic vehicle. It was exactly the type of car the guys went nuts for. The candy-apple red 1969 Camaro had a black interior and looked as though it was in mint condition. He opened the passenger door for me and I dutifully climbed in. As soon as I was seated, he pulled a zip cord out of the pocket of his jacket and fastened my right wrist to the interior door handle. I thought about struggling with him, but knew it would only make things worse. He tested it to make sure it was tight before shutting the door and going around to the driver's side.

Adam climbed into the vehicle, and we were off. My house disappeared behind us and my stomach churned into a tight knot. Part of me was thrilled that we were headed toward Ethan, but the other part was practically paralyzed with terror at the thought that I could be putting him in danger. *What have I done?*

Twenty

It was a beautiful, late-spring day, not a cloud in the sky, and I stared out the passenger window. We were just outside of East Halton on a secluded forested road when Adam suddenly yanked the car over to the shoulder. A shower of gravel sprayed into the ditch, and my heart skipped a beat as I turned to face him. *What is he doing?*

"So, let's lay down some ground rules for this little quest of ours, shall we? First off, you might as well take that free hand of yours and pull your cell phone and ID out of your bag and throw them in the glove box." Adam tapped the top of the dashboard. I hesitated as long as I dared before my shoulders sagged. I had to play along. If I didn't, he would forget about tracking down Ethan and take me straight to the Bana.

Silently I reached into my bag and pulled out both my phone and wallet. I popped the glove box open, and swallowed hard when I caught a glimpse of a large, sheathed knife lying among the title, registration, and other usual glove box items. I threw my stuff in and slammed the door shut.

"Now you can toss your bag into the backseat." Adam waved a hand towards the small area between our seats and the back windshield. Again I followed his instructions wordlessly. My bag landed in a heap behind his seat with the corner of my drawing book peeking out. I stared at it. *Oh no.* I hadn't realized it was still in my bag. Should I try to shove it out of sight? It would be just like Adam to snatch it and scrutinize the pictures, if only to aggravate me. I didn't want to take the chance he would recognize one of the people in my drawings as a protected, but bringing attention to it would probably be worse.

Slowly I turned back around to look at him. "Anything else?" I asked through gritted teeth.

"Yeah, one more thing. If I even get a hint that you're trying to get away from me, I'll knock you out and you'll wake up in the arms of some less-than-charming characters." Adam's dark eyes were as hard as steel, and another tremor of fear ran through me. "Other than that, just buckle up and enjoy the ride." He pulled back onto the road, appearing completely carefree again now that he had established *the rules*.

I slumped against the passenger seat, slowly drawing in a deep breath in a vain attempt to calm the pounding in my chest

Being fastened to the car's door made it hard to get comfortable. As discretely as possible, I slid my arm along the handle, trying to see if there was any spot where it narrowed enough that I could get my hand free. It didn't appear there was.

"That's not a great start at following the rules, is it?" Adam observed, never taking his eyes off the road. He sounded more amused than angry. *Obviously he's got a lot of faith in his tying-people-up skills.*

"I'm just trying to get comfortable," I snapped. Oh, how I wished I could punch him and get away with it.

"Sure." Adam rolled his eyes.

I stared out the passenger window as we traveled farther and farther away from the town I had grown up in, and everything I knew. We'd been driving for over an hour when I straightened in my seat. *I know this road.* I hadn't been paying much attention to my surroundings, just watching trees and fields go by trying to formulate some sort of plan of escape.

I had to believe that Adam would be able to figure out Ethan's location, but I didn't want him to take me to Ethan. The second we figured out where Ethan had ended up was the second I needed to get away from Adam. Ethan had defeated him once, but I didn't want to put him in that position again. Escaping and getting to Ethan before Adam did was my best option. But how? That was the question.

We passed by a road sign, and I smiled. I was almost positive I knew where we were going. I had been on this road only a few months earlier, the day that Ethan had taken me to his family's homestead.

Adam had reacted when I'd handed over the envelope. The return address had been Essex, MA, Ethan's hometown, and Mary's name had been listed as the Dean of Students. Adam must have figured out that this wasn't just a sign to let me know the letter was from Ethan, but some sort of clue regarding his whereabouts, and now we were headed in that direction.

We were almost to the road Ethan's family's house had been on, but instead of turning and heading down it we passed by. My forehead creased. *Where are we going then?* Within minutes I had my answer. We reached the town limits and drove straight to the cemetery. Adam must have reasoned the answers would be at Mary's gravesite instead of the abandoned homestead.

We pulled into the parking lot of the cemetery and stopped under the shade of a large oak tree. Adam shifted in his seat to study me. "I take it you've been here before, from your utter lack of surprise."

I shrugged. "Ethan brought me here once." Now that everyone knew about the two of us, what was the point of concealing how we'd spent our time?

Adam's eyebrows shot up. "Hmm, he really did have a thing for you, didn't he? Ethan didn't let anyone into his world." A cold smile crossed his lips. "Except, of course, for one or two people he was really close to."

My chest clenched at the reminder that Adam had once been a trusted friend before he turned on Ethan and betrayed him. "What now?" I motioned to the gravestones. I didn't want to keep talking about Ethan to Adam. Even the sound of Ethan's name on Adam's tongue sent chills up and down my spine.

"If I cut you free, are you going to run?"

"I'm not going anywhere. I want to find Ethan."

"Fair enough." Adam got out and strolled around to my side of the car. He pulled the door open while I awkwardly stuck half out of the seat with my arm still attached to the handle. "One chance Hannah, just keep that in mind." He pulled a small switchblade from his pocket and cut me free. My jaw clenched, but I held my tongue as I rubbed my wrist.

Once I was out of the car, Adam fell in close step beside me and we walked right to Ethan's family's graves. I gazed across the rows of headstones. What could Adam possibly expect to find here?

The cemetery was basically the way I remembered it, except that the grass was now a lush green, and the trees were in full bloom. Some of the newer graves had bouquets of spring flowers resting on their markers, or lying in front, but all in all the grounds were remarkably similar to when Ethan had brought me here in February. We made our way carefully through the somewhat neglected area of the cemetery to the Flynn family plot.

Adam walked right up to Mary's headstone and began examining it. I let him work and stood staring at Ethan's grave. A name carved on stone, and an empty grave that had been meant for him. A reminder of a life that had once been, and now all that was left was a void. I turned away and wrapped my arms around myself protectively.

Adam had knelt down and was digging around the headstone, apparently searching for something buried near it. After a thorough search, he glanced up with a frown and moved onto the graves of Ethan's parents, and then Ethan's.

After several minutes Adam straightened up, wiping stray grass blades from his pants. "The earth looks untouched. Ethan's good but there's no way the grass would still be grown over perfectly if Ethan had buried something here just over a month ago." Adam surveyed the grassy area in front of each of the headstones.

An uneasy feeling washed over me. I wanted to feel vindicated that Adam's arrogance had been premature, but my continued existence rested solely on the hope that Adam could find Ethan. *Please don't let him give up.*

He pulled the letter and envelope out of his pocket again and skimmed them. I casually maneuvered myself so that I was beside him, the paper at a readable angle to me. I wanted to see Ethan's words again; I needed to feel a connection to him. Had I done the right thing, giving Adam the letter? If I never saw Ethan again this was the last shred of something he'd given me, and I wanted it.

Adam tapped a finger to his chin before folding up the letter and shoving it back in his pocket. He turned the envelope over in his hand. His wheels were definitely going around as he tried to get into Ethan's head and unravel the clue. His head jerked up. "What street is this?"

I glanced around. Because the cemetery was at the end of a dead end road, there was a street sign just off the parking lot. I made a beeline to the green metal sign. From the crunching of grass behind me, I guessed that Adam was following me. Ten feet from the sign, I stopped. "Cemetery Road," I said, turning to look at him. *How does that help us?*

Adam pulled his phone from his pocket and typed Essex, MA into Google maps.

"I tried that when I first got Ethan's letter. There is no 43 Simon Road in Essex, Massachusetts." I shifted my weight from one foot to the other.

"No ..." Adam kept his eyes on the screen as he studied the street names of the town with obvious interest. "But there is a 43 Liverpool Road. Where is Ethan's little helper Simon from?"

My mouth dropped open. *Of course.* I had wondered at Simon's name being in the return address, but hadn't been able to figure out the connection.

"He is from Liverpool." I nodded. A memory of Simon joking about babysitting one of the Beatles when he was just a toddler flashed through my mind.

"Perfect." Adam strode over to the Camaro. I followed and climbed in the passenger seat. *Was Ethan really this close? Would the Hleo do that?*

Adam didn't tie me up again. Either he figured we wouldn't be in the car long, or he actually trusted that I was being honest when I said I was sticking with him until I had some answers about Ethan's whereabouts. Either way I was glad to have my arm free.

We drove to the downtown area of Essex and headed left at the second set of stoplights we came to. The town's main street was a quaint collection of shops, similar to East Halton, but it lacked the tourist appeal of a lakeside town. It felt more like a place whose residents took pride in maintaining a small-town feel. We were only about half a block down Liverpool Road when Adam turned into the parking lot of a stately old building. The metal lettering on the front said Essex Town Hall and Library.

"This is it." Adam threw the car in park, cut the engine, and got out.

"The town library?" I blinked. I couldn't believe Ethan would leave me a clue that would take me back to a library, but then he probably hadn't expected my travel companion to be the person who had tried to end my life in a library less than a year earlier.

We made our way across the parking lot to the building. Adam was walking with purpose, as though the fact that Ethan wanted us to go to a library had allowed him to figure out something that still eluded me. I quickened my pace to keep up.

The library was an older red-brick building, but the inside had been renovated to give the space a modern feel. The walls and ceiling were white, highlighted by glass and well-positioned track lighting. The actual book lending part of the building appeared to only take up the first floor. Just to the left of the entrance, right before the library's help desk, was a wide stone staircase. A sign indicated that the town official's offices were located on the second floor. People looking for licenses and permits should proceed up there, but Adam made his way directly to the information desk, where a gray-haired gentleman was filing away books. "Excuse me sir, I'm interested in some survey and census records for this county, do you keep them here?" Adam pressed his palms to the top of the long white Lucite desk.

The elderly man pushed his glasses higher up his nose with one finger and set down the book he'd been holding before answering. "Is this for that school assignment you kids have?" the man asked, instead of answering Adam's question directly.

I frowned in confusion, but Adam seemed mildly pleased by the man's response. "I'm sorry?"

"You're the second young man to come in here wondering about our old records, although the other one must have been here over a month ago now." The man squinted, as though trying to remember. "You're a little late getting your work done, aren't you?"

My breath caught. He could only be talking about Ethan, which meant we were on the right track.

Adam nodded. "Yes, we are. Really late, in fact, so if there's any way you could help us get the information we need quickly, we'd really appreciate it."

"Well, you're in luck. We do keep the county records here. I'll take you back to the archive room and you can take a look around, as long as you're careful." The man opened a drawer and pulled out a set of keys before making his way around the information desk to join us.

We followed him down the closest aisle of books, all the way to the end, where the man stopped in front of an unmarked, blue door. He selected a key from the ring and unlocked the door, then led us into a small room. Metal shelves, sagging under the weight of cardboard storage boxes, lined all four walls.

"So, do you know specifically what you're looking for?" The guy motioned to the incredible number of records surrounding us.

"Yes. Census records that date from around the late 1800s." Adam eyed the different boxes.

"As I mentioned to the other young man, the oldest census records we have in this facility date from 1902. Anything older than that is kept at the state offices," the librarian explained and Adam's eyes lit up. He was right on Ethan's heels. This guy had just inadvertently confirmed that.

"Do you happen to remember which ones the other guy checked out?"

"Of course." The man looked mildly offended at the question. Clearly he took his work very seriously. He walked over to a box in the corner opposite the door and sifted through it, pulling out a collection of five oversized, leather-bound ledger books. The gentleman set the books down gently on a small table shoved against the far wall of the room.

The librarian rested a hand lightly on one of the books. "I'll give you some time to study them, but as I mentioned to the other young man, these records are very old and somewhat fragile, so please be careful." He walked out of the room and pulled the door closed behind us.

My stomach lurched at being in a confined space alone with Adam again, but I took a deep breath, willing myself to stay calm. I needed to get used to being in close proximity to him. I had no idea how long our little road trip was going to last.

Adam waited a moment to make sure the librarian was truly gone, and then scanned the ledger books' titles. He picked up the second one from the top and slowly flipped through the pages, his gaze intense.

"What exactly are you looking for?" I crossed my arms as he worked.

"I have a theory about Ethan's sappy letter. From what that old guy told us, I'm fairly certain I'm right." Adam didn't even bother to look up. I craned my neck to get a better view. The book he was flipping through was just page after page of lists of names.

When he got to the third page of the F section, an unmarked envelope fell out and slipped to the floor. Adam snapped the book shut and flung it back down on the table with the others.

I winced at the flagrant disregard of the librarian's instructions. Of course, following the rules didn't seem to be anything Adam was overly concerned about.

He stooped down, picked up the envelope, ripped it open, and yanked a piece of paper out of it. My heart jammed in my chest when I saw the handwriting. It was Ethan's. Shoving back my aversion, I crowded in close to Adam to read the words. My heart sank. The letter was the same as the original one he had sent me. "Why would he put a copy of my letter in this old book?"

"It's not the same letter, Hannah." Adam tugged the original from the pocket of his jeans and set the two letters down on the table side by side. As I examined them, I realized he was right; there were a few inconsistencies between the two.

I reached for the new letter, desperate to read it more closely, but Adam grasped my arm firmly. "I don't think so."

"Fine, I won't touch it, but tell me why you think Ethan changed some of the wording in this version of the letter." I pointed to the newer copy.

> *Dear Hannah,*
>
> *I am so sorry I left you the way I did. I know love, that this is all very sudden and frightening for you, and it was always my greatest fear that we would end up separated and I could not be the one protecting you. Please don't lose heart yet. I need you to know that I love you, and have known you were the one for me from the exact moment we met. The time we have spent together has truly changed me, and I am a better person for having you in my life. The circumstances being what they are, I cannot be with you right now, but trust that one day soon we will find our way back to each other. I remain eternally yours.*
> *Love Always,*
>
> *Ethan*

"It's a cipher commonly used by Hleo to send messages to each other. To figure out the message you have to have both letters in your possession. That way, if someone intercepts one of the letters, it doesn't matter. The words that are different or have been added to the second letter are the key to the message. When the letters of each of the words are rearranged, they usually spell out a message, things like letting someone know about a trap, or if a Hleo's been compromised, or, in the case of these letters, the name of a location." Adam ran his fingers across the wording of Ethan's new letter, his voice smug. Had he already figured out the clue? He snatched both letters off the table, folded them up, and stuffed them back into the pocket of his jeans.

"So, what is the location?"

Adam ignored me and headed for the exit.

I grabbed his arm. "Adam, where is he?"

Adam yanked his arm from my grasp. "You really think I'm going to tell you where we're going? I don't even know if this location is where Ethan is, or if it's just another clue to finding him. What I *do* know is that if you know where we're headed, you'll spend the entire trip trying to escape and get there on your own. It will be a whole lot easier for me if you have no choice but to stick with me for your chance to see your precious boy toy again." Adam tapped the end of my nose, a mixture of cheekiness and boredom in his voice.

I recoiled out of his reach. "Fine." My fists were clenched at my sides. *How dare he touch me so casually, as if we are friends?* "Can I have my letter back?" I exhaled slowly and held out my hand.

Adam stared at my palm for a moment. "Yeah, right." He yanked the door open.

Seething with frustration, I followed him back out into the library. He waved to the librarian as we passed by on our way out of the building.

"If you already know the clue, why can't I have my letter back?" I planted both fists on my hips.

"To bug you." Adam unlocked the car doors and pulled mine open for me. "Plus, I can't take a chance you'll remember the extra words when you look at the original letter, and somehow figure out the name of the location. Ethan made the cipher laughably easy, I guess because he thought you would be the one trying to figure it out."

The jab at my deduction skills stung, but I refused to give him the satisfaction of reacting to it as I settled on the front seat. Adam pulled another tie from his pocket. Did he carry an endless supply in there? "Is tying me to the door really necessary?"

"It's going to be a long drive, so yeah, it's necessary."

I worked to keep my breathing under control. Adam walked around the hood, climbed into the driver's seat, and peeled out of the parking lot. We drove in silence. I stared out the window, my teeth clenched tightly together. It was already after three in the afternoon and we were headed back in the direction of East Halton. I watched the highway signs for a clue as to where we could be going, but other than the fact that we were moving west, I had no idea where Ethan's letters could be taking us.

From Adam's mention of it being a long drive, I assumed we were headed somewhere across the country. We weren't driving towards Logan International, the closest airport out of Boston, so I figured no cross-continental travel was planned for the near future.

How long would I be trapped in this car with Adam? The longer Adam and I were together, the more time I had to figure out how to get away from him. If I could discover where Ethan was on my own, then I could try to bolt. I just needed to make sure Adam wouldn't be able to follow me. I had to get my hands on those letters somehow. My heart sank when I glanced over at Adam's unyielding profile. I had a feeling he had no intention of taking them out of his pocket, and I certainly had no intention of going in there after them.

Twenty-One

"Can you answer something for me?" I glared at Adam. We had been driving over two hours, passing right by East Halton and crossing over the New York state border. The sun was still shining, and there wasn't all that much traffic. Wherever we were going, we were making decent time.

"Depends on the question." Adam's brown eyes studied me with restrained curiosity for a moment.

"Do your bosses want me dead or not? When your girlfriend paid me a visit earlier this year with that hulking Russian, they were under orders to bring me in, but then some Bana member cut the brake lines on my car and one of my good friends ended up in the hospital, so which is it?"

"The order for your death was pulled over five months ago, just after my last visit to East Halton." Adam shrugged. "Who tampered with your brakes?"

"I don't know. Ethan was looking into it, and then he was gone. Lucy told me the guy had been dealt with, but she wouldn't give me any more details than that. Apparently it wouldn't be *professional* to share that sort of information with a protected."

"She's something, isn't she?" Adam grinned. He looked over at me as he spoke, and I rolled my eyes before I could stop myself.

I didn't want to bond with Adam, but the words spilled out. "She's just so rigid, takes everything so seriously. She hates me because I made Ethan commit *aliege*." I sighed.

"Aliege. Now there's a term I haven't heard in decades." Adam scratched his jaw.

"She said it's like treason, or something." I shook my head, remembering the contempt in her voice when she spoke to me.

"That's exactly what it is. They apply the term to anyone who's broken one of the significant rules, like killing a protected, or sleeping with them." Adam glanced over at me and arched an eyebrow.

My face warmed. "Yeah, well, her need to follow the rules, combined with her anger at Ethan and Elizabeth for breaking the rules, has caused her to have a less than warm and fuzzy attitude towards me."

"I wouldn't worry about it. That's how most of the Hleo women are. They take the job far more seriously than they need to and they come down on anyone else who doesn't. Man, they were a dour lot from what I remember, although there were a few who knew how to have a good time. There was this one, Lou, or Louise, I guess. I remember once we were both stationed near Greece and we happened to meet up. She had just finished up with this eccentric millionaire, but before heading back to headquarters she convinced the servants at his summer vacation villa in the Greek Islands that she and a handful of us had been invited to spend a week there. Now, she knew how to have a good time. I think your mom may have been around for that one too."

I shot Adam a sideways glance. He had a distant look on his face. My stomach clenched. It felt surreal to hear this person that I had so much dislike for talk about people like Louise or Elizabeth with casual familiarity. It was easy to forget that at one point he had been as much a part of the Hleo world as any of the others I had come to know. *What made you switch sides, Adam Chambers?*

"You spent time with Elizabeth?" It was risky to engage Adam in personal conversation, but the desire to learn more about my birth mother, even from a somewhat untrustworthy source, was overpowering.

"That was a long time ago, it doesn't matter now." Adam shook his head, his tone falling flat. Obviously his past and his Hleo days weren't something he felt like opening up about. He sounded unsure about why he had brought them up in the first place.

"Oh." My shoulders slumped, and the vehicle dropped back into silence. I kicked myself. I shouldn't have expected anything, but

I couldn't help feeling disappointed that he hadn't been willing to share.

"Wait, you said my girlfriend, what girlfriend?" Adam sounded genuinely baffled as a frown creased his forehead.

"Paige." My eyes narrowed. Did he really not know who I meant? A mental picture of her silver, anger-filled eyes crossed my mind.

"Oh, her. Hmm, well Paige is not so much of a girlfriend, as … a good stress release." Adam smirked.

"Gross." I scrunched up my face in disgust.

"She's not exactly the girlfriend kind anyway. What with her still pining for Julian." He turned his attention back to the road.

We merged off the interstate and connected with another one so that we were now heading in a southwesterly direction. I wanted a clear understanding of where we were going, but I forced myself not to look at the signs for too long. I didn't want Adam to know I was paying attention to our travel direction, in hopes that he would let down his guard a little.

"Where is she, anyway?" I asked coldly. There hadn't been any sign of Paige since that day at the mill. Ethan had spent incredible amounts of time and energy hunting for her, but she had been a ghost, able to disappear at will.

"The last I heard she was in the middle of some swamp in Asia. It turns out the higher-ups weren't too pleased at her failure to bring you in. It somehow got back to them that she had you and then defied orders and tried to drown you instead. She's being forced to prove her loyalty by spending time in the truly abysmal parts of this world. A fate that, incidentally, I intend to avoid." Adam wove between two slower-moving vehicles.

I bit my lip. How could the Bana leadership have ever found that out? I shivered as I thought of the cold hatred that had emanated from Paige as she'd held the blade to my neck. She was truly frightening. I was glad to hear that she was on the other side of the world.

Time marched on and the sun started to get low in the sky. Adam eventually pulled off the highway and into the parking lot of a truck-stop diner. "I'm hungry, but I need to know if I cut you free you I'm not going to have a situation where you run off, and I have to chase you, and eventually catch you, and probably do some damage to that pretty face of yours." Adam bobbed his head back and forth as he rhymed off his threat.

My jaw tightened. "I'll behave."

"Good girl." Adam pulled the switchblade from his pocket and reached over the gearshift, leaning across me to cut the zip-tie holding my wrist to the door handle. He moved slowly as he pulled back from cutting me free. A shiver moved through me. A hint of fresh soap mixed with a leathery cologne drifted toward my nostrils. I hated that I found the scent pleasant and pushed myself as far into the seat as I could to create some distance between us.

He grinned, clearly aware of how disconcerting I found his closeness, then got out of the car. I followed his lead, rubbing my wrist. It was stiff and sore from being held in the same position for hours, and I glared at Adam's back the entire walk across the parking lot into the diner.

He pushed open the metal door with ripped screen that led into the restaurant and grabbed a booth near the exit. I slid into the green vinyl seat opposite to him. The truck stop was a typical side-of-the-highway dining establishment, a long narrow room with a counter running the length of it on one side and a collection of booths along the other. Almost everything was stainless steel, the stools, the tables, and the walls. The black and white tiled floor was discolored, and many of the tiles were broken.

When the waitress—an overweight woman with a short bob hairdo—came over, Adam was his usual charming self and soon she was giggling and joking with him.

We ordered drinks and meals and she gave him a little wink as she sauntered away, leaving the two of us on our own again. I didn't bother engaging in conversation with him, instead spending my time distractedly playing with a piece of duct tape that was covering a large rip in the vinyl seat.

As we ate I tried to think of a way that I could get the letters away from Adam. He had them tucked securely into the pocket of his jeans, so my only chance would be if he for some reason took his pants off, an idea I didn't even want to entertain. I picked at the turkey sandwich in front of me while I mused. After several minutes, I realized that quite a bit of time had passed since we had said anything to each other. The silence on his end seemed a little strange and I glanced up. He was facing the counter. I followed his gaze.

Two college-aged girls sat at the bar, shooting flirty looks at Adam and giggling.

One was a brunette in a short plaid skirt and thin sweater, the other a bottle-blonde wearing a pair of tight jeans and a low-cut tank top. My eyebrows shot up as I watched one glance over at him with a coy smile and then turn back to her friend. The two of them burst out laughing.

Adam winked at them, a wide grin on his face.

"You are shameless." I crossed my arms.

"Excuse me?" Adam blinked in mock surprise and innocence as he turned back to me.

"I mean, for all those two know I'm your girlfriend or something, and you're just blatantly sitting here flirting with them."

"You're cute when you're jealous," Adam's dark eyes sparkled mischievously.

"To be jealous would require me to have some sort of emotions towards you other than disgust and loathing."

"Ouch." Adam put a hand to his heart. He turned back to his meal, still grinning. Clearly my comment hadn't fazed him in the least.

I turned and stared out the window. While we were stopped it could be helpful to take in our surroundings. The diner was in a rural area along the highway, with nothing much to observe but fields and open land. Off in the distance a farmer maneuvered his green tractor among rows of leafy green plants.

We were almost done eating when the brunette at the counter got up and ambled over to us. "Hey, I'm Amber. My friend Marybeth and I were just wondering, are you and your sister like traveling across the country or something?" Her tone was flirty and husky, and she rocked back and forth on her heels. I had to swallow back a snicker at her obvious attempt to fish out what sort of relationship Adam and I had.

"I'm Adam and this *is* my sister Hannah. We're on a little road trip, exploring everything the open road has to offer. What are you and your friend Marybeth up to?" Adam inclined his head towards the blonde.

"We're headed home from school, back to Marlboro in Jersey, and we thought we'd do the same. See the sights of this great country on our way." She offered him a suggestive smile.

"See anything good?" Adam looked her up and down. My nose wrinkled in disgust at the cheap flirtation I was being subjected to. How long could they possibly keep this up?

"One or two things." She took a step closer.

"We should probably get going." I threw my napkin down. I couldn't stand it anymore. Adam had more important things to do than waste his time on trashy girls. I didn't need anything distracting him from our quest to find Ethan. I shimmied out of the booth, forcing Amber to step aside, and waited for Adam to do the same.

"You're right, sis." Adam stood and gave the girl an apologetic look.

She glared at me, not even trying to hide her displeasure. "Well, we're staying at the Flamingo Motel down the road, if you're looking for a place to crash. It's not exactly the Hilton, but it's clean, and, you know, we'll be there." She wriggled her eyebrows mischievously at him, and I gagged internally.

"Tempting; we have more miles to cover though, maybe some other time." Adam tugged his wallet from the back pocket of his jeans and dropped some money onto the table. I tried to hide my smile. I enjoyed watching Amber be rejected.

"Well, all right then. If you're ever in Marlboro, here's my number." Amber held out a napkin.

When he reached for it, her fingers brushed his. "Thanks." Adam slipped the napkin into his jacket pocket.

I couldn't take anymore. Spinning on my heel, I headed for the exit, leaving the two lovebirds to say their goodbyes.

Twenty-Two

I was halfway across the parking lot when Adam's arm slipped through mine, and he gripped my elbow tightly "Hannah, don't you think it's a little rude to just leave your *brother* behind like that?" He leaned close to hiss the words in my ear.

"I figured you wanted some alone time with your new *friends*." I stopped in my tracks and turned to stare him down, our faces inches from each other.

He tightened his grip. My mouth went dry, but I worked to keep my face expressionless as he spoke again, his voice hard. "I can't help it if I'm irresistible, but that is no excuse for you to try and ditch me. Do not do it again."

"Fine." I kept my eyes on his, refusing to look away even though the darkness swirling through them sent cold fingers of fear racing up and down my spine.

He didn't move for a few seconds, then he let go of my arm abruptly and placed his hand in the small of my back. "Let's go."

Adam refastened my wrist to the door and we started down the highway again. We drove for another hour, passing by more fields and the occasional grouping of trees, until a neon flashing sign from the side of the highway alerted passing motorists to the fact that a motel was coming up. I didn't know exactly where we were, but we had crossed into Pennsylvania before stopping to eat. I hadn't noticed us come out the other side, so my best guess was that we were somewhere in southern Penn.

The motel was one long L-shaped strip of exterior access rooms, sitting right at the edge of a small town. A coffee shop with the sign half burnt out, and a gas station that looked closed for the evening, even though it was barely ten at night, were the only other establishments within walking distance. It felt a little like something out of the movie *Psycho*, and the fact that no one but Adam had any idea where I was struck me with sickening force.

Adam pulled into the parking lot and headed into the small motel office, leaving me tied to the door. When he came back out, he drove around to the back of the motel, to the spot the farthest away from the main office.

"Did you ask for the most remote room in the place on purpose?" The overhead lamppost had burned out, and a small forest pressed against the back half of the motel, adding to the dark, ominous feeling of the place.

"I asked for privacy for my lady love and myself, since we have a tendency to get a bit rowdy sometimes," Adam replied cheekily. I snorted in disgust and he laughed.

The door stuck when Adam attempted to push it, but he gave it a hard shove and it flew open, crashing against the wall behind it. The room was a decent size, but dated and grungy was an understatement, definitely a sleep-above-the-covers kind of place. *How much did he shell out for these lovely accommodations?* The room had a dresser with a small television chained to the top of it. A round table and chairs sat in the corner of the room, a makeshift dining area. A door in the far wall hung open to reveal a small bathroom. The walls may have been cream or beige at some point, but now they were a faded yellowy color, the smell of stale cigarette smoke masked with air freshener suggesting the cause.

"What now?" I caught a glimpse of the gaudiness of the blue and orange flowered curtains and bedspread, but my thoughts were too frenetic and muddled for the full extent of the ugliness to register. My chest clenched. What were the sleeping arrangements going to be?

"What do you have in mind?" Adam closed the door and slid the deadbolt in place.

Normally locking the door of a motel room made me feel safe. Tonight it made me feel trapped, even more vulnerable than I'd been feeling since Adam showed up at my house. "Let's just get some sleep." A small tremor worked its way through the words and I prayed Adam hadn't noticed.

"If that's what you want." Adam strolled over to me with a wicked smile on his face.

If I can just get to the bathroom, I can lock myself in for the night. I took all of one step before Adam caught me around the wrist. "And where are you going?"

"I'll sleep in the tub." I squared my shoulders as best I could with Adam's grip on me.

"I don't think so." He pulled me towards the bed and forced me to sit down on the edge of it. A wave of nausea hit me. What was he going to do to me? Up until now I had managed to convince myself that Adam was fairly harmless, since he was bound by his contract to keep me alive and bring me in, but as I thought back to that night at the library, it occurred to me that I didn't really know him or what he was okay with doing.

"Come on Adam, let me go." Fear twisted and turned inside me, creating a knot in my stomach.

"I plan on getting a good night's sleep tonight, and I can't do that if you're free to wander around and get your hands on the letters and take off on me." He pulled a zip-tie from his pocket. My heart thudded painfully against my ribs. I couldn't let him tie me up. If he did, he could do anything he wanted to me and I wouldn't be able to stop him.

"You can't be serious."

"And yet I am." Adam yanked my wrist above my head to tie it to the metal railing that ran along the top of the headboard.

"If those letters are in your pants pocket, you have no worries about me going after them."

"Oh really?" Adam's grin was colder now, more predatory. His deep brown gaze traveled from my wrist to my face and then down.

"Really," I spat back, defiant.

"You know, if you're looking for a good way for us to kill some time, I have a few ideas." Adam's fingertips gently traced down my wrist to my elbow.

My stomach lurched. "No thank you."

"Come on, Hannah. I think you and I could have a lot of fun together. Ethan's been gone a while. You must be feeling pretty lonely these days." Adam cupped my chin with his other hand and turned my head until I met his eyes. He leaned in so that his lips were only inches from mine and he was practically lying on top of me. A pulse throbbed in my throat. Everything in me screamed to pull away, but I forced myself to hold his gaze and not move.

After a moment, Adam snorted in amusement and gracefully leapt over me so that he landed beside me on the bed. "Don't worry. Like I told you before, I'm not a monster; I prefer my companions to be willing participants."

I swallowed hard. A gradual awareness that every muscle in my body was aching from being tensed up seeped over me and I forced myself to relax. If what Adam said was true, and I was deeply aware that I couldn't trust that it was, he was only interested in messing with my mind.

He settled in on top of the bedspread, throwing his arms casually behind his head and staring up at the ceiling. "Wonder what those girls we saw in the truck stop are doing now."

I snorted derisively. "Your standards are pretty low if you go for cheap, easy girls like those two." Even knowing it was stupid, given the situation, I couldn't resist taking the shot at him.

"That was just fooling around, giving them a little thrill." Adam picked at a loose thread on the bedspread.

"You really think you're something special, don't you?" I scoffed. *The ego this guy has.*

"Years of validation will do that to a person."

My free hand clenched at my side. "I can't believe you were ever friends with Ethan."

"Yeah, well, that was before." Adam shifted away from me, the lightness gone from his voice. I'd obviously hit a nerve, and I glanced over at him briefly, but he didn't look at me.

We drifted into silence. Eventually his breathing slowed and deepened. I refused to shut my eyes though. Instead, I studied a large water stain on the ceiling in the far corner, too terrified to fall asleep with a deadly killer lying on the bed next to me.

Twenty-Three

Gray light seeped through the crack between the heavy curtains before I finally drifted off to sleep. I awoke what felt like moments later, a sharp pain running up my neck. My arm was asleep, and I felt stiff and sore all over.

    I lay on my side, scared to move in case I woke Adam up. I wanted a few minutes to myself before having to put my guard up again. Eventually, though, the discomfort became too much to bear. Slowly, I shifted on the bed, rolling onto my back in an attempt to find a position that would make my neck stop throbbing. As my peripheral view changed I realized Adam's side of the bed was empty. I pulled myself into a sitting position. *Where could he be?* The bathroom door was wide open, and that was the only place he could be out of view within the room. He must have gone out somewhere.

    I inspected the plastic tie around my wrist. Could I free myself and take off before Adam returned? I slumped against the head board. As terrified as being held captive by Adam was, it would be worth it if he took me to Ethan.

    I froze at the sound of a key being inserted into the door. When it opened, Adam came in, holding a tray of coffees and a brown paper bag. "Morning gorgeous, how'd you sleep?"

    "Like my arm was tied to the bed all night," I replied bitterly, shaking my wrist against the railing.

    "I see someone's not a morning person." He set the food down on the little night table beside me.

    "Only when I've been kidnapped." I squared my jaw.

"Kidnapped? I seem to recall you asking me to take you on this journey so that we could find your long-lost love." Adam pulled the knife from his pocket and reached over to cut my wrist free. I leaned as far away from him as I could. He stepped back and put the knife away before grabbing a coffee out of the cup holder and moving to sit in the dining area of the room.

I shook my arm out, trying to get the blood flowing again, and rotated my shoulder back and forth to loosen up the muscles. I studied Adam through narrowed eyes. How could he look so fresh and well rested? His hair was already styled, and his clothes weren't even rumpled.

I grabbed the other cup and noticed that the lid said double cream, double sugar. My forehead wrinkled. "How do you know how I like my coffee?" I eyed the cup suspiciously. Was there a chance he would drug my drink? I gave the liquid a sniff before deciding it was worth the risk and taking a long sip. I didn't want to be grateful for the warm beverage in my hands, but the shot of caffeine after a day on the road and a terrible sleep was welcome.

"From that day at the coffee shop." Adam tapped the top of the rickety wooden table, as though it was no big deal.

"Oh." I blinked. A memory of how he had bought me a coffee at the Coffee Bean in East Halton, back when I thought he was just a regular decent guy interested in dating me, flashed through my mind. *Boy, had I been wrong about him.*

"Hannah, you would be amazed to learn what I know about you." He turned his gaze to me.

I looked away and jumped to my feet to stride over to the bathroom. Without a word, I closed the door behind me and rested my head against it.

"We need to get going, so don't take too long." Adam called through the door.

"I won't," I snapped.

I studied my reflection in the cracked mirror above the sink. My ponytail was matted from rubbing against the pillow all night, and my eyes had dark circles under them. I quickly splashed some water on my face and pulled my hair out of the elastic, running my hands through it in an attempt to dispense with the worst of the tangles. I smoothed out my clothes and took a deep breath. Would we find Ethan soon? I really didn't want to have many more nights like that one.

I joined Adam in the bedroom area again and we headed out to the Camaro. The temperature had dropped overnight and now, although it was a sunny day, the air was cool and a white mist hung close to the earth. My breath swirled in a cloud and I shivered, wishing I had remembered to bring a jacket with me. Adam didn't seem to notice the cold as he checked us out of the motel and we hit the road again.

We had been driving for quite a while when I noticed a sign for Richmond. At some point we must have crossed into Virginia. Green rolling pastures stretched out as far as the eye could see on both sides of the highway. From my best guess, it appeared that our course was shifting more south than west. I kept quiet while Adam drove, having no desire to engage him in conversation.

Adam had re-tied my wrist to the door, and I slid my arm forward, trying to find a more comfortable position.

"You said your brake lines were cut."

"What?" My head snapped up.

"Your car. You said someone tried to kill you by tampering with your brakes." Adam glanced over at me.

"Yeah, Ethan told me that they had been cut in a manner that could be dismissed as mere mechanical failure, nothing more than an accident. And whoever did it disabled the sensor so it wouldn't alert me of the problem." I tapped my finger on the door handle as I repeated what Ethan had told me in the Connie's Coffee parking lot after he had investigated my wrecked car. I shut my eyes and frowned as the image of Ryan lying in a hospital bed, tubes and cords attached to him, played through my mind.

"Huh. I think I can guess who did it then." Adam merged onto a different highway.

I straightened up in my seat. "Who?" My excitement at Adam's ability to solve this mystery overshadowed how much his confident grin irked me.

"A guy named Donatello. He's big into causing motor vehicle accidents, and cutting brake lines just happens to be a trademark of his. I also know that he doesn't pay much attention to current orders, so there's a big chance he didn't know about the hit being pulled."

My mouth dropped open. "He didn't know?" How could such a stupid mistake have occurred?

"It happens. We don't exactly have monthly staff meetings." Adam slipped a hand off the steering wheel and casually rested it on the driver door.

His cavalier response sent heat coursing through my chest. "So, you're telling me that the reason Ryan ended up lying in a hospital bed with critical injuries is because of miscommunication?" I waved my free hand through the air.

"Is Ryan the short dark-haired one, or the lanky blond one?"

I blinked. How did he remember what my male friends looked like? I frowned. He must have been watching me much more closely in the fall than I had known.

I clenched my teeth. I would not discuss my friends with him. He waited in silence until I couldn't take it anymore. "The dark-haired one." I blew out a breath. "He suffered internal bleeding and had to have surgery. What would have happened to this Donatello person if I had been in the car and had died?"

"With how much they want you, let's just say Donatello's career would have come to a crashing halt, as would his life." Adam switched lanes. He sounded amused by the possibility.

"They really want me that badly?" My stomach flip-flopped hard. If things didn't go as I hoped, Adam would be taking me right to these people.

"You're one of the Bana's top priorities right now. Alexander has big plans for the future, and apparently he's going to use you somehow to accomplish those plans."

I sighed and shook my head in frustration. "I'm sick of the Bana and Hleo. I just want all of this to be over."

Surprise flashed across Adam's face. "Really? I thought you were the number one cheerleader on Ethan's team destiny."

"I guess; I don't know. I can accept the idea that something bigger than us is in control. It makes sense when you look around and see all the intricate details that are in the creation and framework of our existence, but I don't know about the Hleo. I mean, I keep getting told that they want what's best for everyone, but I can't understand how taking Ethan away from me could be what's best. Just look at what's happened to me in the weeks since his disappearance. First I have to deal with Lucy, and now you." I shot him an annoyed expression, not even trying to hide my contempt. "Plus, I thought that the Hleo were supposed to be superior moral beings, but Miriam bold-faced lied to me." I fiddled with the seatbelt strap. Why was I telling Adam any of this? He wasn't exactly a confidant, and yet it felt good to open up and say exactly what I was thinking to someone who knew the whole story, even if it was him.

"Okay, I'll bite; she lied to you?"

"She knew about my relationship with Ethan when we went to Veridan. When it was just her and I talking, she told me it was dangerous to love a Hleo. I asked her point blank if she was going to rat on us and tell the others, but she said it was our information to share and she would keep quiet. I thought she was being serious, but it was only a little more than a month later that they took him away from me." Both my hands closed into fists.

"So, that's why you want off the destiny train, because they took your boy-toy away?"

"Not just that. All of this has been thrown at me. From the moment I learned the truth, I've felt all this pressure. You, Ethan, all the Hleo, you all got to choose whether you wanted to be part of this world. I've never felt I've had a choice, and I'm finding it all a little suffocating." *Stop talking Hannah, you're telling him too much.* I ignored my inner voice. At this point, what did it matter what I told Adam?

His knuckles went white as he gripped the steering wheel. "Maybe it was a choice to get in, but that's the last choice I ever made. From that moment on I've belonged to someone else. Good, bad, right, wrong, it doesn't really matter which side you're on. It's still someone else calling the shots in your life."

I was too stunned to respond. Was there a chance that Adam was just as sick of the world of destiny as I was?

His eyes locked with mine for a second. Something flashed through them that took me a moment to identify. Disillusionment. He cleared his throat and focused back on the road.

"I may not have any choices now, but there are certain benefits to the life I've chosen." The swagger was back in Adam's voice. He stepped on the gas of the muscle car and we shot past the car ahead of us while taking a curve. Although I couldn't see the speedometer, I was sure we were well over the speed limit. I gripped the door handle.

We wound our way down the steep mountain, towering walls of rock lining either side of us. I planted the palm of my free hand against the dashboard. "That's something you actually have in common with Ethan, you both like to drive crazy fast."

Adam whipped in front of another car, pressing his foot even harder against the accelerator. "It's the adrenaline; our kind tends to crave it. When you're in this form you can start to feel a little like you're frozen or something, so you need to do things that make you feel alive." He looked over at me with a mischievous grin on his face. "Although from what I understand, Ethan's shown pretty strong restraint in that area."

I groaned inwardly. *Why did Adam have to hear Katie's mention of my inexperience with Ethan?* I had hoped he would just let it go. I should have known better.

"Please don't," I appealed weakly, knowing that my plea was futile.

"So, you and Ethan really never …?" Adam made a lewd pounding gesture with his hand.

I pressed my lips together, refusing to answer.

"I can't believe it. What is wrong with him? If you and I were together, we'd never get out of bed." I could feel his eyes roaming over me, but refused to look over as we exited the highway and headed down a more rural road.

"You're the last person in the world I would ever be with," I muttered, sending him a dark glance.

"Really?" A smirk crossed his face. "Because I have it on good authority that before I tried to kill you, you were very much into me."

"Only because I was confused about how Ethan felt about me, and I didn't know who you really were. Also, you were pretty much throwing yourself at me," I shot back indignantly. I desperately wanted to cross my arms, but my wrist was still firmly attached to the door handle.

"And it worked, didn't it?" Adam was still smiling.

"Yeah, well, you're not nearly as charming as you think you are." I shook my wrist in a futile effort to get it free. The action was more a show of defiance than any real attempt at escape. Adam watched my useless struggle in obvious amusement, and allowed the conversation to drop.

I hated that he was right. At one point I had wondered about dating him, and had been attracted to him, but that was before I knew the truth. If I had known who the real Adam Chambers was, I never would have had any sort of romantic notions towards him.

Adam pulled off the road into a gas station. The temperature had risen during the morning and I rolled down the window to get some fresh air while he pumped gas.

"Can't get enough of me, huh?" He cocked his head to one side to study me.

I'd reached my limit of tolerance for his smugness. Not even caring if it made him mad, I twisted the window crank of the classic vehicle and closed the window in his face.

Twenty-Four

"I guess there are just some rules Ethan refuses to break." Adam glanced into the rearview mirror. I couldn't tell if he was talking to himself or me. We were once again back on the highway, but had gotten caught in stopped-dead traffic. Flashing lights quite a ways up the road suggested an accident of some kind.

"What is that supposed to mean?"

"The Hleo leaders, The Three, have a set of ridiculous rules they make all their followers live by. The number one rule is not to get into a romantic relationship with a protected, but it's a two-part rule. Getting into a relationship is forbidden, but sleeping with one is unforgivable."

"Really?"

"You mean Ethan, your soulmate, the one you share your every bit of being with, didn't explain this to you?" Adam batted his eyes condescendingly. I wanted to hit him, but he continued before I could react. "The Three have kind of an old-world view about sex. They believe that sex is more than just, well, what it usually is. They see it as two souls joining together and becoming one or some gibberish like that. I know this because it's something they drill into us right from the beginning of training. The idea goes that a protected has a unique essence or calling imprinted on their lives, and that goes right down to their soul, so for a Hleo, with their altered less-than-worthy being, to sleep with them would defile them, taint their calling."

I bit my thumbnail. Adam couldn't be trusted, but I didn't know why he would bother lying about something like this. And as I thought back to Ethan and I, and every time we had gotten remotely intimate—Simon's warning the night he'd caught us, Ethan pulling away at Veridan, and again at the pond—Adam's explanation fit. Maybe that was what Ethan had been going to explain to me that day, when we were interrupted by the news of Ryan's accident.

Adam pulled a quick maneuver, cutting off an SUV to swerve into the closest exit lane. I winced when the large vehicle laid on its horn, but we left it and the traffic jam behind us as Adam sped down a service road that shouldered the highway.

"So, Hleo aren't allowed to have sex?" *So awkward.* Talking to Adam of all people about this subject was beyond weird, but I was too curious to stop myself.

"Not with protecteds, not if they want to keep being Hleo. Technically they can with regular humans or with each other, but I think The Three are happier if a Hleo remains celibate. Focused one hundred percent on the job is their motto, which doesn't leave a lot of time for extracurricular activities. Of course, there were always creative ways to take care of those needs, for those of us who wanted to."

Heat flared in my cheeks. I really did not want to continue this conversation, not with Adam, anyway. "Okay, then."

His laugh was harsh. "Am I offending your delicate sensibilities? Don't worry, your precious Ethan is not like that. I doubt he's ever scratched that itch. He's too by the book. Then again, I never thought he'd get into a relationship with one of you, so what do I know." Adam tilted his head from side to side as if he was deliberating. "Although, if he believed his time with you was temporary, that there was always going to be a point when he would have to leave, then it makes sense that he wouldn't allow himself to break that one final rule. He wouldn't want to destroy his chance of staying on as a Hleo if he did get caught. Plus, he's too much of a gentleman to sleep with somebody and then ditch them."

I bristled. Adam spoke as though he knew Ethan better than I did, explaining his motivation to me with such certainty.

I opened my mouth to argue with Adam, to say that I knew Ethan, and I knew he would never leave me, but shut it again. Here we were on a bizarre road trip together to find Ethan because, in fact, he *had* left me. *Where are you Ethan?* If only I could talk to him. Then maybe I could understand how I had ended up alone in the first place. We were driving along a riverbank and I watched a guy in a small motorboat cast a fishing line into the water.

"I'm surprised they kept Ethan after finding out the terrible truth about you two starting up a romantic relationship," Adam mused.

"What do you mean?"

"I've never heard of anyone doing what Ethan did and being allowed to stay on as a Hleo. I'm surprised they didn't get rid of him right away, but then I suppose he is considered to be the best, especially since I left."

"Get rid of, like kill?" The blood drained from my face.

"What? No!" Adam scrunched up his face, as though I was being ridiculous. "They don't kill their own, even when they break the rules. I'm proof of that, aren't I? That's not the way they do things. It would go against their precious virtues. No, they would strip him of his Hleo abilities and he'd go back to being a regular old human." Adam shook his head and grimaced, as though that would be a more terrible punishment than death.

My breath caught in my throat. "They can do that?" I felt like I'd been punched in the stomach. Adam's admission was earth-shattering. If what he was saying was true, it *was* possible for Ethan to become like me again, and that meant it was possible for us to grow old together, something I had believed was impossible. *Why did Ethan keep that from me?*

"Something else Ethan neglected to tell you?" Adam's tone was mocking.

I didn't respond. It was none of his business what Ethan had and hadn't told me.

"Well, it's basically the same as sentencing someone to death, so I can see why he'd avoid mentioning it. I've heard it's one of the most painful processes a person can endure. It's why most of the Hleo that have screwed up, leave and join the Bana before they can be reverted. There are very few who would be willing to stay and take their punishment." Adam drummed the steering wheel with his hands. Was he sharing a personal experience with me?

"Why is it so awful?" I turned to face him straight on.

"The body gets used to its new form as a Hleo, the strength, the speed, the sustainability, and when a branding is reversed it shocks the system drastically. To go back to needing food, and air, and other normal bodily requirements is hard. Apparently, as the serum is drawn out of your body it's like being lit on fire and thrown into ice all at once. Every one of your cells is being pulled apart and reassembled as your blood starts pumping normally again.

"I don't know exactly what Ethan told you about being branded, but it's like being infused with a special type of steroid that makes every bit of you stronger, faster, and immune to disease and aging. To have all of that taken away, well, it's not something many would choose."

"Ethan would be willing to do that for me, no matter how awful it might be, I know he would." My chest tightened. *But do I have any right to ask him to?*

"He didn't even tell you he *could* become a normal human again, Hannah! You need to ask yourself why that is. Ethan is all about duty; don't fool yourself into thinking he will choose you over being a Hleo, that he would be willing to give up the one cause that has kept him going all these years for some tryst with a high-school girl. The only reason we're even on this journey, besides to rub it in to Ethan how easy it was for me to get to you, is to show you just how wrong you are about his loyalty. I know you think we'll find him, and you'll come up with some magical plan to get away from me, and then the two of you can go back to playing house together, but you're wrong. Ethan has been reassigned. Even if the two of you did somehow manage to escape, your time together would end when your destiny moment came. Then they'll call for him again, and he'll go. Ethan is loyal to the Hleo above all else; why do you think he could so easily turn on someone he had called brother for years?" Adam turned to look at me, his voice full of hurt and betrayal. His usual casual demeanor was gone and he appeared completely rattled. Even his eyes were far darker than normal.

I shrank back in my seat, stunned and unsure of how to react. Adam had verbalized my deepest fear, that Ethan was going to choose the Hleo over me, and the more Adam talked, the more it seemed he was right. Why had Ethan allowed himself to be reassigned? Why hadn't he told me about being able to change back into a normal human, or about the intimacy stuff? Even though I wanted to be furious with Adam for bringing all of those issues up, to yell at him and tell him how wrong he was, I couldn't bring myself to do it. His rant had clearly been more about the two of them than about Ethan and me, and I thought of all Ethan had told me about their relationship.

"For what it's worth, I know Ethan regrets how he handled things with you." I looked down at the hand clenched in my lap while I spoke. I didn't want to make the situation worse, but it felt like something Adam should know, and that Ethan might wish he could share under different circumstances.

Adam didn't react, so I turned to stare out at the expansive gorge we were currently crossing by bridge, figuring silence was best. After a few minutes of silence, I thought I heard him mutter, "A lot of good that does me now."

Twenty-Five

It was early afternoon when Adam stopped so we could get something to eat. We had just crossed over the Tennessee state line. I couldn't believe how much ground we'd covered in less than a day. *Where are we going, and how much longer will it take us to get there?*

The sun beat down from a blue sky and the temperature had risen substantially. When Adam cut me free from the zip-tie, I immediately discarded my sweater into the backseat so that I was only in a tank top and T-shirt.

"Hope you like subs." Adam held the door open so I could walk into the sandwich franchise next to a gas station.

"They're fine." I eyed the menu board, trying to decide what to get. It was the first thing he'd said to me since his explosion about Ethan. I couldn't help but wonder at the lack of usual charm. Had my admission about Ethan's regrets shaken him that much?

We ate fairly quickly, and then were back on our way. I got in the car and held out my wrist, ready for Adam to zip-tie it to the door handle once again, but he didn't. I watched him warily as he crossed over to his side of the Camaro and climbed in. *Did you forget, Adam, or have you decided to trust me a little bit more?* I hastily tucked my arm into my stomach to make it less noticeable in case he had simply forgotten. He stuck the key in the ignition and we drove off, away from the rest stop area. I tried not to react, but I was so glad to be free. It meant a better chance of escape later.

Adam was still quiet, and I set my mind to trying to recall Ethan's letters. If only I'd been paying closer attention to the differences in the letters upon my cursory glance of the second one.

Ethan had used the word love more than once in the new letter, and I couldn't be sure, but I thought I had caught the word scared, or frightened maybe. *Think Hannah, think.*

As we passed by a cutoff for Knoxville, I had a flash. A little blonde girl peering over the side of an old stone well. She was leaning forward on her tippy toes, as though looking down into the gaping hole to search for something specific. A pile of broken boards sat beside the well, perhaps at one time the cover for it, but even in my mind's eye they were rotten with decay. The well was positioned at the bottom of a gradually sloping embankment that bordered a forest. A road ran along the top of the hill, and some sort of parade or street fair was going on in the background of the scene. There were all sorts of people milling about on the street, and a huge banner hung overhead. The weather appeared to be about the same as what Adam and I were traveling in, a beautiful cloudless day, but my mind kept focusing in on the little girl. She must have been about eight years old, with a light blue summer dress on.

Her position was precarious, and a ripple of fear for her surged through me. There was an urgent feeling to the image I didn't normally experience, and I mentally cataloged its details. From the style the people wore, and the few cars that lined the street, the image was clearly relatively recent. I studied the banner. Something about it struck me, the town name, and the date on the banner; Madison City, TN - May 26-28. I took a slow breath and allowed the scene to fade to black in my mind, thankful that I'd only received one image this time. I didn't need the overload of multiple images causing me to pass out in front of Adam.

"Are you okay?" Adam's gaze darted from the road to me.

"What day is it?"

"What?" His brows furrowed together.

"The date, what day is it?" I demanded, more urgently.

"May twenty-seventh, why?"

I bit my lip. *What if my vision is happening right now?* That little girl could be in serious danger; she could easily slip into that old well at any moment. *I have to do something.*

"How far is Madison City from here?" I glanced out the window at our surroundings, a stretch of green, rolling pastures.

"What? How should I know?" Adam blinked, sounding completely baffled by my strange questions. He kept looking at me as if I had come completely unhinged.

"Come on Adam. You haven't consulted a map once on this trip; you obviously know the towns and roads across America really well. How far is Madison City, Tennessee from here?"

Adam studied me for a moment, then shrugged. "About fifteen minutes."

My mind raced. *Fifteen minutes. She's at that well, I know it.* "Can we go there?" I tried not to sound too desperate. I didn't want Adam to immediately dismiss my request just to spite me.

"No," Adam declared matter-of-factly.

"Look, there's something I want to check out there. Just one small thing. It's really important, and then we can continue on our way. I promise I have nothing shady planned."

He pursed his lips. "I'm not sure if you realize it, but this is not a taxi service. We are already on a crazy, person-finding mission as per your begging request, and I'm taking a risk I won't make my superiors mad if they find out I have you off course, so I'm going to need more than 'you just want to check something' before I will even consider another detour."

My stomach churned. I had to convince Adam to give in. "I have a feeling that an innocent person is in life-threatening trouble. I hope I'm wrong, but I need to check to make sure. Please Adam, it's really important."

His expression softened a little. "A feeling, huh?" Skepticism dripped from his voice, but I thought I detected a hint of curiosity.

"I just want to make sure she's safe, and it's only fifteen minutes." I clasped my hands together, not caring if he realized I was free from the door handle.

"No funny business?" He pointed a finger at me.

"I promise." I held my breath.

Adam didn't speak for long enough that I was sure he was going to refuse. Finally, he sighed. "Fine."

Relief coursed through me. "Thank you."

He pulled off the interstate at the next exit and we started east, changing course from the southerly direction we had been heading. Adam was quiet as we drove, likely attempting to figure out what I was up to.

I didn't bother trying to explain further. Even if he didn't understand it, ultimately he was taking me to Madison City, that's all I needed from him. I shut my eyes and brought the image into the forefront of my mind, attempting to commit every single detail I could to memory. I wanted to get a feel for what we would be looking for when we arrived.

Twelve minutes later we were approaching a small town and a crowd of people in the streets.

"Is that a street fair?" Adam twisted to look at me incredulously.

"I guess so." I tried to sound innocent, while I kept my eyes on the crowds, banners, and balloons.

"And this isn't a trick?" Adam's jaw tightened. The car slowed down.

My pulse sped up. "Please Adam, I swear, no tricks." I gripped his arm to implore him to keep driving, but stopped and dropped my hand. I couldn't let him see how desperate I was or he might pull a u-turn and speed away without giving me a chance to make sure the old well was empty, and the little girl was safe. I also didn't feel comfortable touching him. He clutched the wheel tighter for a moment, and then the engine revved as we resumed speed.

We were coming into town from the angle my vision had come from. Madison City was small and scenic, tucked into the mountains. And from the size of the crowd, most of its townspeople were at the fair.

The main street had been blocked off with wooden barricades, forcing Adam to turn down a residential street. "Where to, *boss*?"

"Pull in there." I pointed to the parking lot of a small medical clinic. Adam followed my instructions and stopped the car in a spot well away from the four other vehicles parked in the lot. He cut the engine and lifted both hands, palms up, in a 'what now?' motion.

"We need to walk back to the main street, cross over it, and head down the ditch to the edge of the forest. I'm telling you exactly where I'm going so you know that you can trust me. I am not going to run." I kept my eyes locked with his.

Adam studied me for a moment, then nodded in clearly reluctant agreement.

We climbed out of the car and I was hit with the sound of lighthearted country music and the aroma of French fries and cotton candy. I strode towards the fair, practically running, with Adam close enough that if I did try anything he'd be able to grab me. In a matter of minutes we had made our way through the colorful throngs of people enjoying the festivities and beautiful weather, and stood at the top of the embankment. At the bottom was the forlorn-looking well, exactly as I had pictured it.

I ignored the eerie sensation that pricked the hairs on my arms from seeing in person something that had only been in my mind twenty minutes before. I tamped down the emotion, determined to keep focused on the task at hand.

I took a step down the hill, but Adam gripped my elbow to stop me. "Where are we going?"

"I told you I want to check something." I tugged my arm from his grasp and carefully traversed my way through the long grass of the hill.

"You realize you're a freak, right?" Adam trotted along beside me.

"I'm well aware," I replied wryly, as my pants snagged on the coarse grass. Adam was right. My ability was purely the stuff of freaks.

I hoped I would be proven wrong, that the well would be empty, and Adam would think I was crazy, but the gut feeling that the little girl was in danger wouldn't go away. If I could actually save someone by having arrived in the right place at the correct moment because of one of my flashes, it would make some of the turmoil worth it.

"You wanted to make a wish?" Adam mocked as we approached the cavernous stone structure.

"Shhh." I waved my hand at him. We were within a few feet of the well when I heard a soft, quivering cry.

He stopped and stared at the well, then rushed forward. He must have heard the same sound I had. When he reached it, Adam peered down into the well. His head snapped back up. "There's a little girl down there!" His eyes were wide.

I rushed to his side and glanced down. Fifteen feet below me, I caught a glimpse of the girl in my vision. She was wearing the same summery blue dress, although it was now tattered and dirty. Her hair was matted and there were streaks on her face from dirt mixed with tears. She was crying, but looked up at the sound of our voices.

"Hi, we're going to help you, okay?" I called down to her in my most reassuring voice. She nodded in response, her breath coming in small gasps.

"How did you know?" Adam grasped my shoulders and stared at me in bewilderment.

I shook out of his hold. "Later. Right now let's just get her out of there." I motioned to the well, and he nodded.

"I'll be right back." He ran back up the embankment and disappeared.

"It's going to be okay." I told the girl. She nodded again and looked up at me, complete trust on her face. I craned my neck to search the area Adam had disappeared. *Hurry, hurry.*

Adam returned minutes later, clutching a yellow-corded rope he must have pilfered from one of the fair's booths.

He flung his coat to the ground and quickly looped the rope around one of the large trees that stood close to the well. He then wrapped it around his waist, and tied a series of knots in the rope. "I'm going to get the girl, you wait here." Adam swung a leg over the side of the old stone well. The hole was about four feet across, giving him ample room to lower himself down. I watched him slide the knots in a manner that allowed him to drop slowly into the damp dark space. It only took a few minutes for Adam to reach the bottom.

"Hi sweetheart, my friend Hannah and I are here to help. We're going to get you out of this well and back to your family safe and sound, okay?" Adam crouched down beside the little girl, his voice bouncing off the rock walls.

My throat tightened. How could such a cold-blooded killer be so kind to a small child?

"Okay." She managed to get out through shaky breaths.

"My name is Adam, what's your name?" Adam asked.

"Laney," she replied.

"All right Laney, I'm going to help you get out of here." Adam picked her up and held her tight against his chest. She wrapped her arms around his neck and he let go of her and used both hands to haul them both up the rope, planting his feet against the sides for leverage as they rose.

"You know, it's a little dirty, but that's a very pretty dress you have on. Is blue your favorite color?"

"I like pink." Laney tipped back her head, an uncertain expression on her face as she looked up at me.

"That's my friend Hannah up there. Pink is her favorite color." Adam clutched the rope, the muscles in his arms bulging. "You're holding on very well, nice strong grip. How old are you?"

"I'm eight. I'll be nine in a month." Laney gave him a small smile, beginning to perk up.

"Nine, wow! So what do you want for your birthday?" Adam kept his attention on her as he slid the rope through the knots. They were a little over halfway up the shaft now.

"I asked for a puppy. I have a cat named Trixie, but mom says I can have a dog as long as I promise to walk him and feed him." Laney shifted in Adam's grasp, her voice growing animated.

"Dogs are a big responsibility, but I think you'll be able to handle it." Adam's voice was smooth, calm. I had to admit I was impressed with his ability to distract Laney from the situation.

They reached the top and Adam threw one arm over the edge and wrapped the other one around Laney's waist. "Okay Laney, I'm holding on to you nice and tight so you don't have to worry about falling. I need you to stretch your arms up as high as they will go, and Hannah is going to grab you, can you do that?"

She clutched the collar of his shirt tighter. "I'm scared."

"I know sweetheart, but I promise I won't let anything happen to you."

"Okay. I think I can." Laney's blue eyes were wide as she stared up at me, the confidence in her voice wavering.

"Hi Laney, I'm Hannah. It's very nice to meet you." I held out my arms and leaned over the thick stone perimeter wall.

"Nice to meet you too." Laney looked from me to Adam. He nodded and she took a breath before reaching up. I slid my hands under her arms so I could lift her over the top of the well wall and set her down on the grass. She had scrapes on her hands, elbows, and knees, but none appeared super deep.

"My leg hurts." She rubbed her eyes with the backs of her dirty little hands, wiping away stray tears.

Adam hauled himself up and tossed one leg over the stone wall so he was straddling it. A moment later he had scrambled over and joined us on the grass. "Where does it hurt, Laney?" Adam knelt down beside her.

"Here." She pointed just above her left ankle.

He examined the leg carefully. "Well, the bad news is I think it's broken, but the good news is, you're probably going to get a really cool cast that all your friends can sign."

"Could it be a pink cast?" She gazed up at him adoringly.

Adam grinned. "I think that could definitely be arranged. How about we get you back to your mom so she can take you to the hospital."

Laney nodded her little blonde head in agreement.

Before we started up the hill Adam grabbed the boards that had once sat across the well and dropped them back into their original position. Then he wrapped Laney in his coat and scooped her up in his arms.

I trailed along behind them as Adam made his way up the embankment towards the fair, reeling from what I had just witnessed. *He is so good with her*. I hadn't expected him to respond well to children. How could someone so capable of violence display such gentleness?

When we got to the top of the hill we wandered through the crowd for a few minutes, hunting for Laney's family, until finally she pointed to a frantic-looking woman by the cotton candy stand. As soon as her mother's eyes landed on Laney she ran over to us, arms outstretched

Adam passed Laney back to her mother, and explained what had happened. Then he firmly advised that the town needed to do something about boarding the old well up, or filling it in. The mother thanked us repeatedly, hugging her injured daughter tightly to her chest while doing so. "How can I ever thank you?"

"No need." Adam rested his hand on Laney's head for a moment. "We're just glad she's okay. Better get her to the hospital and have that ankle checked out. She wants a pink cast."

The mother smiled up at him, her eyes filled with tears as she nodded. Before she could say more, Adam grasped my elbow and turned me toward the car.

He didn't speak the entire way back, but I braced myself, knowing that, as soon as we were alone, he'd have a whole lot of questions for me that I had no idea had to answer.

Twenty-Six

Adam held the door open for me, his jaw tight. The tension between us was almost palpable. I climbed in and he slammed the door behind me. After sliding into the driver's seat, he sat with his hands gripping the steering wheel. I stared at my lap, feeling more and more uneasy as the silence stretched on.

"Okay, tell me."

I hesitated. Should I lie? My shoulders slumped. What did it matter if Adam knew the truth? It didn't make any difference to my situation. "I see protecteds." I focused on a family walking down the sidewalk in front of the car, heading home from the festivities. They looked happy, and I envied their ability to spend the afternoon together enjoying a simple town fair. Would I ever be that carefree again? A pang shot through me.

"*See them?* What does that mean?"

I drummed my fingers on my knees. "I get random visions of protecteds. They pop into my head from time to time. It's been happening since I was twelve. For a long time I was under the impression that they were simply flashes of inspiration, just my imagination creating images for me to draw, but then Ethan recognized someone in one of my drawings. It was his sister—who, as you probably know, was a protected—and since then Ethan and other Hleo have been able to confirm that all of my flashes are different protecteds from different points in time.

"For some reason, today I got a vision of this little girl hanging over the edge of a well, and I could see the town name and a date on a banner that hung at the edge of the image. This is the very first time since I've started having these flashes that my vision has actually coincided with a time and place I could get to." I exhaled slowly.

Adam's eyes narrowed. "If your visions are random, how is it that you just *happened* to see a town that was less than half an hour from where you were?"

I shook my head. "I honestly don't know. It's possible the images aren't actually random, but Ethan and I have been analyzing them for months, and we've never discovered any sort of pattern or way to control when I receive a flash, who it will be of, or from what time period. It's been so frustrating, and now, with what just happened, I'm more confused than ever." I sighed bitterly.

"So that little girl, Laney, she's a protected?" Adam's grip on the steering wheel tightened.

"If she's the same as every other person in my flashes, then yes." My stomach churned. I hadn't really thought this through. Had I just put Laney in danger by revealing to a Bana member that she was a protected?

To my relief, Adam started up the car, backed out of the parking spot, and peeled off in the direction we had come from. He appeared agitated, continually glancing into the rearview mirror.

I clutched the door handle. "What's with the speed?"

"If she's a protected then there could be a Hleo somewhere nearby. I don't need him or her spotting us and thinking I was after that little girl, slowing us down."

My mouth dropped open. He was right; if it was close to the time in her life when Laney would make her big decision, there could have been a Hleo around. Someone I might have been able to question about Ethan, but it was too late now; we were already ten minutes out of Madison City. I slumped back against my seat.

"So what is her destiny then?" Adam broke through the silence as we approached the highway.

I shrugged. "I don't know." Adam narrowed his eyes again. "Really, I don't." I held out my hands, palms up.

"I don't get it. I thought Miriam was the only one who could see protecteds. You're the same as her?" Adam forehead was creased as he again reminded me that he was once part of the Hleo world.

"I'm not the same as Miriam; my visions work like photos, hers are like videos."

"How do you know that?"

"She told me."

Adam stared at me. The car drifted across the center lane.

"Watch out!" I pointed to the oncoming pickup truck hauling a trailer full of hay bales. Adam swerved, narrowly missing getting side-swiped by the farm vehicle. He slowed the vehicle slightly and ran a hand down his face.

I straightened up in my seat. "Ethan took me to Veridan in the winter to talk to The Three. While we were there, Miriam explained how her visions work, and how they differ from mine. It was while we were on our way back from Veridan that Paige and Uri came after me. Did you really not know that?" Now it was my turn to stare skeptically at him. I couldn't believe he and Paige had had no contact in the last few months.

"Like I said, Paige and I have no obligations to each other. After what happened in the fall I was going to drop coming after you. Ethan deserves hurt and anguish for what he did to me, but after my defeat my pride was a little wounded. I figured I'd wait until he got reassigned to come after him again. No sense dragging you into our feud twice. I'd go directly after him the next time. But then Alexander put me on this assignment, so here I am."

My chest clenched. "Alexander put you on this assignment directly?" Just the mention of the ominous leader of the Bana put me on edge.

"Well, one of his henchmen did, a guy named Muirhead. He's like Alexander's number two, so an order from him is essentially an order from Alexander himself."

"Muirhead?" My mind spun. Muirhead was the name of the gentleman Milton had mentioned who bought the Glain Neidr back from around the turn of the century.

"You know him?"

"Only by name." *I wonder if he's responsible for the destruction to poor Milton's store.* I gulped at the thought. I glanced over at Adam. *Or maybe it was you.*

"Did you destroy Milton's store?" My tone was sharp as anger welled up inside me.

His head jerked. "What?"

"You know very well what. Milton's Oddities and Rarities in Hartford. I went there a few weeks ago to talk to the owner about …

something, and someone had trashed his store. It was you, wasn't it?" I pointed an accusing finger at him.

"I have no idea what you're talking about." Adam pushed my hand away.

"Well, if it wasn't you, then who was it?"

Adam shrugged. "Alexander has numerous schemes going on at any given time. I'm sure it was another one of his toadies, doing his bidding."

I eyed him for a moment. *Are you telling the truth?*

He didn't look at me, just turned the steering wheel slightly to merge onto a different highway. "That's why he wants you so bad."

The knot in my stomach twisted tighter. What he was saying had to be true, Alexander wanted me because of my ability to see and draw protecteds. But why? Until we had some idea of how and why I could do what I did, what good was it to anyone? I played with the ring on my pinky finger. As far as I was concerned, the far bigger question was why I had this ability in the first place. Except for the fact that it had brought Ethan into my life, I'd give anything to have never seen a flash in my life.

"Alexander must have learned what you can do, and now he wants to use it for himself somehow."

"I don't know how he could have. We've been pretty careful about keeping it quiet." I bit my lip.

"He has ways. If Ethan's been contacting people trying to figure out if your images are protecteds, it wouldn't take long before a Bana got wind of it. Trust me, we are more linked with the Hleo than they'd like to admit," Adam said wryly.

"I guess that's it, then. Why else would he want to bring me in, instead of just killing me? If only he understood how little control I have over my visions, he wouldn't care about me. I can't do anything to help him with whatever his plans might be."

We continued to wind our way through a mountainous area, on roads that cut through the towering limestone embankments. Were we still in Tennessee or had we crossed into another state? I hadn't been paying attention so I wasn't sure exactly where we were. I kept my eyes on the road signs, trying to figure out our location.

"Was there a year on that banner?"

I turned in his direction. "What?"

"You said there was a date on the banner you saw in your mind. Did it have a year on it?"

"No. Only a month and day."

"Then why did you do it?" Adam shifted gears as he picked up speed.

I frowned. "Why did I do what?"

"Why did you talk me into going to that well? If what you've told me is true then there was only a chance she was going to be down there. Your vision, or whatever you call them, could have been from a hundred years ago, for all you know. Even if the scene looked relatively modern, it could have been ten years in the past or in the future, you had no way of telling. And you had to be aware that I would ask how you knew she would be there, which meant telling me the truth about yourself. I'm the Bana, I'm the bad guy; it doesn't seem smart to let me in on your ability to see protecteds. So why did you do it?"

"If there was a chance that we could help that little girl, then it was worth telling you about my ability."

"How did you know you'd be able to talk me into the detour?"

"I didn't, I was just banking on the hope that you aren't a complete monster."

Surprise flashed in his eyes. "Well, thanks for your faith in my humanity." His tone was wry. He obviously didn't like it when the conversation got too deep, or touched on his capacity for good. Was that because he didn't believe he had such a thing anymore, or because he was afraid that he did?

"You're welcome." I settled back in my seat.

A hint of a smile crossed his lips.

Twenty-Seven

Adam rested an arm casually on the door's window frame. The sun had just dipped below the trees as we moved into the second evening of our journey together. He shifted in his seat. "So, I'm curious about something."

"What?" I straightened up, bracing myself for whatever topic he had come up with that I probably wouldn't want to discuss.

"What is your plan when we get to Ethan? Suppose, by some miracle, you are able to get away from me, what happens next? He's still someone else's Hleo now." From his tone of voice, Adam relished relaying that fact to me more than was necessary. "You must have some sort of plan, right? You naively got in the car with a known dangerous threat and allowed yourself to be dragged across this fair land, just hoping that I'm not lying to you in order to make this trip easy on myself. For all you know I took one look at Ethan's letters, realized he's in Jakarta and thought, well if she thinks we're going to Ethan she won't try to escape. Meanwhile, we're headed right for Alexander."

"You wouldn't do … that's not what's happening, is it?" The blood drained from my face.

Adam studied me for a moment, his expression unreadable, before his lips curved up into a grin. "No."

I scrutinized him. Was he telling me the truth and we really were headed for Ethan? Or were we actually going straight to Alexander and he was just toying with me, messing with my mind again. I wasn't as naïve as he'd accused me of being; I knew he couldn't be trusted to do anything I wanted him to do, not unless it served his best interests. In this case, I was counting on the fact that he believed finding Ethan did just that. Coming with him had been a calculated risk, but one I was willing to take. I needed to see Ethan. Even if Adam believed it was nothing more than a detour before my inevitable fate of being handed over to the Bana, I had faith in Ethan's ability to come to my rescue, if given the opportunity.

"So what's the plan then? I mean, I get it. You think you're going to reach Ethan, he's going to abandon his new protected, sucker punch me, and you'll run into each other's arms and head off into the sunset. But then what?"

My brow furrowed. "Why would I tell you?"

"Because I don't think you have a plan." Adam's tone was smug.

I squared my jaw. *Maybe I don't, but I won't give him the satisfaction of knowing that.* "Well, I do."

"Uh huh."

I bit my lip. I hadn't really given it that much thought. All I had been focusing on was getting to Ethan. To look into his emerald eyes once again and feel his arms around me. "Maybe I don't have all the particulars worked out, but so what? It's romantic."

Adam shook his head. "It's foolish, is what it is."

I narrowed my eyes. "What would you know about romance anyway? You've probably never even been in love."

The question was met with silence. After a moment I crossed my arms and stared out at the dense forest, full of moss-covered trees, that we were passing through. *I am so done with talking to him.*

"I have, twice actually."

"Oh." I dropped my arms to my sides, feeling chastised.

"Allison Chambers. She was the absolute love of my life."

My forehead creased. "Chambers, so she was—"

"My wife. Allison was my wife, and the reason I accepted when Victor came calling all those years ago." Adam pressed his lips together.

I blinked. "What happened?" What sort of person could fall in love with someone like Adam?

"Allison was a neighbor. I grew up in Mt Vernon, Illinois, and her family lived down the street from mine. I fell in love with her the day her family moved into the big two-story colonial house three doors down from the one I lived in. I was eight years old. She was seven. I still remember thinking her hair was like sunshine, and her smile was the most beautiful thing I had ever seen. She was soft-spoken and gentle, with a loving nature, always wanting to help others, always motivating me to be a better person. We were married when she turned eighteen, in a small summer ceremony in her parents' backyard."

"Eighteen?" I couldn't even imagine getting married at my age.

"That was the norm back then. We weren't considered too young for that sort of commitment. We were happy together and completely in love. I worked for her father as an apprentice in the pharmacy he owned. I enjoyed the work, but I really enjoyed the way Ally made my life whole," Adam recalled, sadness and longing thick in his voice.

I swallowed hard. It startled me to think of Adam as a vulnerable being, capable of such deep emotions.

"In that time it wasn't uncommon to start a family right away. The more children you had the better, was the logic. Allison loved children. She had been the eldest in her family of seven brothers and sisters, and dreamed of having a large family. She and I tried for years to have a baby. She was disappointed when it looked like she wouldn't be able to have children. I knew she thought she was failing me in some way. I never seemed to be able to convince her that she was all the family I needed." Adam's grip on the steering wheel tightened. "Allison had three miscarriages, each one more devastating than the last, until finally she got pregnant, and it appeared as though she would be able to carry this baby to term."

A sick feeling developed in the pit of my stomach.

"Ally died giving birth to our one and only child. She only got to hold our little girl in her arms for a moment before she closed her eyes and never opened them again. She had asked me to name the baby Lily, but Lily had come too early and was very weak. She only lived a day longer than Allison. Her family and I buried them together in a little plot under a big old shade tree. That's where my family still lies to this day." Adam's eyes were glassy.

I fought against the feeling of sympathy that threatened to well up in my chest. Adam had almost killed me. He wanted to destroy Ethan and he planned to turn me over to the Bana. I couldn't feel sorry for him. I wouldn't. If I allowed myself to feel anything but loathing for him then I wouldn't be able to fight him when I needed to.

I chewed on the inside of my cheek. What a terrible thing to have to live through, no one deserved that. Of course, for all I knew, he'd made up the whole story. After all, it didn't seem possible that Adam, this superficial, uncaring human being, could have cared so deeply for another person and had been a *father*. Although, if it were true, I guess I could see how enduring such a tragedy might have caused him to become such a closed-off person. Shallow behavior was a safer choice than human connection.

I felt his gaze on me and turned my head slightly.

"You don't believe me, do you?"

I lifted my shoulders. "I don't know what to believe."

Adam gave a slight nod. "I guess I don't blame you. It's all true though. After I lost Ally, I found myself in a very dark place. Everything in my existence only served to remind me of her so I left, took off for a completely different part of the country, determined to leave all of my hurt in the past. I made my way to New York and got a job in a factory there. I was practically living in squalor when Victor came to see me. Somehow he knew my story. He told me that I had been chosen to serve a higher calling in this world, and by serving that calling I would be able to see the plan that exists for all of creation, and find reason for the unexplainable tragedies that occur. I don't know how well you know Victor, but he can be very charming and persuasive when he wants to be. He has an incredible talent for knowing the exact thing a person needs to hear. I had nothing to lose, so I went with him, and that's how I got sucked into the world of the Hleo." Adam glanced over his shoulder as he merged onto a new highway.

We were taking a bypass around Birmingham, Alabama. I hadn't even noticed us leave Tennessee; Adam had completely distracted me. I knew I should be paying more attention to my surroundings, but, in spite of myself, his story drew me in.

"You said you fell in love twice." The words were out before I could stop them. Judging by his drawn face, sharing his past had definitely taken a toll on Adam. I didn't want to be insensitive, but after the way Allison had died, what could the other woman who had managed to reach Adam's heart be like?

He sighed. "When I signed up for the life of a Hleo, I signed up completely. Their unspoken expectation of a life of celibacy was completely fine with me. Allison was the only soul mate I had ever known, and the only person I could ever conceive of loving.

"I served the Hleo loyally for years, but as I protected different people I became more and more jaded. For every person I protected who was a good and decent person, worthy of having someone looking out for them, it seemed there were two more who were worthless excuses for human beings, whose deaths would actually make the world a better place. And that leads us to the second woman I fell in love with, and the events that caused Ethan to turn on me." Adam's grip on the wheel tightened, his knuckles going white.

I forced myself to play it cool so he'd keep talking. I had always been really curious to learn the exact details behind Ethan and Adam's relationship falling apart, and now that I knew there was a girl involved I was dying to hear more.

"I was stationed as a Hleo for this guy in Savannah, Georgia. He was a human piece of garbage. He spent his days getting falling-down drunk, while I spent my time pouring drinks down his throat. My cover position, conveniently, was as a bartender at the local pub he frequented. I had been told by the town locals that he'd had a rough time since coming home from the war. Day in and day out I watched him get black-out drunk, then I would help him stagger home when he couldn't get there himself. After all, I couldn't take a chance that some Bana member would choose that vulnerable moment to assassinate him, or worse, that the stupid moron would stumble into traffic and get hit by a car.

"I'd take the guy back to his lovely residential bungalow on his nice quiet street and see the black eyes and bruises on his wife's face and arms, the look of fear in her eyes when we entered the house. I'd bring him in and get him settled on a bed for the night. Occasionally she'd ask me to stay for coffee, or a piece of pie, anything to keep from being alone in the house with him in case he came to and decided to knock her around a little more. I was supposed to watch over this guy, protect him from getting hurt, and in the meantime I had to stand by while he did that to his wife." Adam's voice was practically shaking with rage, and I wrapped my arms around myself.

"I'd stick around a few times a month. Then it became once a week. And eventually I spent the better part of most evenings with her. Nora Ostrowski. I remember her dark brown eyes matched her hair perfectly. She was a little older than me, technically speaking, but we had each endured a lifetime of heartache in only a short amount of time, and it connected us somehow."

We passed a sign for a service centre. I couldn't remember the last time we'd eaten, but I was too afraid that if I interrupted Adam to ask him to stop, he'd never finish the story. I pressed a hand to my stomach and kept my mouth shut.

"At first it was just two people keeping each other company. She'd tell me about the years before he went off to war, the hopes and plans they'd had. How she had wanted a big family, and to grow old with her high school sweetheart, but when he came back he was a different man, and now she didn't know what to do. I mostly just listened to her, gave her a comforting shoulder to cry on over her frustration and disappointment with how her husband treated her. In those days you just put up with an unhappy life, it never even occurred to her that she had the option of leaving him." Adam shook his head in disbelief.

"It was late one night, later than I usually stayed. He was blacked out in the bedroom, and I was about to leave. I was on my way out the door when she slipped her soft, gentle fingers between mine and just stood looking up at me. I knew from the expression on her face that she had the same feelings for me that I'd developed for her. I cupped her face in my hands and kissed her, my first kiss since Allison. It was warm and welcoming and we both found comfort in having found another damaged soul in this world. I held her in my arms for a while, and promised her that I would never let him hurt her again." Adam's voice sounded far away, as though he were back in that house with her again.

I held my breath, desperate to know what happened next.

"A week later I saw Julian Monteiro, a notorious member of the Bana at that time, sniffing around. I knew what he was there for, so I made it easy for him. I talked Nora into going out one evening to spend time with her sister, something she didn't normally do. Once I saw that she had safely arrived at her sister's home on the other side of town. I doubled back. I got there just in time to see Julian suffocating the life out of my protected. He was good, made the whole thing look the stupid scum had choked on his own vomit, something he very easily could have done.

"Julian had just accomplished his goal when Ethan showed up. It turns out he was stationed in some nearby town, and had come seeking my advice on what to do about his protected falling in love with him. That's fair, isn't it? Ethan gets infatuated schoolgirls"—Adam shot me a pointed look—"and I get abusive drunks. I'm sure there's some sort of justice in that."

I opened my mouth to defend myself, but he continued before I could.

"He caught me watching, failing to carry out my sworn duty by allowing a protected to be murdered. I tried to explain, to make him understand and see my point of view, but he was so self-righteous, so convinced of the rightness of the cause, that I couldn't make him listen. He accused me of slipping, told me that he'd seen a change in me, and that I wasn't the person he had trained with and considered a brother all these years. I knew that after he left it would only be a matter of time before The Three would call me in, but I hoped I would at least get a chance to say goodbye to Nora." Adam's voice held the edge of old hurt that hadn't healed.

"When she found out about her husband's death, she wouldn't see me. She was racked with guilt and thought it was her fault. If she hadn't gone to see her sister, she would have been there and been able to prevent him from choking. I couldn't tell her the truth, that she had nothing to do with how he'd died, and if anything I had kept her from getting killed by getting her out of the house." Adam ran a hand over his face, as though to wipe away the pain he was reliving.

"The Three sent for me only days later, forcing me to leave her there, in emotional shambles, unable to be the one to comfort her. I was locked up at Treow, the Hleo's European base, for almost a year while they tried to decide what to do with me. And then came their judgment: I would be reverted back to my human form and thrown into regular society to try to survive on my own. It had been over sixty years since I had attempted to function as an ordinary person, and the thought terrified me. I took the first opportunity I could to escape.

"Once I managed to get away from the Hleo, I spent the next six months holed up as a fugitive. Having someone on the loose with

Hleo abilities and agelessness was too much of a liability for the society, and I had to stay on the run while they hunted me. I was in some small town in the Midwest when Julian sought me out. He knew what I had done for him that night, and how the Hleo had decided to punish me, so he came to find me and extend an invitation to join the Bana. By this time I was completely disillusioned with the Hleo and their *glorious cause* and I knew the Bana would provide me with a certain amount of protection. I couldn't care less who was in control of the world anymore, as long as they left me alone for the most part."

In spite of all my efforts, empathy tugged at my core. To a certain degree, I could understand Adam's frustration with the Hleo. I was in the situation I was because of their ideals and rules. I readjusted the strap of the seatbelt, feeling uncomfortable suddenly. *Is it because of being in the car so long, or because I have something in common with Adam?* My emotions were in such turmoil, I couldn't be sure.

"I headed to a Bana compound for their programming and training. I was there over a year, becoming part of their world, receiving the proper amount of brainwashing to make sure the Hleo way of doing things was out of my system for good, before they felt they could trust me to do what they wanted." Adam wove his way in and out of highway traffic. The needle on the speedometer slowly rose.

"Their ultimate test of loyalty, before they would consider me one of their own, was for me to take out Ethan's protected. They knew the sort of relationship we'd had, and I guess they assumed it would be the perfect way to determine whether I was really on their side. They obviously didn't realize that, by the time I got through their training, I had spent months letting my anger towards Ethan's betrayal simmer.

It took me less than a week to track Ethan down and take the guy he'd been protecting out. After my first hit, the Bana rewarded me handsomely, and gave me some time off. Their style is to supply work on more of a contract basis, instead of the all-encompassing servitude the Hleo require. They'd contact me next time they needed me, otherwise I was free to do whatever I wanted, on their dime. I took off to find Nora. It had been almost three years since I had seen her, and she had moved from Savannah to Charleston." A sad smile crossed Adam's lips, and I swallowed hard.

"I remember driving up her street, my heart bursting at the thought that I would have the opportunity to be with her. I didn't care about secrecy; I was going to tell her the truth and ask her to be with me for however long we could be. I parked the car across from her house and saw her, as beautiful as ever. It was a warm summer day, and she was in her little, perfectly-manicured yard hanging laundry. She stood there amongst the fresh white linens, the same dark brown hair and beautiful small frame in a blue gingham dress." Adam was fully gone now, lost in the memory of that time.

I clasped my hands in my lap to keep from reaching out to touch his arm. If Adam's plan in sharing all this with me was to get me to lower my guard around him, I had no intention of letting him know it was working.

"Something stopped me from running to her. I stood across the street, watching her. She had just finished hanging the last of the laundry when I noticed a bassinette sitting beside her on the ground with a smiling baby boy inside. He wore a little blue baseball cap, and was gazing at her with complete adoration. She scooped him up in her arms and kissed him as only a mother can and took him into the house. I took off and left the two of them, confused by what I had witnessed and my heart once again broken."

I repressed a sigh, realizing I had been hoping for a happy ending. *Stop it. Remember who he is, and why you are on this road trip with him. He betrayed Ethan and, given the opportunity, he will do it again without hesitating.* I gripped my hands together so tightly my knuckles ached.

"I learned afterwards that she had remarried and started a family. This time she had picked a good man, I made sure of that before I even considered leaving her again. If she was happy, how could I come in and disrupt it all? She finally got the life she deserved, so I let her go, and didn't look back."

"Adam, I—"

He lifted a hand from the gear shift. "You don't have to say anything. I didn't tell you any of this to glean sympathy from you. I just wanted you to know that your hope that I'm not a complete monster, like I keep telling you, isn't completely unfounded. There was a time when I was capable of loving someone else."

Before I could answer, or maybe to prevent me from doing so, Adam pressed down on the gas pedal and we shot forward. Over the roar of the engine, I barely managed to catch the words he muttered, as if to himself, "Who knows, maybe I could again someday."

Twenty-Eight

Clouds had slowly rolled in while we were driving. The sky had grown darker until now there was a very real threat of rain overhead. It was hard to tell what time it was from the weather and I glanced at my watch. *Eight o'clock*. It had been awhile since we'd passed any gas stations, restaurants, or motels, but up ahead the neon sign of a dive motel pierced through the grayness.

I flexed my ankles back and forth trying to work out some of the stiffness from sitting in a vehicle for so long. "You know it's not too late for you to make a change." I was taking a risk making such a suggestion, and I wasn't even sure if it was a true statement, but after Adam's confession about his past it felt as though things had changed between us slightly. Would he actually be receptive to what I was saying?

"Yeah, right." Adam forced a laugh. The look he threw me suggested I was truly naïve. He pulled off the highway and into the parking lot of a two-story motel. The sign said *The Flamingo*, and boasted a bright pink neon bird beside the lettering.

Adam left me in the car while he ran into the office to get us a room. I wasn't ready to give up, and as soon as he was back I kept pressing. "Why not? Why don't you just start a new life away from all of this? What's stopping you?"

"The Bana don't exactly have an open resignation policy. They aren't big on just letting people walk away. Besides, I've become pretty accustomed to the lifestyle the Bana provide." Adam drove the car across the parking lot and pulled into a spot about halfway down the length of the building.

"Clearly." I couldn't help but laugh as I scrutinized the cheap motel we were parked in front of. The paint was peeling, and two of the rooms on the lower level had broken windows boarded up. Half of the letters under the neon flamingo were burnt out, and although a little less shabby than the last motel, it still gave off the overall impression that staying here could give a person tetanus.

Adam sneered. "This is work. In my off hours I wouldn't be caught dead in anything less than five stars on the beach, just soaking up the sun." We climbed out of the vehicle and made our way to our room.

Sounds nice. There's not much I wouldn't give right now to be lying around on a beach, far away from all of this. I kicked at a pebble on the sidewalk in front of our room.

Adam stuck the key in the lock and pushed the door open to reveal a fair-sized room with a double bed and pullout sofa. He held out his hand in an 'after you' motion and I walked into the incredibly dated motel room. Adam followed, shutting the door behind us. The room must have been decorated in the eighties and not retouched since. Everything was done in pastels, from the peach and pink bedspread to the creamy-pink furniture and pale blue carpet. The bedding had a zigzag pattern, and the couch was a yellow and peach patterned number. I ran a finger along the top of the long dresser pushed against the wall opposite the bed. A large television sat on it, but thankfully my inspection revealed no dust. A small area at the back of the room, just outside the bathroom, contained a dressing mirror and sink. I caught a glimpse of Adam's expression in the glass. He still stood by the door, eyeing the bed with a deep frown. *What's wrong with him?*

"I think I saw a restaurant down the road, are you hungry?" Adam reached for the doorknob.

"Sure, that sounds good." My stomach rumbled at the mention of food.

He held the door open for me and we headed out to get a bite to eat. We were both quiet as we sat in the booth of the Mexican restaurant Adam had chosen. The stories he had shared with me played over in my mind. There was so much more to Adam Chambers than I could have ever imagined. I picked at the rice on my plate. The most startling thing for me to grasp was that we actually had some things in common. I sensed he was struggling with the same realization, although he seemed focused on his burrito.

The rain had started shortly after we entered the restaurant and was coming down hard. I stared out the window, waiting for it to let up a little, as drops formed on the glass and rolled down. The clouds were thick, with no breaks in sight. *This could go on for hours.*

"I don't think it's going to stop anytime soon." Adam nodded outside. "The air was pretty heavy; it's the sort of rain that lasts. I wouldn't be surprised if it pours all night."

"I was thinking the same thing." I wiped my mouth and dropped my napkin onto my plate.

"We might as well face it." Adam shimmied out of the booth, reaching into his wallet and depositing a few bills on the table to cover the cost of the meal.

We stood under the overhang of the restaurant for a moment, looking up at the sheet of rain that stood between us and the car, before making a wild dash to the vehicle. As I dropped onto the leather seat of the Camaro I wished I'd thrown my sweater back on. It was still in the backseat, and in the seconds it had taken us to run across the parking lot I had managed to get soaked. I rubbed my arms, trying to wipe away the worst of the moisture, while Adam ran a hand through his hair, sending beads of water scattering across the dashboard.

Adam pulled into the motel parking lot and we made a beeline for our room, running along the sidewalk and standing under the second floor walkway to keep from getting any wetter. Adam unlocked the door and pushed it open for me to go in first. I stepped into the dark motel room and someone grabbed my wrist and twisted my arm hard into a hold behind my back, spinning me around. I screamed out in surprise and pain, and Adam quickly flipped on the light.

"Hello, you two," a female voice greeted us.

My heart sank. "Paige," I breathed. I stood on my tip-toes, trying to relieve some of the pressure she was applying to my upper arm and shoulder blade, but she simply squeezed tighter.

Adam closed the door and casually sauntered into the room. "I thought that must be you. You've been following us since Tennessee, right?" He leaned against the dresser and crossed his arms, appearing completely indifferent to Paige's painful grasp of me.

"Virginia actually," Paige replied smugly. "Aren't you two a little off course?"

"I thought we'd take the scenic route. Aren't you supposed to be in a swamp somewhere?" Adam shot back. His eyes met mine for a brief second, then fell back on her. The usual look of boredom was on his face, but the tension between the two of them was building.

"I've decided to go a different direction. I'm more than a little tired of following orders, of having someone else tell me what to do. It's time to break free from all of this and go my own way, start living my life the way I want." From the corner of my eye I saw her lift her chin defiantly.

"And you wanted us to be the first to hear the good news?"

"Very funny. Obviously Alexander isn't the live-and-let-live kind. If I'm going to have any chance at leaving safely I need some leverage, a reason for them to let me go." Paige's fingers dug into my forearm as a growing terror churned in the pit of my stomach.

Adam cocked his head. "What does that have to do with us?"

I tried to twist around far enough to read her expression, but the action put too much pressure on my arm and I was forced to keep looking helplessly at Adam as I waited for her to explain.

"They want her, are desperate for her, both sides. We can take her far away from here and lock her up in some hole. Then, when we are safely tucked into the Italian coast, or at one of the South American jungle resorts, or wherever you want, somewhere we can't be found, we'll contact them and use her to barter for our freedom. You want free of all of this too. I know you do. Come with me now, and we can live however we want, for however long we want." Paige held a knife to my side with her free hand. Clearly she meant business.

Adam listened to her plan, his features neutral, but his glance grazed the knife. A wave of dizziness hit me as I tried not to let the fear of spending my days in some dark box somewhere overtake me. *Things are really bleak if I need to rely on Adam not to be tempted by Paige's plan of escape.*

"You really think that would work?"

My stomach clenched. Was he actually considering joining Paige and using me as a pawn to gain their freedom?

"It's worth a try. Better than being part of the endless game they have going on. Destiny, it's all just a waste of time and energy, but they are all so wrapped up in it, take it so seriously. I know they would give us whatever we want in exchange for her." Paige took a step closer to him, forcing me forward.

Adam shook his head. "You wouldn't get across the border with her, let alone get away with stashing her somewhere on the other side of the globe."

A twinge of hope rippled through me. *Maybe he isn't just going to hand me over to Paige.* I glanced up at him, and for a second I could see a sober expression in his eyes, behind the mask of boredom and disdain. The knot in my stomach tightened. *He doesn't have a way out of this.*

"You don't know that." Paige's grip on my arm loosened a little as she pled her case.

"I do. Alexander is a whole other level of extreme; you don't want to cross him. And speaking of which, what exactly are you planning to do with the knife? You know you can't hurt her, so you might as well drop it; she isn't going anywhere." Adam held out his hand for the weapon. Paige hesitated. I couldn't see her very well, but she'd gone completely still so I guessed she was at least contemplating what Adam had said.

"Maybe we can't kill her, but I'm sure they'd overlook a few cuts and bruises."

She's testing him, but why?

"We get it, Paige. You're a dangerous assassin who likes to hurt people, we're all impressed, but it's not worth testing your theory." Adam still sounded indifferent, but he'd taken a step towards us.

Paige tightened her hold on me again. "You don't want me to hurt her, do you?" Wicked amusement dripped from her voice.

"I couldn't care less." Adam still seemed unconcerned, but his voice lacked enough conviction to be believable.

My forehead creased. *He doesn't want her to hurt me.* Why did he care? Was he only worried about what Alexander would do, or was it something more?

"Did she get to you too? What's with this girl?" I felt the heat as Paige's gaze burned into the side of my face.

I concentrated on a bleach stain on the pale blue rug. *Well, this conversation has taken an awkward turn.*

"Don't be ridiculous."

"So, you don't care if I do this?" Paige ran the blade just under my ribs. I cried out as fire tore across my abdomen.

Before I could react further, Adam grabbed Paige by the wrist and twisted, forcing her to drop the knife. As it thudded to the floor, he yanked her off of me and dragged her to the motel room door. "Stay here," he commanded me from the doorway. He slammed the door shut, but I could see the two of them through a gap in the curtains of the large window beside the door.

I stood frozen, trying to get my brain to work, I needed to attend to the gash Paige had inflicted on me. I pressed my hand against my stomach, and blood stained my fingertips.

"You're going to screw everything up. They're going to want to know how she got that cut." Adam's voice was loud enough to carry through the glass. He gestured wildly, his usual cool demeanor completely gone.

"You're in love with her too, aren't you?" Paige yanked her wrist from his grasp and studied him with her mysterious silver eyes.

Adam drove his hand through his hair. "I'm as in love with her as you are with me. Your plan is brainless and it won't work. They'll track us down and kill us for causing them trouble. Just forget it and get out of here before we both get caught and they want to know what's going on."

"I don't buy it. You've never been scared of them before. She's really gotten to you, hasn't she?"

I should have been checking the bathroom for something I could use to patch myself up, but their conversation was too intriguing to walk away from.

"Get out of here, Paige, or I swear I will call Antonio and tell him exactly how to find you, and your secret accounts."

I frowned. *Who is Antonio? What secret accounts?* There was silence for a second and I took a small step forward to see Paige more clearly. Her tan complexion had gone pale.

She stumbled back. "You wouldn't do that." She didn't sound nearly as confident as she had only seconds earlier.

"Just try me." Adam stared her down.

Paige's hands balled into fists. "Fine, but I'm still getting out. You're on your own from here, so don't come looking to me for any favors." She spun on her heel and stalked off, then stopped and whirled back around. "I never thought I'd see you turn down such a golden opportunity to gain full control of your life again, but have it your way, stay their little puppet." She walked through the rain to a silver sedan, yanked open the door, and slid behind the wheel. As she sped away, her tires kicked up a spray of wet gravel.

Adam disappeared from view. He returned minutes later carrying a half-empty bottle of rubbing alcohol, a few separately-packaged gauze bandages, and other miscellaneous medical items. "She's gone." He walked over to me and set the medical supplies down on the bed.

"Good." I exhaled with relief.

"How deep are you cut?" Adam closed the gap between us.

"I'll be okay." I tried to sound convincing while holding my bleeding stomach.

"Hannah, let me see. If you're cut too deeply you're going to need stitches." Adam held out a hand towards me, but I took a step back. Adam trying to be helpful was just too weird.

"No, I'm fine," I stressed again, but my side was throbbing, and the patch of blood on my shirt was spreading.

"Come on. I've patched myself up thousands of times. Let me see how bad it is."

I nodded, reluctantly, and pulled my hand away to reveal a three-inch gash through a hole in my blood-stained T-shirt. Adam tilted the shade of the floor lamp in the corner of the room up so that light shone directly on me.

I hesitantly lifted my shirt up enough that my stomach and the wound were visible, feeling completely exposed in the glow of the lamp. Adam knelt down so that he was at eye level with the cut. His thumb slid across the skin just under the wound. The soft motion caused unexpected tingles to run up my spine.

I loved Ethan with every fiber of my being. My body's reaction had to be a result of Adam's touch being the most intimate contact I'd had with another person since Ethan had left. I was sure of it. "So, will I live?" I forced myself to speak lightly and focus my attention on a faded watercolor painting on the wall.

"It's actually not that deep, and it looks like a clean wound. Let me just grab a cloth from the bathroom to wash off the worst of the blood." Adam's fingers still rested on my stomach. As if he'd just realized he'd left them there longer than he needed to, he jerked back his hand and strode over to the bathroom.

Adam returned in seconds, and handed me the warm white cloth. "You can clean up the blood and then I'll close the wound."

I took the cloth and wiped it across my side as he rifled through the supplies on the bed. "So who's Antonio?"

"You heard us?" Adam's grip on a little medicine bottle tightened.

Crap. I didn't want Adam to know I'd overheard Paige accusing him of being in love with me. "Um, just that name. It seemed to really upset Paige."

"Antonio's the Bana's money guy. He handles the payment side of things. The Bana don't mind you living it up on their dime, but they aren't big on you trying to establish your own financial security. They want everyone completely dependent on the organization. Makes us much easier to control. If they find out you've been stashing funds on the side, there's only one way they'll deal with you." Adam made a slashing motion across his throat. "Antonio runs spot checks every once in a while to see if anyone's breeching the agreement. He's not someone you want to cross."

"So far, none of the Bana I've met are people I want to cross." I pulled the cloth away as the flow of blood seemed to have slowed.

Adam opened his mouth, then shut it without speaking and picked up the bottle of rubbing alcohol. "Let's get that cut dealt with."

I nodded and he knelt down in front of me again. I bit down on my thumb when he ran a cotton ball soaked with the alcohol over the wound, the sting of the liquid shooting pain across my midsection.

"You probably could have used a few stitches, but this will have to do." He pressed the edges of the wound together and applied a sticky clear salve to it.

"What is that?" I watched him carefully make sure the whole cut was covered.

"Liquid skin." Adam grabbed a gauze bandage and applied it over the injury.

"Ew." I made a face and Adam laughed.

He looked up at me for a second; his hand still on my stomach and his expression serious. "I'm just glad I had this stuff with me."

"Me too."

He stood up and backed away and I pulled my shirt down. *Why are things so awkward between us?*

"I'm just going to run these back out to the car." Adam gathered all the supplies up off the bed.

"Thank you," I murmured as he headed for the door.

"No problem."

It was getting late, and I was ready to sleep. Since I had no idea where we were going, I didn't know how far we were from our destination, but I knew Adam only had a limited amount of time before he was supposed to deliver me to Alexander, so I assumed we were getting close.

I still had no plan of escape, but the longer we traveled together, the more I wondered if Adam's heart was really into handing me over to the ominous Alexander.

Adam walked back into the room and slid the chain lock on the door closed. "I'll sleep on the pullout."

I wrinkled my nose, studying the shabby-looking sofa.

"Better than the bed, believe me. You kick in your sleep." Adam pulled the cushions off the couch and tossed them to the ground.

"I do not," I scoffed indignantly, although I couldn't be sure. I'd never shared a bed with anyone besides Katie before, and she hadn't mentioned anything.

"Whatever you say." Adam tugged the bed frame out and flopped down on the mattress. "Goodnight."

I drew the covers back on the bed and slipped under them. *What is going on with you Adam?* Paige's words had rattled him. I was certain that's why he was electing to sleep on the sketchy-looking sofa-bed instead of beside me. Because her words were true, or because they just bugged him I didn't know; either way it didn't matter. My focus was on getting to Ethan.

"Goodnight." I reached over to turn off the bedside lamp. *Wait a minute. Adam forgot to tie me to the bed.* I glanced over at him. Was there any hope of being able to get my hands on Ethan's letters? Adam was lying with his back to me, on the side with the pocket I'd seen him stuff the letters into. Maybe if he rolled over there would be an opportunity for me to go after them, but that was risky. If he woke up and found me hovering over him in the middle of the night I wasn't sure how he would react, nor was I sure I wanted to find out. *I better not take the chance.*

I closed my eyes. *What a difference a day makes.* Adam Chambers was a far more complicated individual than I had originally thought, and I felt a certain amount of pity for him. He was a prisoner, trapped in his own life, having made some very poor decisions after being marred by tragedy. Decisions that had landed him on a path he didn't appear to be overly interested in being on.

I rolled over and punched up the nearly flat pillow. The sooner I got away from him and found Ethan, the sooner I would be able to leave the conflicting emotions he was causing behind.

Then I could focus completely on Ethan and me, and figure out where the two of us were going to go from here.

Twenty-Nine

I woke slowly, the sound of the shower running in the bathroom gradually pulling me back to consciousness. Disoriented, I bolted upright. Pain from the cut on my stomach coursed through my side and I pressed my lips together to keep from crying out again. I tentatively touched the gash site, but Adam's fix was holding. Surveying the motel room, I noted that everything looked the same as it had the night before, except Adam had obviously gone into the bathroom and closed the door. A T-shirt and a pair of jeans hanging over a chair outside the bathroom door caught my eye. Something was sticking out of the pocket. *Ethan's letters.*

    I raced over to the pants and slipped the pieces of paper out of them. Then I scrambled back to the bed and grabbed the motel pen and paper off the bedside table. Scanning the letters, I jotted down all the differing words, finishing just as the water stopped. My heart drummed in my chest as I vaulted from the bed and crossed the room, folding the letters before shoving them back in Adam's pants. I strode back to the bed, jamming the piece of paper I'd written the words on into my own pocket. I had just gotten settled back under the covers and closed my eyes when Adam opened the door. I jumped, as though the noise had startled me awake, and ran my hands over my eyes before looking over at him. Still wet from the shower, he had a towel wrapped around his waist and another around his neck that he was using to rub his hair.

    "Morning, sunshine." He greeted me casually as he stepped into the room. Apparently it was no big deal for him to be standing half naked in front of me.

"Hi." I glanced away and examined the flecks of paint on the ceiling. I had to admit, Adam was in great shape, but this was incredibly uncomfortable, and I wished that he would just get dressed. I had a feeling his hesitation to do so was on purpose though.

"Sleep well?" He picked his pants and shirt up off the back of the chair.

"Yeah, fine, I think I'll have a shower too." I jumped off the bed and brushed past him, shutting the bathroom door behind me before he could respond.

I locked the door and turned the water on so Adam would think I was showering. Then I lowered the lid on the toilet and sat down to study the words I had carefully written out.

love, and, frightening, always, yet, exact, terrifically, totally, eternally, love, always

I stared at them, looking them over and over, trying to decipher what they could mean. There was no way to make a workable sentence out of the words, which meant there was a good chance I was supposed to rearrange all the letters. I sighed. I had limited time before Adam would expect me to finish my 'shower,' but nothing would come together, no matter how I rearranged the words. Adam said Ethan had made it easy for me, but I couldn't see it. I glanced at the bathroom door, nervous he would knock at any second. In one last ditch effort, I scribbled the words out in an acrostic.

Love
And
Frightening
Always
Yet
Exact
Terrifically
Totally
Eternally
Love
Always

My lips spread into a grin. The answer was clear and I shook my head, mad at myself that I hadn't thought to do this sooner. It wasn't a matter of rearranging the words or letters, I just needed to use the first letter of each word. When I did, they spelled Lafayette, LA. My heart soared. I could get away from Adam and find Ethan on my own. I just had to figure out how. Adam knocked loudly on the door. "That's long enough."

"Be right out," I called, ripping the piece of paper into tiny pieces and wadding them up in Kleenex before throwing them into the wastebasket. I stuck my head into the shower so my hair would be wet, toweled it off, and straightened myself up as best I could with a slashed and bloody T-shirt.

When I pulled the bathroom door open Adam was dressed and stretched out on the bed watching television.

"Let's get a move on." He threw the TV remote down and hopped off the side of the bed.

I was getting a little tired of following his orders, but, not wanting to make him angry when I was so close to my goal, I followed him in silence.

Back in the front seat, I buckled my seatbelt and grabbed the door handle as Adam peeled out of the lot. *How am I going to get away from Adam long enough to put a little distance between us?* If I could get to Ethan first, warn him what Adam was up to, we could devise a plan of attack. Maybe I could even keep Ethan from having to fight Adam altogether. We had to be getting close to the Louisiana border, I needed to think fast. I couldn't tuck and roll from a moving vehicle, not at the speed Adam drove. If we stopped for gas or to eat I would have to just make a break for it and hope for the best.

Adam was being strangely quiet. I glanced over, but his attention appeared to be on the road. He'd been so open yesterday; was there any chance he'd answer the question I'd been dying to ask him since he'd first brought it up?

"You really knew my mom and dad?"

He drummed his fingers on the steering wheel. "Yeah, they were quite the pair."

"I don't know very much about them."

Adam pursed his lips as he shifted gears. I clasped my hands together. *Please Adam, tell me about my parents.*

"I knew Elizabeth back in the Hleo years. She was an incredible fighter. We were sparring partners once and she managed to get me on the mat more often than I got her, and she was a risk taker too. It's funny, I remember her being somewhat of a contradiction, always willing to put herself out there to get done what she needed to, but not reckless. Her mind was always going. She had no time for the frivolous activities some of the rest of us were into." Adam sounded distant, as though visualizing another time and place. His appreciative tone made me wonder. Had he been interested in Elizabeth?

"Did you and she ever …?" I ran my hands along my knees.

"I asked her out once when we were both stationed in France, romance capital of the world and all, but she shot me down." Adam gave me a lopsided grin. He sounded more amused by the memory than hurt by the rejection.

I wrinkled my nose. It was weird to think this guy, who looked only a few years older than me, had asked my biological mother out on a date.

"So you were friends?"

"Friends? Hmm, I don't know if that's what you'd call it. Your mom, me, Ethan, we were always the faces on assignments, the personality takers. We were always partnered with some techno geek that handled the behind-the-scenes stuff. Because of that, we didn't have many opportunities to hang out together; we were always off on separate assignments. The only time we would do things with each other was if we happened to be stationed in the same part of the world, or ended up back at Veridan or one of the other headquarters at the same time, which didn't occur very often. So I don't know if you could say friends. I probably knew Noah better actually." Adam pulled out to pass a slow-moving tractor-trailer.

"Really?"

"Yeah, his nickname was *The Artist*. The leaders of the Bana don't always use us as assassins. If we have some sort of other ability they can exploit for their gain they will. Your dad had a gift with a paintbrush, and Eric and Alexander picked up on this. His talent was useful for forging artwork and bonds, or he sometimes pretended to be a famous artist to get in with prestigious political and social circles the Bana wanted to connect with. And, on a less professional note, I know it helped him with the ladies. I remember hearing him brag that David's Oath of the Horatii, hanging in the Louvre, was actually his handiwork, but I have no idea if that's true or not."

My mouth dropped open. "None of that was in the file the Hleo have on him."

"I doubt they knew. The Hleo's main concern is always watching the Bana to see what they are doing with protecteds."

"So Noah was an artist?"

"Yeah." Adam shrugged. "That's probably where you got your ability from."

So I got my drawing skills from my father. "Can you tell me anything about how he and Elizabeth got together?"

"No. I was underground at the time." Adam's tone fell flat, and I grimaced.

"Right." I nodded sheepishly. We traveled in silence while I stared out at the increasingly marshy-looking forests we were passing by. The rain had stopped sometime during the night, but it was still an overcast day and a dampness hung in the air.

"I heard about them once I was back. They were long gone, but I overheard someone talking about how they had spawned a child, and I remember thinking that Noah Carter and Elizabeth Seaton would have made one odd couple." Adam ran his hand along his jawline.

I frowned. "Odd?"

"Yeah, Elizabeth was driven, serious, and headstrong. I thought for sure she'd see through Noah's charm, but I guess there weren't many women he couldn't get. Your mom must have intrigued him as well, for him to want to settle down in a relationship with her." Adam arched his eyebrows.

I twisted the ring on my finger as I thought about the idea of opposites attracting. This adage was especially true for my adopted parents, Richard and Julia. They were so different and yet they'd had a happy marriage.

I inhaled slowly. "I wish I could have met them."

Adam cleared his throat. "I'm sure they wish they could have seen you grow up as well."

"Thanks." I shifted in my seat. The last thing I should be feeling for the man who had taken me from my home and threatened to turn me over to the leaders of the Bana was thankful. Still, he had given me a gift—another piece of the puzzle I was fitting together about my parents—and I couldn't repress a flicker of gratitude.

A road sign caught my eye. We were less than a hundred miles outside of New Orleans. I had been so distracted listening to Adam, I had neglected to come up with a way to escape from him.

We had only been on the road a few hours, but Adam turned off the interstate into a busy service station. He pulled up to the gas pumps and hopped out to fill the gas tank.

When he'd finished and replaced the nozzle, he stuck his head through the open driver's side window. "I'm going to get a coffee, do you want anything?"

I shook my head. "I'm good."

"Stay here," he commanded before striding over to the convenience store connected to the gas station. He didn't even bother to turn around to make sure I obeyed. *Does he really believe he can trust me now?* It didn't matter. This was my chance. I scanned the service station for viable escape options. A charter bus was parked on the far side of the parking lot. The sign above the front window said New Orleans.

"Good enough," I whispered to myself. I grabbed my bag and sweater from the back seat, then opened the glove box and snatched out my phone and wallet. The knife caught my eye. I studied the building he'd disappeared into, but didn't see Adam anywhere. It was now or never. *I need to slow him down or he'll catch me for sure.* My heart racing, I grabbed the weapon, pulled it from its sheath, and shoved open the car door. I slid out, crouching down so I couldn't be seen from the store, then slashed the blade across the passenger tire. A hissing sound accompanied the rush of air brushing over my arm. *Perfect.* I dumped the knife in the closest garbage can then, with a final glance at the building, I wove my way through the parking lot, using vehicles, columns, and gas pumps to block me from view, until I got around to the far side of the bus.

The door was open, and the bus driver, a gentleman, strands of white streaking through his close-cropped afro, sat behind the wheel reading a newspaper.

"Excuse me, sir." I peered up at him.

He closed the paper and turned to look at me. "Yes?" He had a thick southern accent, and wore a nametag that read *Russell*.

"I was just wondering if this bus is going to Lafayette." I glanced over my shoulder in the direction of the store.

"As a matter of fact it is, after it stops in New Orleans and Baton Rouge." Russell gave me a warm, grandfatherly smile.

"I'd like a ticket then; how much is it?" I opened up my wallet.

"Well, from here to Lafayette, I believe that would be ..." He ran a finger down the price chart pasted to his dashboard, "... $16.50 sugar."

"Okay." I snatched the bills out of my wallet and counted them. I didn't have enough.

"I only have seven dollars." I held up the bills in my hand dejectedly, my heart sinking. There was no way I could go get money out of an ATM without getting caught, and if I couldn't get on this bus how was I going to get away from Adam? I looked over at the store again with a frown.

Russell's gaze followed mine, and he seemed to catch on that I was trying to get away from this service station as fast as possible. "You know what honey, you climb on and we'll sort out the money thing later." He beckoned me onto the bus with a wave.

"Really? Thank you so much." I flashed him a grateful smile and climbed the deep staircase onto the bus.

"You just grab a seat anywhere."

I chose one near the front of the bus, on the side opposite the convenience store. Sliding down low, I clutched my bag to my chest. *Please go. Please go.*

There weren't that many people on the bus; a mother and her young children had settled near the back, and a college-aged couple sat up a few rows from them. There was an elderly woman right in the middle and an equally elderly man a few rows up from her. Two rows behind me, on the opposite side of the aisle, a slightly heavy woman in a ball cap met my quick glance with a warm smile.

Russell closed the door and I let out the breath I'd been holding. Slowly, the big coach bus pulled out of the service station and onto the interstate. *Did he leave quickly for my benefit?* I straightened up in my seat, watching the scenery change from shops and restaurants to fields and countryside.

I pressed my forehead against the cool glass of the window as a sense of relief washed over me. I wasn't fully in the clear. Adam was still headed to Lafayette, and if he had noticed the bus, it wouldn't be hard for him to figure out my escape method. The flat tire would slow him down at least a little, so for the moment, I was free.

For the first time since I had left my house with Adam I dug into my purse and pulled out the letter stamp. *Okay Ethan, what is this for? And why did you send it to me?* I set my belongings down on the empty seat beside me and rolled the little object between my palms, tracing the circular symbol with my thumb. Maybe once I got to Lafayette the answer would become clear.

We had only been traveling an hour or so when we pulled into the New Orleans bus station to let passengers off and receive new ones. Other than the elderly gentleman, all the people I had shared the ride with exited the bus.

I slouched back down in the seat, out of view of the window, waiting nervously for the bus to be on its way again. We sat there idling for about fifteen minutes while a group of twenty or so travelers boarded. I was about to jump off the bus and start walking, when Russell closed the door and we were on the road again, heading for Baton Rouge. When we reached it, we pulled into the station and Russell put the bus into park and yanked on the big silver knob to open up the doors. Several people boarded the bus. I watched each of them warily as they made their way up the stairs and settled into different seats around me, but none of them even spared me a glance. My pulse raced. I was scared that each new passenger would be Adam, but he never appeared.

As Russell pulled out of the bus station my muscles relaxed again. Had I actually been successful in getting away from Adam? About five minutes outside of Baton Rouge, exhaustion took over. I shut my eyes and drifted off into a much-needed deep sleep.

Thirty

I awoke to the sensation of someone gently shaking my shoulder. I had forgotten where I was and jolted awake in my seat to see Russell looking down at me, his dark eyes warm.

"We've arrived in Lafayette, Miss."

I rubbed my eyes with my palms. "Thank you so much for waking me up." I'd slept the entire trip from Baton Rouge.

"No problem, sugar." Russell offered me a sympathetic smile. "You know, lots of people got someone they just got to get away from." He took a step back so that I could move into the aisle.

I stood and grabbed my purse from the seat beside me. "Thank you for your help. I really appreciate it." I nodded in his direction, grateful that he'd helped me get closer to my goal. I needed to see Ethan. If I could just get to him everything would make sense again.

"You sure you're okay?" Russell gripped the seats on either side of him, studying me.

"Yes, the thing I need most is waiting for me here. As soon as I get to it everything will be just fine again. By the way, do you know where I can find an ATM around here so I can get you the money for my ticket?"

Russel shook his head. "Don't worry about it, this one's on the house. You just take care of yourself, you hear?"

My chest squeezed at this man's kindness. "Thank you. That's so nice of you." When he stepped to one side, I slipped past him and off the bus.

Standing in front of the Lafayette bus terminal, I carefully scanned my surroundings for any signs of Adam or his Camaro.

Other than a few parked cars, the street was deserted. I checked a map of Lafayette on my phone for what seemed to be the city's center and started down the sidewalk in that direction, keeping a wary eye out for Adam just in case. About four blocks away from the bus station I reached a cordoned-off street that hosted a bustling market.

Crowds of people milled around, wandering among the vendors' booths that displayed an array of goods. Food tables and makeshift tents set up with clothes, jewelry, antiques, and artwork, lined both sides of the street. I scoured the tables for anything that even closely resembled the letter stamp, but nothing stood out.

I reached the end of the market. *Now where?* I couldn't just wander the streets of Lafayette aimlessly. I veered towards an iron bench at the edge of the sidewalk, planning to sit and regroup, when a banner draped across the front of the building on the opposite side of the street, advertising a historical reenactment event, caught my eye. The evening was being hosted by the Hamilton family the following month, and in the background of the banner was a familiar-looking symbol. My eyes widened as I dug into my purse and pulled out the letter stamp to compare the two. The symbols were exactly the same. I flipped the stamp over to examine the scrolling letter H. *For Hamilton?*

I jumped off the bench and crossed the street. The lettering stenciled on the glass doors of the tan brick building read *Lafayette First National Bank*. I gingerly pushed the door open and walked inside, not entirely sure what to do next.

The old, gothic-style bank had clearly been in business a very long time. The ceiling soared above the large decorative columns that lined the marble foyer leading to the counter along the back wall. I made my way past the rich mahogany tables between the teller wall and the front entrance, and joined the line of people waiting to do their banking. As I stood there, I glanced around for any clues that would help explain why the H symbol had been on the banner outside, but there were none.

When it was my turn, I approached a friendly-looking teller in her mid-fifties.

"I was wondering if you might be able to help me with something." The counter was so high I practically had to stand on my tippy toes as I rested my elbows on it.

"I can certainly try. What do you need, honey?" The woman, Carol, according to her nametag, had a thick Louisiana drawl. She flashed me an encouraging smile with lips a shade too red for the workplace.

"I noticed the banner hanging outside the bank and wanted to know if you could tell me what the symbol on it means." I bit my lip, feeling awkward for asking such a random, non-money-related question.

She frowned. "I'm sorry. I'm not sure what you're talking about."

I pulled the little stamp out of my purse and set it on the counter in front of her. "I'm playing a little game with a friend of mine. He sent me this letter stamp in the mail, and now I'm trying to figure out the significance of it." I placed a finger on the top of the stamp. "Your bank has a banner outside advertising an event hosted by the Hamilton family, and the banner has the same symbol on it."

"Oh my gracious, of course, the Hamilton banner. I forgot they put that up last week. I walk by it every day so you'd think I would know what you were talking about. Well honey, the Hamiltons are one of Lafayette's oldest and most respected families. They have tons of money, and give lots of it back to the city in different ways. I believe the symbol comes from their family crest. They use it to let people know when they are involved with some project or event in the city, like the bash they're hosting next month."

"The Hamiltons? Would you be able to tell me where they live?" I shifted my weight eagerly, trying to keep from getting too excited. Could I possibly be closing in on Ethan?

"Sure can. Their estate is over on Hamilton Lane. Fitting name, huh? It's a private manor though, so you won't be able to go inside, if that's what your game is leading to," Carol warned in a motherly tone.

"Oh no." I held my hands up, palms toward her. "I just needed to find out whose family the stamp belonged to, that's all."

"Okay then." She nodded, seemingly satisfied with my answer.

"Thanks for your time." I started to leave, then thought of one more question. It couldn't hurt to ask. I turned back. "Do you know the Hamilton family?"

"Me? No, not personally, but pretty much everyone in town can point out who they are. Why?"

"I'm curious about whether a young guy has been staying with them recently."

"Hmm." She wrinkled her nose uncertainly. "They all do their banking here, and are usually in a few times a month. Occasionally they have someone new with them, a family member visiting from out of town or something. What does this guy look like?"

I pulled my cell phone out of my pocket. Ignoring the thirty-seven text messages and fifty-three missed phone calls from Katie, as well as the two percent battery life warning, I found an image of Ethan that showed his face clearly and held the screen up to the teller. "Do you recognize him?"

She scrutinized the picture for a moment, staring at the screen before shaking her head. "I'm sorry sweetie, I don't."

My shoulders drooped. "Thanks anyway." I attempted a smile before walking back outside.

The Hamilton family was the reason Ethan was here in Lafayette, I could feel it. I looked at the little stamp one more time, now positive that the H on the bottom must stand for Hamilton.

An available taxi was parked about halfway down the block, and I strode over to it. I would check out the Hamilton estate, and hopefully talk to someone in the family. Maybe he or she would recognize Ethan's picture. The driver lowered his window as I approached. I stopped beside the vehicle. "I'd like to go to the Hamilton estate please."

The man inclined his head in the direction of the backseat and I climbed in. He took off and we drove for about five minutes, making our way ten blocks or so from the bank. I studied the property, surrounded by a thick ivy hedge, as we turned onto Hamilton Lane and he parked across the street from a huge set of iron gates. If this was the home of Ethan's latest protected, he'd definitely gotten an upgrade. I swallowed hard. Maybe he wouldn't be as eager to give all that up and come back to East Halton as I'd hoped.

Thirty-One

The cab driver pointed to the entrance. "Hamilton Estate."

"Great, thanks." I tugged a five-dollar bill from my pocket, but froze when the gates parted and a black town car pulled out and turned onto the street, heading the way we had come. "Follow that car." I pointed before I could even think it through.

The taxi driver pulled a U-turn and took off behind the car. We drove across town, keeping the town car in view until it pulled into the parking lot of a large building. A large marble sign on a small lawn out front read *Hamilton Convention Center*.

A well-poised, middle-aged woman with a silvery blond bob and a younger, very elegant woman in four-inch heels, exited the town car and clicked their way into the banquet hall.

"Let me out here, please." The taxi driver stopped at the curb across the street from the convention center. I handed him all the money I had before stepping out onto the sidewalk and staring at the building. Should I follow the two women into the hall?

I had spent the ride debating the best way to handle this situation. I didn't want to blow whatever cover Ethan had established here in Lafayette. If he had pointed me in the direction of the Hamilton family, it likely meant that he was protecting one of them. If that was the case, it shouldn't take long for me to find him. I just had to figure out which Hamilton Ethan was shadowing.

I wasn't sure what I would say if I got caught sneaking around inside, but if I was close to finding Ethan, I couldn't stop now. I crossed the street and walked up under the overhang at the front door. I took a steadying breath and pulled the large wooden door to the hall open, peering inside cautiously. No one was in the main foyer and the lights were off, so I slipped in and silently closed the door behind me. Even in the dimness, I could see that the foyer was decorated in neutral browns and beiges. Voices drifted from a hallway to the left, so I crept in that direction.

I peered through the little round window of the door on the right side of the hallway as I passed by. Behind the door was a full-sized industrial kitchen. No one appeared to be in the room, so I kept moving down the hall to a set of double doors. Women's voices filtered through the crack between the doors. I was about to peek inside when I noticed another door just a little farther down the hall marked *Balcony* in fancy gold lettering.

I made my way to it and tugged the door open. The women's voices grew more distinct. Directly in front of me, a staircase led to an upper level. The stairwell was dark as I made my way up, testing each step for creaks before putting my weight on it. When I reached the top, I stopped to take in my surroundings. A wide carpeted hallway ran in a rounded arc with sets of deep purple curtains lining the inner wall every twenty feet or so. Were those box seats? I walked over to the closest one to see if my guess was right.

I slid the fabric along the rod. Sure enough, tucked in behind the curtain was a little area with angled rows of seating and a curved railing at the bottom. There were only two rows, with seating for four in each. Decorative columns separated the boxed area I was in from the ones on either side of it. The creamy, rounded marble was wide enough to conceal me from the women, but allowed me to peek over the railing in front of me and get a good view of the room below.

I gazed down, expecting a theater with rows of seats, but was surprised to see a beautiful marble floor in a space that looked more like a ballroom. A stage had been built against the far wall. Apparently this massive, impressive room had multiple purposes. It was designed in browns and creams, with hints of gold and purple throughout. It had a yesteryear feel with lots of carved wood, hanging chandeliers, and rich-colored tapestry curtains.

The women stood in the middle of the empty room about fifteen feet below me. The elder woman glanced at her watch every few seconds, more in control than the younger one, who paced in front of her. "Where could they be? They knew what time we were supposed to meet, didn't they?" the younger woman asked in a beautiful, husky, southern accent. She was the epitome of chic in a black, knee-length pencil skirt, white blouse, red heels, and matching red handbag. A ribbon of jealousy ran through me at the thought that Ethan might be spending his days with her. She was likely only a few years older than his perpetual age of twenty-one, and I wondered if she or the other woman—who had to be her mother, based on the resemblance between them—could be his new protected.

"I told them specifically that we needed to meet for one, because I have an appointment with the caterers at two," the older woman replied, in a voice that almost matched her daughter's, but pitched slightly lower. She smoothed out the light cream-colored pantsuit she had on with both palms.

"We'll give them a couple more minutes then. Do you have the specifications ready?"

"Of course. I'm hoping he'll be able to complete the work at least a week before the dinner so we'll have enough time for any last-minute changes or additions." Her mother removed a plastic file folder from her bag, opened it, and rifled through the papers inside.

What and *who* are they talking about? A door opened from underneath me. Two men appeared from under the balcony, walking towards the women. My heart leapt into my throat. The man on the right had snowy-white hair, but the man on the left was Ethan; I would know him anywhere. I pressed a fist to my mouth to hold in my cry of joy.

"Hi Daddy, what took you two so long?" The younger woman walked over to the men with arms outstretched and gave the gentleman with Ethan a kiss on the cheek.

"Sorry sugar pie, Ethan and I were going over the blueprints for the back balcony and lost track of time." The older man pulled away from his daughter and walked over to the woman who must be his wife. I bit down on my knuckle to keep from making a sound at the mention of Ethan's name.

"Well, that's okay, you're worth the wait." The younger woman took a step closer to Ethan. Even from up in the balcony I could see her batting her eyelashes flirtatiously. Heat flooded my cheeks. *Who did this woman think she was to act that way with my Ethan?* I dropped my hand and drew in a calming breath. Just because she was acting that way didn't mean Ethan returned her feelings. I'd watched many girls at East Halton High flirt with Ethan for months, and he remained politely disinterested in all of them.

"Shall we get down to it?" Ethan addressed the older woman. I could hear in his voice the complete indifference to the younger one's advances. I let out my breath in a rush and smiled.

They started talking about the plans they had for the room, and it became obvious that Ethan was here in the capacity of a building contractor, or perhaps an architect. Some sort of construction designer in any case, hired to work with the Hamiltons to complete renovations to the ballroom for the upcoming fundraising event. As they walked around the vast space, the older woman pointed to the areas she wanted changed, and described what she had in mind.

Ethan, dressed in more sophisticated clothes than he'd usually worn in East Halton—a button-up shirt and brown suede blazer with dark jeans and boots—listened intently. His hair was styled differently as well, cut a little shorter on the sides. It made him seem much older, and for the first time since I left home I felt a little unsure about my decision to travel across the country to find him.

I tried not to move as I watched the four of them interact, but my foot was falling asleep and I needed to shift my weight. As soon as I did, Ethan's gaze darted upwards and locked with mine. No one else had noticed my subtle movement, but he had, and as our eyes met I felt the same spark of electricity I always felt when we looked at each other.

Ethan managed to keep his features composed, but his eyes held a mixture of relief, curiosity, and most of all, love. I gave him a big smile. The corners of his mouth lifted slightly, but then his expression changed. His focus shifted to something behind me, and a dark cloud swept over his face. Before I could turn around, an arm wrapped around my waist, and a strong hand covered my mouth, keeping me from crying out. I'd been caught.

Thirty-Two

"Hi gorgeous. Did you enjoy your brief taste of freedom?" Adam's breath was warm against my ear. "I have to say I'm the tiniest bit disappointed in your underestimation of my skills. Although the tire was a nice touch, I'll give you that. Let's really get Ethan's blood boiling, shall we?" He took his hand away from my mouth and greeted Ethan with an insolent wave.

Anger flashed in Ethan's eyes as he helplessly stood and listened to Mr. and Mrs. Hamilton debate the height they felt was appropriate for the new stage construction. Ethan answered their questions without ever taking his eyes off of Adam and me. My back was to Adam, but I felt him motion something to Ethan before he dragged me back into the shadows at the rear of the theatre box.

I had to get away; if Adam got me back to his car, I would never see Ethan again. I started struggling, wriggling, and trying to claw my way free, but to no avail; Adam had me in a tight hold. *Come on Hannah, remember your defense lessons from Lucy.* I stomped my foot down hard on the top of his, and his grip loosened. I managed to break free and run for the balcony stairs, but he lunged forward and grabbed my waist and wrist again before I had even made it down one stair.

"Fighting is useless," Adam assured me as we wrestled. He sounded more amused by my struggle than anything.

"Please, Adam, don't do this." Even knowing his words were true, I continued to resist his efforts to tug me farther down the curved hallway, to a different set of stairs than the ones I had used.

We made our way down them and out the back door. Adam's car was parked in a back alley behind the convention centre. I continued to try to free myself from the grip he had on my wrist, but instead of throwing me in the passenger seat of the car, as I had expected him to, he stopped and stared at his vehicle. A garbage truck had stopped inches in front of his Camaro, and the driver was nowhere in sight. Since Adam had backed right up to a dumpster, he was completely boxed in and unable to get out of the alley.

Adam slammed his free hand down on the hood of the car and yelled out in frustration. Then, with a quick glance back at the door we'd just come out of, he tightened his grasp on my wrist and abandoned the car. He strode out of the alley, jerking me along with him.

"I hope that was a satisfying enough reunion, because that's the last time you're going to see him." Adam dragged me down the sidewalk of a residential street, his voice callous.

"Adam please, please don't do this." We'd shared some pretty intense moments on our trip. He'd even opened up a few times, let me see the pain that drove him. Could I reach him again? "You told me you weren't a monster, here's your chance to prove it."

I had slowed a bit, hoping he would stop and listen to me, but he yanked on my wrist and increased his speed until I was practically running to keep up. He gave no indication that what I'd said affected him. There was a cold efficiency to his actions. As though the part of him capable of humanity—the not-a-monster part, as he'd called it—had been shut down, replaced with an implacable determination to complete the assignment he'd been given.

Terror swelled inside me. Where had that Adam gone? And what was this robotic Adam going to do to me?

We sprinted down the road, crossing at an intersection and heading down a street that led to a well-established neighborhood with towering trees. Adam kept checking behind him every few seconds, presumably for any sign that Ethan had managed to get away from the Hamiltons, but no one appeared to be following us.

"You know what's going to happen; you have to know what they're going to do to me. How can you just hand me over to them?" I forced my legs to keep pace with him. What could I say that would get through to him?

"They aren't going to hurt you. If that was the plan, they would have just had me kill you right away." Adam stopped at another intersection and glanced to the left then right.

Where are we going? "There are lots of things they could do to me that would be far worse than killing me," I shot back.

He frowned, but didn't respond.

We crossed the street and sped along a sidewalk, passing by a collection of older homes with newer ones dotted here and there between them. My legs ached, but Adam just kept going. A few passersby shot us questioning looks, but no one attempted to help me.

"Where are you taking me anyway?" I asked bitterly.

"One thing about the Bana, they always have a back-up plan," Adam replied matter-of-factly.

Too out of breath to speak, I gave up arguing for the time being as we hurried another three blocks, until we came to the last house on a dead-end street. It was a big old Victorian set on a large lot, painted in a variety of colors. It looked to be at least three stories, maybe even four with the attic. Adam pulled me along a stone path, across an overgrown yard, and up the stairs at the front of the house.

"Adam please, all I want is to be free from all of this. Please just let me go," I begged. I felt like a broken record, but I didn't have any other arguments. He stopped on the porch and turned to study me, loosening his grip on my arm just slightly. He had a strange expression on his face. Was I finally getting through to him?

"You want to be free? That's what you want, your freedom? Then let's go. You're just as much a victim of all this destiny nonsense as I am. With your special ability, it won't really matter whether you end up with the Bana or Hleo, they're going to poke and prod your mind until it's gone and all that's left of you is a shell. Paige's idea of just disappearing and living the good life on a beach somewhere wasn't completely terrible. I can make sure we are never found. If you want freedom, then let's go be free; you're as good an insurance policy for me as any." Adam watched my face closely.

I blinked. "Adam, I ..." I didn't know how to respond, his offer had caught me so off guard.

"Yeah, that's what I thought," Adam scoffed. "You don't want to be free, Hannah; you want to be with *him*. Well, he can just watch and see how things turn out for the girl he dragged into this world." Adam turned his attention to the electronic lock on the door.

My shoulders slumped and I didn't bother responding. There wasn't anything left to say that would help, and my mind was still reeling over his proposal.

Adam punched in a code and pushed the door open. Still gripping my wrist, he walked inside and the two of us stood in the middle of a house that was nothing but bare rooms, plaster walls, and plywood floors. The outside was merely a façade. A plain set of wooden stairs loomed in front of us and Adam dragged me up the staircase to the second floor.

This one matched the first floor in its stark emptiness, and we continued to the third floor of the house. It had no interior walls either, just two dormer-style windows facing the road, and basic plywood floors. Random wooden and metal chairs and a card table were set up in the one corner, and a ratty-looking couch with blankets folded up on it had been pushed against the wall. My stomach clenched at the sight of a coil of rope under one of the chairs.

Deliberately turning away, I frowned at an old-fashioned claw-foot bathtub in the corner across from the card table. There must have been a bathroom there at one time. Glue marks on the plywood in the shape of bathroom tiles surrounded the tub.

"Charming," I observed sarcastically, as Adam pushed me down on one of the metal chairs.

"I think they were going for open concept," Adam replied dryly. "It's just a shell because it's a Bana trap house."

I furrowed my brow. "A trap house?"

"Yeah, the entire house is rigged with explosives. If you don't disarm the house before you enter, an alarm is triggered, causing an explosion. The subfloor is wired, so if there is an explosion the basement blows, causing the house to implode, crumbling and killing anyone unfortunate enough to be caught inside."

My eye widened. "Are you serious? Why are we here then?"

"Don't worry, I disarmed it, we're all good." Adam crouched down and grabbed the rope out from under the chair.

I cocked my head. "You know you're faster than me. Do you really need to tie me up?"

"I need to make sure you stay here while I find us another ride. I can't go back to get the car. I'm sure Ethan immediately figured out whose it was. I should have dumped it a long time ago, but it was just so nice." Within minutes he'd wrapped the rope around my calves, tying them to the legs of the chair, and fastened my wrists behind my back. Once he was done, he flopped down on the couch. A cloud of dust billowed up into the air, but Adam didn't seem to notice. He pulled out his cell phone and started scrolling through information on his screen.

"Make yourself comfortable. I guess we'll just hang out here for awhile." I clenched my jaw and glared at him.

"Don't worry, we'll be on our way as soon as we have a new vehicle." Adam kept his eyes on his phone.

I examined the space. If Adam did leave me to go steal another car, could I get out of here? I glanced in his direction. He still seemed engrossed with his phone screen and I wriggled my hands a little to see if there was any way of squeezing out of my constraints. *Too tight, now what?* If only I could convince him to let me go. Adam had actually been nice to me at moments during our trip, and from what both he and Ethan had told me, at one time he had been a decent person.

"You don't have to do this, Adam."

He lifted his head, his eyes narrowed. "I don't have to do what?"

"Hand me over to them. I get that you've had some really terrible things happen in your past, but it's not too late. You can make amends for your actions." I kept my eyes locked with his. I meant what I said; after everything Adam had shared, it seemed he wasn't completely incapable of redemption, there was always a chance.

"Hannah, be serious." Adam got up off the couch and walked over to the corner, pressing both palms to the trim around the window and staring out the glass.

"I am serious; you can just let me go."

"Don't you think I tried?" He whirled back around to snap at me, his brown eyes sparking intensely.

"What?" I blinked again as shock rippled through me.

He strode over to me, gripping the arms of the chair and leaning his face in close to mine. His expression was incredulous as he studied me, as though he couldn't believe I hadn't picked up on it.

"I don't understand." I tilted back, his closeness intimidating.

Adam stepped away and drove his hands through his sand-colored hair. "Come on. You really think I'm so bad at what I do that I would just leave those letters lying around for you to find? You really think I just happened to leave you alone in the car, untied, with enough time to get away at a gas station where a bus was parked? You think I just forgot to take your cell phone out of the glove box so you'd be able to grab it?"

"But ..." I stuttered, not even sure where to begin questioning him. Getting away *had* felt a little too easy, but if he wanted to let me go, then why was I in the situation I was now?

Adam rubbed a hand across his jawline. "I gave you the best opportunity to get away. I thought you'd just grab the letters and bolt from the motel room. Imagine my surprise when I emerged from the shower and there you were, still cuddled up on the bed waiting for me."

"Why would you do that?"

"Why do guys ever do nice things for girls?" he responded flatly.

I swallowed hard. "So when I got on the bus, why didn't you just let me go? Why did you follow me to Lafayette?"

"Because the second after you got on that bus I got a call, wanting to know what was going on." Adam shook his head.

"And?" I shrugged.

"They were watching. They've been watching the whole time, which means I'm stuck. There is no abort option with this directive." Adam sighed and turned his gaze to the window again.

"So you have to choose between my life and yours, and naturally you choose yours." I rolled my eyes. Of course Adam's selfishness would trump any feelings he may have developed for me.

"They aren't going to kill you, Hannah. They wouldn't go to all this trouble if that's what they wan—"

"You said it yourself, Adam. They're going to prod at my brain until there's nothing left. *I see protecteds.* They're obviously going to try to use that knowledge to their advantage, and somehow I doubt I'm going to be able to convince them I have no control over how my brain works, which means my life is about to become very terrible, very quickly," I shouted at him in frustration.

Adam's dark eyes softened. He took a hesitant step in my direction. Was I finally getting through to him? "Maybe you're—" He stopped and his head snapped towards the window. He strode back to the dust-covered glass and peered down into the front yard.

My chest tightened. What now? Had the Bana sent someone to make sure Adam brought me in? "What is it?"

Adam spun back around, his gaze boring into me. "He found us."

Thirty-Three

For a few, wild seconds, all I could think of was that Alexander had somehow tracked us down. I struggled to draw in a breath. "Who found us?"

"Your precious boyfriend." Adam spat out the words.

"Ethan," I whispered, my heart rate speeding up. Even if Adam had been about to confess some sort of romantic feelings towards me, it meant nothing. At the end of the day he had still been prepared to hand me over to pure evil, and that made it no contest between the two guys.

"Looks like you'll have another chance to catch up after all." Adam moved away from the window, to the top of the stairs. His expression had hardened again. I bit my lip *He can't let Ethan win under any circumstance.* There was too much conflict and hatred between them. I was out of luck appealing to him for freedom now.

We waited silently, until the sound of the door swinging open could be heard.

"We're up here, old chum," Adam called down the stairs, the smug tone back in his voice. My stomach churned, and I redoubled my efforts to loosen the ropes around my wrists.

Ethan's head appeared at the top of the stairwell, his gaze shifting from me to Adam as he assessed the situation.

"Well, this seems familiar, doesn't it?" Adam swept a hand toward me. "Me, standing between you and your lady love."

Ethan kept the same hard stare on his face. He took another step up to join Adam and me on the third floor.

"Although, I can't help but question your devotion to her. I mean, you just up and disappear on the poor girl, leaving her on her own. Defenseless and vulnerable, giving her a few measly clues to try to track you down." Adam twisted to grin at me. "Hannah, why don't you tell Ethan about our road trip and the nights spent sharing a hotel bed together?"

My fists clenched. *Why are you goading him, Adam? Talk to him. Maybe the three of us can figure this thing out.*

"You know, she really is nice to cuddle up to. I definitely get what you see in her. I especially like that little freckle on her stomach, adorable. Although from what I hear, you haven't had a chance to see that yet." Adam winked at me.

It was all Ethan could stand. He cried out and ran at Adam, spearing him and slamming him against the rough plywood floor.

The two rolled around on the ground, punching and kicking, each of them trying to do as much damage to the other as they could. They were pretty evenly matched, and for several moments neither seemed to be able to get the upper hand.

I watched helplessly from my position on the chair, fighting with the ropes, desperate to be able to spring into action, no matter who the victor ended up being. My wrists were chafed raw from rubbing against the rough cords of the rope. A fine sprinkle of dust landed on my arms. I looked up and froze. More dust was shaking off the walls. My breathing sped up. A low rumble came from under us, and the windows began to rattle. Definitely more movement than the house reacting to the mayhem Adam and Ethan were causing. Had the charges Adam mentioned somehow been detonated?

Ethan and Adam were so busy fighting they failed to notice the commotion. "Stop!" I screamed as loud as I could. Both of them turned to stare at me. "Look." I jerked my head towards the windows. The glass was now rattling so hard I couldn't believe it hadn't broken yet. The guys scrambled away from each other.

"The charges; they must have been set off somehow." Adam scanned the room. The plaster on the walls was cracking, coming apart at the seams.

"This is a Bana trap house? Why would you bring her here?" Ethan gaped at Adam. He was obviously familiar with the ways of the Bana, and understood perfectly what was happening now.

"I didn't have a lot of options, and I disarmed it. You must have triggered something," Adam shot back at him. The glass in the windows finally gave in to the pressure and shattered into pieces. I turned my head to protect my eyes from the shards hurtling through the air and scattering across the plywood floor. Thankfully I was far enough back from the dangerous spray to avoid being hit.

"I didn't touch a thing, the door was unlocked; you mustn't have disarmed it correctly." His focus still on Adam, Ethan inched closer to me.

Adam flung both arms in the air. "I locked the door behind us, so how exactly was it open?"

"Actually boys, that was me."

My head whipped in the direction of the female voice. Paige stood at the top of the stairs watching the three of us, seemingly amused by the scene. "See, here's the thing. I've decided if you guys won't make it easy for me, play by my rules and let me have her, then it's best to just be rid of the two of you. Then no one can stop me from taking off with my little insurance policy." Paige strode over to us. My gaze dropped to her hand. She held a small crossbow, aimed directly at my chest.

"A crossbow, really?" Adam's fists clenched as he edged closer to her.

"Ah, ah, ah." She wagged a finger at him with her free hand. "Not one more step." She lifted the weapon slightly. "I think you know my accuracy with one of these."

I swallowed hard at the coldness in her eyes. I doubted that she cared in the least if she did me serious harm. She'd take me with her, dead or alive. The only thing in my favor would be the inconvenience of having to carry my body out of the house.

"Are you insane?" Adam yelled. "If you touch her, they will kill you."

Paige just smiled.

While the two of them were busy with each other, Ethan moved to stand between Paige and me.

Paige didn't hesitate, she immediately pulled the trigger and an arrow soared through the air, narrowly missing Ethan's head and sailing above mine. He didn't even flinch.

"That was your warning, Ethan. Now get out of my way." Paige's voice was as cold as her eyes.

"You'll have to come through me to get to her." Ethan's tone matched hers, hard as nails. He took another step forward, slightly to the side so that to aim at him she could no longer point it directly at me.

"I'd rather have you watch me whisk your fair Hannah away, then allow this house to collapse around you, but have it your way." Paige pulled the trigger again. With more speed than humanly possible, Ethan jerked his head to the left, skillfully avoiding the arrow. Adam rushed Paige, slamming her to the ground, but not before she had pulled the trigger one more time. The arrow pierced his shoulder, sticking out just below the collarbone, and Adam cried out. He rolled away from her, grasping the shaft.

In a quick spin motion, she pulled herself back to her feet, tossing the now-empty weapon to the ground and setting her sights on Ethan. The two of them began exchanging blows in the unstable house.

"The second set of charges will go off any time now," Adam called to Ethan as he tugged the arrow free, grimacing in pain. "It's a failsafe in case the first ones don't work. Once they blow, we only have about thirty seconds before this place becomes rubble." He waved a hand in my direction. "Get her out of here. I'll deal with Paige."

"Fine." Ethan continued to duck and weave against Paige's furious attack, until he was able to toss her over his shoulder and flip her to the ground. Adam sprang on top of her, trying to subdue her, but she went after his injured shoulder. He couldn't quite contain her and she slid away from him back to her feet. The two of them attacked each other. Paige had a graceful fighting style, almost like a dancer, and was very quick, but Adam was stronger. I had no idea which of the two of them would win.

Ethan lunged at me, over floorboards that had begun to buckle. Plaster was crumbling off the walls in large chunks, sending clouds of dust into the air. The rumbling grew louder.

"I'll have you out of here in a few seconds." Ethan slid a knife from the sheath around his ankle and sawed through the strands of rope Adam had wound around my wrists.

"Ethan—" The floor splintered and the boards dropped, slanting into the middle of the room. Ethan stumbled backwards, towards the crack. My chair slid and tipped forward, and I leaned back as far as I could to right myself. Ethan managed to recover his balance and scramble back over to me, but his knife had fallen through the gap in the collapsing floor. His eyes frantically searched the area until he found a large shard of glass from the window. He picked it up and slashed through the remaining rope around my wrists and ankles, sucking in a quick breath when the glass cut into his palm. He tossed the shard to the ground. The floor continued to cave in, forming a v-like configuration. The walls and ceiling buckled around us; all the plaster on the walls had shaken completely loose, and now the exposed rafters above us were starting to crack from the pressure of being pushed in on themselves.

Adam and Paige were over near the bathtub area. He picked her up with his good arm and threw her into the old claw-foot tub. She grabbed some sort of plumbing pipe out of the tub and smashed it against his face. He staggered backwards, blood trickling down his cheek. It looked like he was about to retaliate when there was a loud crack and the ceiling beams above them finally gave in. Adam glanced over at Ethan and me, and we locked eyes one last time before he disappeared beneath the wreckage and dust of the collapsing house.

Ethan grabbed my hand and we sprinted for the staircase. The stairs were shaking so hard I almost fell down them. The banister and its spindles came apart beneath our hands as we ran down the first flight and dashed to the stairs that led to the main floor. The dust was getting thick, and I pressed the sleeve of my sweater to my mouth to keep from coughing while we crawled over the debris littering the floor.

We stopped at the top. If we could get down this flight, it was only ten or so steps to the front door. From our vantage point, I could see that the main floor had all but given in, buckling and bowing heavily, and collapsed into the basement in most sections. The staircase appeared to be the only part of the house still somewhat intact. Ethan tugged on my hand and we started down. Halfway to the bottom, a large cracking sound split the air and the stair beneath me gave way. My scream was cut off when Ethan flung an arm around my waist and lifted me onto the next step.

We reached the bottom, and darted across what was left of the main floor towards the front door. Hope sparked within me. *We're going to make it.* I reached for the doorknob just as another huge rumbling sound came from above us. Before I could react, the ceiling came crashing down around us. The force of the collapsing floor from above ripped Ethan and I apart. A large beam plunged down onto my leg, pinning me under it. I cried out as all around me drywall, plaster, and wood came rushing down. I couldn't see Ethan anymore, and was quickly becoming encased in a debris cocoon, but there was nothing I could do about it since my leg was trapped. From my peripheral, I sensed something falling above me, but before I could cover my head it struck me hard and everything went black.

Thirty-Four

I woke up coughing. My eyes stung and I blinked rapidly in an attempt to see through the dust. A heavy silence blanketed the building; the house appeared to be done collapsing in on itself. I tried to move, but couldn't. The space was too small and my leg was still stuck. An intense throbbing pain ran up my leg from my foot, I was pretty sure my ankle was broken. I pulled at it, trying to free myself, but the beam was too heavy.

Panic crept over me, rising in my throat, tightening my chest. Would I die here? Was Ethan already dead? A piece of broken drywall beside me started to shake. "Hannah, Hannah, can you hear me?" Ethan was yelling, the desperation in his voice mingling with the sound of rubble being frantically torn through.

"Ethan," I called out, and then choked on the thick dust in the air and began coughing again.

"I'm coming. Are you all right?" Ethan's fingers appeared around the edge of a piece of drywall as he gripped it and yanked it away from me, creating a small opening between us.

"I'm okay. My leg is stuck, but I'm okay." I twisted my body as much as I could so I could watch him work.

Within minutes Ethan had managed to shove enough debris aside that I could see his face. "Hi." My voice was weak, but I managed a faint smile.

"Hi." He stopped what he was doing for a few seconds to look at me. His face and clothes were coated in dirt and sweat, and blood dripped down the side of his head from his hairline. His eyes were wild with worry, but the corners of his mouth turned up in response, and even given the situation we were in, my heart melted all over again at the sight of that perfect smile and deep-green gaze.

He reached forward through the small opening and cupped my face in his palm, stroking my cheek gently with his thumb. I closed my eyes and leaned in, grateful for the contact. I had missed him so much. After a few seconds he set back to work and managed to clear enough space to maneuver himself into the opening beside me. He examined the heavy wooden beam pinning my leg, then tried to lift it. It shifted ever so slightly, but not enough for me to move.

"Do you think you can pull your foot free if I can get this beam up high enough?" Ethan adjusted his grasp.

"Yeah, I think so."

Ethan took a deep breath and pushed up on the wooden plank. His arm and neck muscles strained from the effort, and I yanked my foot away. "Ah!" Intense pain shot from my ankle all the way up my.

The beam came crashing back down as Ethan's strength ran out. He scooped me up in his arms and carried me out of the little tunnel he'd managed to create. When he climbed off of what was left of the front porch, he lowered me down gingerly to sit on the ground in the front yard.

As I sprawled out on the grass, trying to find a comfortable position, I surveyed the wreckage and shuddered. It was only by sheer luck that we were still alive. Where had Adam ended up in all that rubble? The Hleo and Bana couldn't die from natural causes, but there was nothing natural about the way that house had crumpled. The upper floors had been demolished; there was no way he could have lived. The twinge of sadness that coursed through me surprised me. Even after all he'd done, I couldn't help feeling that, if Adam had only been given a chance, he might have found a way to turn things around. He had, after all, sacrificed himself to Paige so Ethan and I would have a chance to escape. It was an action I didn't fully understand, but as Ethan gently took my ankle in his hands to examine it, I was grateful.

"I'm just going to move it a little, try to assess how badly you're injured." Ethan rolled my ankle slowly to the left, but paused when I couldn't repress a whimper. "I'm fairly certain it's broken. We'll get you to a hospital and have it taken care of right away." Ethan bent down to pick me up again, but I lifted a hand to stop him.

I brushed a strand of hair off his forehead and slid my palm to the side of his face, studying him intently. He gazed back at me, a mixture of worry, relief, and affection in his eyes as they searched mine. His hands were cut up, his face and clothes were dirty and bloodstained, but it was still so amazing to see him. Part of me had begun to believe this moment would never happen, that I would never get to see Ethan Flynn again, and in this first opportunity we had to stop and just take each other in since reuniting, I wanted to be able to push back the fear and uncertainty that I'd made the right decision to find him once and for all.

"I missed you." I gave him a tentative smile.

He reached up to stroke my hair, which I could feel was dirty and matted, probably with blood. He brought his lips to mine. They were soft and warm, and tingles of electricity rippled through me. I wrapped my arms around his neck and clung to him.

"How did I ever live a second without you?" Ethan breathed, pulling away and running his fingers through my hair again. I wanted him to explain everything right then and there, but my ankle was killing me, and I wasn't sure I was completely ready to have the discussion about his sudden departure from East Halton and from me.

"I'm so glad to see you." I reached for him again, then winced as I repositioned my ankle slightly.

"We should get you to a hospital." Ethan glanced down at my foot. "Are you injured anywhere else? Did Adam hurt you at all?"

Thoughts of Paige running her knife blade across my stomach and Adam coming to my rescue flashed through my mind. I shook my head. "No. He didn't hurt me. I did get a cut on my side, but that was thanks to Paige, not Adam." I patted the spot where the liquid skin was still holding firm.

Anger flashed in Ethan's eyes. "Paige." His teeth were gritted.

I grasped his arm gently. "Let's just get out of here. We can talk more later."

He nodded and crouched beside me to slide his arms under my knees and back to pick me up. He carried me to his Jeep, parked halfway down the block, and set me down carefully on the passenger seat. Sirens pierced the air off in the distance, likely headed for the wreckage we had just managed to escape from. Ethan threw the Jeep in gear and we drove off. From my view in the passenger side mirror I could see smoke and clouds of dust billowing into the sky as we drove away, leaving Adam and the rubble behind us.

Twenty-Nine

Ethan took me to the closest emergency room, where a doctor confirmed that I had indeed broken my ankle. They casted it and gave me crutches and painkillers. Ethan and I cleaned ourselves up the best we could in the hospital washrooms, then we were on our own, left to figure out the next step.

We sat in Ethan's Jeep in the hospital parking lot. I tried to find a comfortable position for my bulky ankle, while Ethan watched me. "I guess we only have one option now." The key was in the ignition and he gripped the wheel with both hands, but seemed hesitant to begin driving.

"And what is that?" My stomach twisted into a tight knot. *What is he going to say? That we have to separate again?*

"We need to go to The Three and explain to them that us being apart isn't going to work, and they are going to have to accept that." Ethan let go of the wheel and took my hand in his. He looked at me expectantly, as though he needed me to confirm that this was what I still wanted.

"Oh yes, of course." I let out a huge sigh of relief. I'd been terrified Ethan was going to send me back to East Halton alone. The muscles in my shoulders I hadn't even realized had tensed up started to relax. I was so happy he wanted the same thing I did.

"Okay good, because I've already called them to let them know we're on our way."

We left Lafayette, our course set northeast as we drove towards Virginia, and Veridan. It would take us almost a day to get there, and I was ecstatic we'd have a chance to be alone together.

"I have to admit Adam was probably the last person I ever expected you to show up with. I still don't fully understand what happened there. Did he kidnap you, and you managed to elude him for a little while?" Ethan's grip on my fingers tightened at the word *kidnap*.

"Sort of." I squeezed his hand back and then proceeded to fill him in on the details of my journey from East Halton to the Hamilton Conference Center. I told him about playing on Adam's ego and using him to sort out the clues Ethan had left me, our trek across several states, Paige's chaotic plea to drag me away to some jungle as leverage for her freedom, and my learning more about Adam's past, which helped me to understand how bitterness had taken such a hold of him. I omitted the part about Adam developing feelings for me. I was still sorting out what that meant, although, since he was dead, it might be something better left buried.

"When I saw you standing in that balcony I thought I was hallucinating. I couldn't believe I would be so fortunate to actually see you this soon. But when Adam appeared behind you, well, then I knew it was really you."

"*Soon?* It's felt like forever," I murmured.

"Believe me, I know." Ethan nodded, but kept his eyes on the road.

I studied his profile. Something stronger than relief flooded through me. I'd missed him, I was acutely aware of that, but it was more than that; I'd been caught in the grip of some restricting force in Ethan's absence, and now it had dissipated and I could finally breathe again.

We made our way east, the vehicle slipping into silence. I was so happy to see Ethan, and pleased that he was just as glad to see me. I didn't want to wreck the moment, but I needed to know. "You left." I stared down at our linked hands. I tried not to sound hurt, but my voice betrayed me. I could feel his gaze on me.

"I left." He released my hand to tilt my chin up so I'd meet his eyes. "Let me begin by saying I'm so sorry for letting things happen the way they did. You have no idea how tortured I've been for the last month, how many times I wanted to just come back to you—"

"So why didn't you?" Being pulled between his loyalty for the Hleo, and his love for me, was a terrible position for Ethan to be in, especially with his inclination to follow the rules. I hated that it had to be one or the other, that I had put him in that spot, but I struggled with why it appeared he had chosen loyalty over love.

Ethan ran a hand over his face. "The night of Ryan's accident, when we got into that fight, I got a call from Bridget after you had headed home, informing me that my presence was requested in front of The Three immediately. I knew from your words that you needed some time to yourself, and I wanted to honor your request, so I gave Simon strict instructions to keep a close eye on you and inform me right away if anything unusual happened. I drove down to Veridan, figuring that whatever they wanted to talk to me about would be brief, and I would be able to get back before you ever had a chance to know I was gone." Ethan returned his attention to the road. "When I arrived at Veridan, I learned that The Three had discovered the truth."

I snorted.

His forehead creased. "What?"

"Sorry, it's just you said *discovered*, as if they'd just stumbled on the truth about us, when Miriam knew all along. She promised not to say anything, and then just over a month later, all of a sudden they're calling you in." I shook my head, not even trying to hide the bitterness I felt about being lied to.

Ethan's frown deepened. "Miriam knew?"

"Yes." I arched a brow. "Didn't she rat us out?"

"No, she didn't. It was Travis. He saw me kiss you when we were at his house, and he went to Victor with the information. I never did trust him. It was stupid and careless of me to be so openly affectionate around him. I was just so relieved you were okay." Ethan exhaled slowly, and my lips curled up in a small smile as I remembered that stolen moment at Travis's house.

"I can't believe Miriam knew." Ethan shook his head.

"Why not?"

"Because I would have expected her to confront me about it. Miriam and I have always had a very honest and close relationship. She's been a lot like a mother to me in many ways. I wonder why she was going to let it slide." Ethan shifted gears to pass around a slow-moving sedan and the Jeep's engine revved loudly.

"Maybe she doesn't care if we date." I pulled at the leg of my pants, trying to rearrange how it was wrapped around my cast.

"Maybe." Ethan didn't sound convinced.

I bit on my thumbnail as a thought buzzed around my brain. I'd been wrongfully blaming Miriam for the last month. I'd built up a case against The Three and the Hleo, especially Miriam, and now I needed to accept that perhaps my animosity had been a little misguided. They *had* separated us though. I just hoped we would somehow be able to unravel this mess and make them see our point of view when we got to Veridan.

"So what did they say to you?" We had always known this was a possibility, but I'd always believed if The Three did find out about us that Ethan would defend our relationship and choose me over duty if it came down to that.

"They called me in to respond to the accusations Travis had laid against me. I don't think they could fully believe I would ever break the Hleo's most sacred rule, and they needed to hear it directly from me. There's no way of lying or hiding how I feel about you, so I came clean. I'll never forget the look in Gabriel's eyes; it wasn't anger, it was crushing disappointment. Miriam didn't seem as upset as the other two, which makes sense now. They reluctantly charged me with committing *aliege*, the Hleo's word for treason, and told me they would allow me to stay on as a Hleo, but I was never to see you again."

I clenched my fists. Heat coursed through my veins, pulsing like blood. *How dare they tell him that?*

Ethan rested his fingers over my fist. "I tried to make them understand, to convince them I needed to be the one protecting you. You are vitally important and no one else is able to guard you as well as I am, but my protests only led them to give me an ultimatum." He circled my thumb protectively with his.

"An ultimatum?" I chewed on the inside of my cheek.

"Either I accept an immediate reassignment and allow another Hleo to guard you, without contacting you myself, or, if I really felt so vehemently that no one else could protect you, then they would immediately transfer you to Veridan for your own protection, and I would be removed from Hleo service permanently." Ethan shoulders sagged, the burden of disappointing his superiors clearly weighing on him.

"Those are awful choices." The hurt of his leaving was starting to soften as sympathy for the tough spot he had been forced into washed over me.

"I know how much your family and your life mean to you. I understand that you just want to feel normal again and to put this world behind you, and I couldn't be the one responsible for letting you be taken away from all you know. I tried to do what I thought was best, and agreed, unwillingly, to be reassigned. As soon as I was given my new assignment in Lafayette, I drove right back to you. I couldn't just leave without saying good-bye. I didn't care that it was direct defiance, I needed to at least explain what was happening and make you understand that as soon as I could, I would come back to you."

"You drove back to Easton Halton even after you were reassigned? Why didn't you talk to me?"

"I got there Saturday evening and found out that Simon had been called back to Veridan as well. Lucy was already in East Halton."

"Oh no! Lucy." I suddenly remembered Adam's admission that he'd locked her up.

"What about her?"

"Adam tied her up in an old cabin. If she's still there, she won't be doing too well. I know Hleo don't need to eat and drink, but this is going on day four." Lucy may not be my favorite person in the world, but I didn't want to see harm come to her.

"She's fine. She got herself free from the cabin. She was at Veridan when I called, strategizing how to track you down and get you back from Adam. I'm not sure if she was relieved or angry to hear that you were safe and sound with me." Ethan managed a lopsided grin.

"She was probably furious that she allowed herself to be bested by Adam." I rolled my eyes, but I was glad to know that she was okay.

"Probably. As I'm sure you're well aware, Lucy's incredibly by the book. If she knew I'd come back to East Halton, she would have gone straight to The Three. They would've placed you in protection for sure, and barred me from ever seeing you again. I couldn't let her find me there, so I waited for a moment of negligence in her surveillance, but she was more than vigilant. Even when you didn't see her, she was there watching you, always watching you.

"By Monday afternoon I needed to get going to Louisiana or The Three would have become suspicious, so I left the letter at Katie's for you. It was the hardest thing I've ever done, disappear without getting one last chance to talk to you. I was so worried about what you must be thinking, and whether or not you would be kept safe in my absence. I hoped that because Lucy was your mom's partner she would take care of you."

"She didn't even admit to being Elizabeth's partner. I found that out from Lou."

Ethan blinked. "Lou?"

"Yeah, remember how she gave me her phone number when we were at Veridan? I called her, hoping that she might be able to give me a lead to your whereabouts. She told me all about Lucy and Elizabeth and how hurt Lucy was when Elizabeth ran off with Noah. I'm pretty sure Lucy channeled that bitterness into how she treated me." I squared my jaw.

"I'm sorry you had it rough. She was so attentive while I was still in East Halton, I figured she would be capable. I should have known better."

I shrugged. "She tried."

Ethan slid his hand across the back of my neck, rubbing it softly with his thumb. "I was always coming back; I just had to figure out a way. The letter was meant as a beacon, a sign that I wasn't deserting you. I sent the Hamilton stamp for the same reason, so you would know I was still out there, still desperate to be with you. They were really only meant as clues to find me as a last resort, in case you were able to figure them out and needed to get to me. Or maybe, selfishly, part of me was always hoping you would try to find me, I don't know."

"I'm sorry you were put in such a terrible position. Everything's gotten so screwed up. You weren't supposed to have to choose between me and the Hleo. I know how much serving them means to you. I do love my family and my friends, but I would be willing to go live at Veridan if you were there with me, even if it was just as a regular human being and not a Hleo anymore. Be honest with me; is part of the reason you allowed yourself to be reassigned because you don't want to give up being a Hleo? Adam explained to me that you could have the branding process reversed. He said it wasn't very pleasant, but if it meant we could be together, live our lives together …"

"Hannah, no, it had nothing to do with me. Even if I did become a normal human again and you went to live at Veridan, they wouldn't have allowed me to stay with you. I would have been banished from the Hleo's world completely, as though I had never been a part of it. I sincerely thought that you being able to stay where you were and continue to live your life would be what you would want, even if it meant that I had to leave you for a while."

"Nothing is worth being separated from you, even for a second. Part of me has been missing for the last month and a half. All I could think about was finding you, even if that meant trusting someone who once tried to kill me." I shifted in my seat to face him squarely. "Ethan, I love you, I want us to be together, but I need answers from you. Adam told me all this stuff, and now I'm so confused. He said that you're a Hleo, and leaving is what you do, that you're loyal to the cause above all else, even personal relationships. He said it's why you haven't explained everything to me, like being able to revert back, or why we haven't … *been* together. He said you wouldn't get intimate with me because you know you're eventually leaving, and you don't want to hurt me or break any rules that aren't worth breaking." I was rambling and my face felt like it was on fire, but I needed to know what was going on in Ethan's head. I wanted to get everything we had been avoiding out in the open. If I could talk about these subjects with Adam, then I needed to be able to talk about them with Ethan.

Ethan frowned. "Why would you listen to Adam? He would only ever take what you told him and twist it to play mind games with you. He may think he knows me, that he has me figured out and knows the choices I'll make, but he doesn't understand me at all, not anymore."

"So, tell me what you're thinking about us then," I pressed.

"Okay. Let me start with the most important belief I have. Hannah, you are the very reason I exist now; every action I take, every decision I make, is with you in mind. It's true, I've hesitated in certain areas of our relationship, and it does have something to do with the rule Adam told you about. At first it wasn't an issue. I haven't been in a hurry to rush the physical side of our relationship because I wanted you to know I love you on a much deeper level than just that, and I didn't want you to feel pressured to do anything you weren't ready for. It's been an awkward topic of conversation for us, and easier to set aside than to confront, but you deserve a complete explanation. It's what I was going to share with you at Veridan and again at the pond the day of Ryan's accident.

"As a Hleo, I believe protecteds are sacred individuals, it's how I've been programmed and how I've seen them for as long as I can remember. I can't help but look at you as a special, unique being, and I do contemplate whether my actions could be harmful to you in some way. But there's more to my hesitation than just the Hleo rules. I've been around for a long time, and my mindset was formed years ago. When it comes to the ultimate expression of intimacy between two people, I believe it isn't something that should be rushed into." Ethan tapped the top of the gearshift with his finger. "I know I should have shared all this right from that night Simon walked in on us and our physical relationship started propelling forward, but I wasn't sure how you would react. I didn't want to make you feel more unusual than you already feel, and truth be told, I did avoid the topic. I kind of hoped I'd be able to keep my desire for you in check until we had some concrete answers on your ability and a better idea of what the future is going to hold."

My pulse raced when Ethan admitted he'd fought his desire to be with me. If anything, it only made me want him more. "So you think we should keep taking things slowly?"

"I know I don't always act like it—that day at the pond was a particularly weak moment for me—but yes, until we know more about our future I am totally fine with taking things slowly. And Hannah, it's going to be *our* future; I'm not going anywhere without you from here on out."

"I'm thrilled to hear you say that, but how are we going to make it work?"

"What Adam told you is true. It is possible for me to revert back to a normal human being, and yes, it is a painful process, but that would never stop me if it meant being with you. There wouldn't even be a moment of hesitation."

"So, are you planning on changing back?"

"I don't know."

"You don't know." I slumped back in my seat, feeling the unexpected words like a slap. How could he and I possibly stay together if he didn't change back for me?

Ethan touched my arm. "Wait, before you take that the wrong way, let me explain." He pulled away and ran a hand over his face. "I knew The Three would be watching my every move, making sure I was complying with their command that I stay out of your life, but I was desperate to know if Lucy was able to help you where I had failed."

"She wasn't," I commented wryly.

"I know. I had Simon hack into Lucy's communications with The Three to see if you'd had a breakthrough and to make sure you were okay."

My chest squeezed that he would go to that much effort for me.

"The five images you had all at once—"

"That was fun." I recalled passing out and my dad finding me on my bedroom floor. "It was actually six. I didn't quite get the last one completely sketched out before Adam appeared on the scene, so Lucy didn't have a chance to send that one out to other Hleo."

"Well, the five Lucy did share were all accounted for almost immediately. And they were all moments that had occurred some time in the two weeks before you saw them."

"The sixth one was too. It was an image of a man on a fishing boat and I recognized Lou in the background of the image. When I called her, I asked her about her latest protected and it was the guy from my image."

Ethan pressed his fingers to his temple. "That fits with everything else then. I know it feels scattered, but I think your images are starting to sharpen and hone in on specific timelines that would allow you to pinpoint current protecteds."

I swallowed hard and thought of Laney. The image of her at the well had been perfect timing.

Ethan dropped his hand. "I haven't shared this with anyone. I didn't know how to tell you, or if I even should, but from all the research we've done, from everything we've looked at and from all the information I've found—or rather haven't found—about anyone else with your ability, I've come to a conclusion. I don't know how or when, but I think you might be meant to be Miriam's replacement." Ethan carefully studied my face for my reaction. My breath hitched.

"From the time The Three began, there has only been one person who can see protecteds at any given time. It seems to be a protective measure created by The Metadas, so that protecteds are kept just that, protected. It makes me wonder if your ability has presented itself because Miriam's time is coming to an end. And I learned something else while I was in Lafayette that sort of confirms my theory." Ethan turned his attention back to the road while I worked on continuing to inhale and exhale. "Remember when we were at Veridan and we found that strange blacked-out report in Elizabeth's file?"

All I could do was nod.

"Well, I looked into it, and found some information you need to hear. While I was still at Veridan after facing The Three, I ran into an old colleague, James McCormick. He worked at Veridan in a position very similar to Bridget's at the time that report would have been filed, which meant he knew the personal going-ons of The Three. At first he wouldn't talk to me, he called me a traitor and vowed to have nothing to do with me, but I kept bugging him, positive he would have some useful information. Last week he finally agreed to talk, and shared what he knew. I outlined the report as best I could remember and he immediately knew what I was talking about.

"James told me that about thirty years ago The Three were antsy about something. They refused to give him any details, but every time one of them would come out of the circular room, he or she would be agitated. Then one day they asked him to call your mother in for a secret meeting. They didn't tell him why, but he put the clues together and suspected that Elizabeth was being trained by Miriam.

"When Elizabeth took off, The Three had James take care of the files on her training sessions. He's the one who blacked out the information on the sheet we saw. The files recorded Elizabeth's progress through multiple training sessions, during which she went into the circular room with Miriam to learn how to wield the power of seeing protecteds.

"James told me that The Three had become fearful of a threat on Miriam's life and wanted to take the precaution of having a replacement ready, should such an attack occur. There is a very intricate anointing process when one of us becomes one of The Three, something I didn't really know, but James outlined for me. He explained that a Hleo has to go into the circular room four separate times to be rebranded with the Hleo's serum. Each time this happens, a new element is added to the serum to change its organic properties. James didn't know what was added or how it worked, all he knew was this was what needed to happen for one of us to be gifted with the divine abilities of The Three. James couldn't be entirely sure, but he believed that Elizabeth had conducted two or three of these sessions before she disappeared, which means ..."

"Which means she had almost had the same power as Miriam, and she could have somehow passed it on to her daughter."

"Yes. I think so." Ethan's face was drawn, as though he wasn't sure he should have shared this news with me.

"But Miriam's fine and guarded extremely well. Plus, she doesn't age. I mean, why would I need to replace her?" I rubbed my forehead with the side of my hand, finding this new information too hard to accept.

"I don't know, and maybe I'm wrong." Ethan shrugged, but he didn't sound overly convinced.

"Ethan, I can't be Miriam, how could I be Miriam?" I found breathing difficult and tried not to hyperventilate, as the overwhelming wave hit me the same way it had when I'd first learned of the Hleo world.

Ethan rubbed my shoulder soothingly. "Maybe we're jumping the gun. There haven't been any signs that Miriam is in any sort of danger, and until we talk to The Three and try to get them to open up, we won't know anything for sure. I mean, even if it does turn out that Elizabeth somehow passed on a remnant of Miriam's ability to you, it doesn't necessarily mean you are meant to be her replacement. That plan was put in place for Elizabeth and a lot has changed since then."

I looked down at my casted ankle, shifting my foot to find a more comfortable position. *I can barely keep myself alive, how can I take on the responsibility of trying to keep protecteds safe?* This was just too big, a life-altering responsibility that would require me to give up everything and hide myself away in seclusion. I would watch generations come and go while I would never age. It was something I couldn't wrap my mind around.

"This is why I wasn't sure how to tell you, because I know it's too much to take in. I don't want you obsessing, especially when we aren't sure that's where things are headed. I only told you so I could explain why I'm not sure about becoming human again.

"If, for some reason, you are meant to take over for Miriam, then I would ask to stay by your side, to be your faithful servant for however long this life existed for us. If you were one of The Three, you would no longer be a protected, and the rules would be different. It's never happened before, but there is nothing specific prohibiting a Hleo from being with one of The Three."

My heart leapt. That idea definitely brightened up the picture. The constriction in my chest eased a little.

"But if a different purpose for your ability becomes clear and you're freed from the entanglements with the society, I'll leave the Hleo and be changed back in a heartbeat to be with you. If you'll have me." Ethan gave me a hopeful smile.

"Of course I'll have you. If it's for the next 80 years or 800, I want to spend my life with you. Why do you think I was willing to take such a risk to find you?" I slipped my arms around his neck, burying my face against his shoulder.

He kissed the top of my head. "I still can't believe you drove across the country with Adam to find me, and that he helped us escape. It just doesn't make sense to me."

There was a question in his voice I wasn't prepared to answer. I settled back against my seat. "Adam's an enigma."

"I guess that's true. I'm just glad his car got blocked in." Ethan ran his thumb down my cheek, giving me a relief-filled smile.

"Me too." I leaned into his hand.

We were already out of Louisiana and traveling through southern Mississippi. The air was humid and sticky, and the sky was dark, as though it might rain at any moment, but I kept the window down, enjoying the feeling of the breeze on my skin.

We drove in comfortable silence for quite a while. I was lost in thoughts of my possible future as Miriam's replacement. *It can't be that. It must be something else.* I repeated that statement over and over in my head, but couldn't stop myself from wondering, what if?

Ethan pulled onto an interstate, getting off of the back roads we'd been driving down. He would glance over at me every once in awhile while he drove, as though he was worried I would disappear into thin air. I smiled at his rare show of insecurity.

We'd made our way through Mississippi and had crossed into Alabama when Ethan looked over at me with a different sort of frown on his face. "I want you to be prepared. It's going to be hard to make The Three accept us as a couple. There has never in the history of the society been an exception to that rule. That's not to say the rule has never been broken. It's just that, the few times it has, the offending Hleo has immediately been changed back and kicked out. When they called me in and told me why I was standing in front of them, I assumed that would be my fate too. I'd already decided that once I was changed back to a normal human again I would find a way to be with you. There are very rigid protocols in place to keep reverted Hleo from getting back to the protected they have gotten into a relationship with, but I wouldn't have let that stand in my way." He reached for my hand again and held it in his.

"But then they didn't remove me from the Hleo. I'm pretty sure the only reason they gave me a second chance was because of the extenuating circumstances surrounding you. I think they're leery of doing something that will push you away from them, especially since they still aren't sure what to do with you."

"If they tell us we can't be together, that's exactly what they'll do." I straightened up in my seat.

"I'm not sure we're going to convince them to bend on a centuries-old rule."

"What will we do if they don't?" I wanted the turmoil in my stomach to die down, but Ethan wasn't painting an overly positive picture.

"I have an idea, but it's pretty extreme. If The Three are determined to separate us, we could take off. We would leave our lives behind us, just like Elizabeth and Noah did, and find somewhere secluded to live, just the two of us."

I bit my lip in a moment of hesitation, then nodded. "Okay, if it comes to that, that's what we'll do."

"Really think this through though, Hannah. It means saying good-bye to Katie, and all your other friends, to your dad. I never want to have to ask you to do that, but ..."

"But it might be the only way you and I can have a future together."

He nodded. "Yes."

"Who knows, maybe we'll be able to persuade them."

"Yeah, maybe. I guess we'll cross that bridge when we come to it."

The sun dropped below the horizon. My ankle was killing me, so I finally gave in and took one of the painkillers the doctor had prescribed. Before long I drifted off into a deep peaceful sleep. For the first time in a long time I felt completely safe.

Thirty

The Jeep hit a pothole and I woke with a jerk. The sky was tinged with the faintest orange and pink hues of the breaking dawn. "How long have I been asleep?" I rotated my shoulders and turned my neck trying to get my tensed muscles to loosen up.

"Almost eight hours," Ethan glanced down at my cast. "How are you feeling?"

At the moment I was pain free and I tentatively swiveled my ankle to see how it was doing. A dull ache spread up my leg, but nothing too sore to handle. "It's better."

"Good, and the rest of you?"

"A little stiff, but considering a house fell on me, I really can't complain." I grinned and Ethan rolled his eyes.

I glanced out the window at the lush green forests we were passing by. The surroundings felt vaguely familiar. It took me a moment to figure it out, but then I realized we were less than an hour from Veridan Manor. We were traveling on the same road Ethan and I had taken from the train station only a few months ago on our first trip to Hleo headquarters. Nervous butterflies fluttered hard in my stomach as I mentally tried to prepare for what was to come.

When we reached it, Ethan pulled off the road and turned in at the guardhouse, stopping to check in with security.

"Ethan?" An older gentleman dressed in a security uniform poked his silvery head through the open window of the Jeep, obviously surprised by our arrival.

"Hi Charles. I called ahead; they should be expecting us at the main house." Ethan spoke to the guy politely enough, but there was a strained formality in his voice. *He's not looking forward to this visit.*

"I'll have to verify that." The security guard's dark brown eyes trailed from Ethan to me before he retreated into the guardhouse. Was that a slight hint of hostility in his gaze? "Go on through." Charles waved from the building's window, lifting the gate so we could pass.

Ethan took a deep breath before shifting the Jeep back into drive. We wound our way up the narrow road that led to the manor and pulled into a parking area to the right of the large iron entrance doors. Ethan helped me out of the vehicle and we slowly made our way inside, since I had to hobble across the stone terrace on crutches.

Bridget, The Three's personal assistant at Veridan, came to greet us as we walked into the grand front foyer. "Good morning Ethan, Hannah." She shook our hands politely, but there was a definite coolness in her tone.

"Bridget." Ethan nodded curtly.

"I'm afraid you've chosen a very busy day for your … meeting." Bridget stumbled over the word. "The Three won't be able to speak with you for another hour or so."

"That's fine, we'll wait." Ethan's posture was very straight, as though he was determined not to let this petite girl make him feel inferior.

"They'll meet you in the library board room at two." Bridget consulted the screen of her phone, which appeared to be open to a schedule app of some kind.

"Perfect. We'll just entertain ourselves until then," Ethan replied.

"Great. If you'll excuse me." Bridget turned on her heel and strode off in the direction she'd come, her blonde ponytail swishing with the motion.

"Is it just me, or was she mad at us?" I watched her until she disappeared into one of the many hallways leading off the great hall.

"Yeah, I'm a bit of a pariah around here these days. You should have seen her the last time I came here. I'm sure she assumed, understandably, that The Three were about to strip me of my right to be a Hleo, and she gave me a wide berth, as though my traitorous tendencies might be contagious. Like leprosy." Ethan lifted his shoulders slightly.

I frowned. How could he take the contempt so easily? "I'm so sorry I've put you in this position."

"You didn't put me anywhere. As much as I care about you, Hannah, I make my own choices. And I accept the responsibility for them." His voice was gentle, taking any possible sting out of the words. "Now where would you like to go? Are you hungry?" Ethan asked.

"I'm okay for now. Some fresh air might be nice, though."

"Outside?" Ethan glanced down at my cast doubtfully.

"I'll be fine." I repositioned the crutches under my arms.

"Okay, outside it is." Ethan held up his hands in surrender and we made our way deeper into the manor, headed for the library and the back exit. We passed a handful of people while we walked. Some of them nodded at Ethan, but none of them said hello, and I thought I saw one of them sneer. *Is this how it will be with The Three?*

"Hey, you two." A familiar voice called out from behind us. I turned around. Lou came down a narrow set of stairs towards us, and a smile spread across my lips. I was so glad she was at Veridan.

"Lou, hi." I hobbled over to her.

"What did you do to yourself?" She eyed my leg with an amused grin.

"It looks worse than it feels; just a bout of clumsiness." I shrugged. I was too on edge to get into the whole story at the moment.

She nodded with an impish smile. "So, the two of you, huh?"

"Lou." Ethan's voice held a warning tone.

She put a hand on his arm to stop him. "Don't worry, I think it's great."

I sighed. "You might be the only one." I glanced around to see if anyone was listening.

Lou studied me for a second, and her lighthearted expression sobered. "Hey, can I talk to Hannah for a second, just us girls?"

Ethan turned to me for approval, and I nodded. "Come find me on the terrace when you're done." He went out through the back door that led to the garden area.

Lou motioned to a delicate-looking settee propped against the hallway wall and we walked over and sank down onto it. "I know you're scared of what people around here think, but don't give them a second thought. The guys can't believe Ethan got away with it for as long as he did when they haven't been able to, and the girls are just jealous." Lou shot me a knowing look.

"Jealous?"

"Yeah. See, Ethan's choice is a bit of a puzzle to everyone. He's beloved around this place. He's a natural leader, has one of the best protecteds' survival records ever, a great take-down tally for Bana, and the boy is just skilled. He's never done anything remotely close to defying Hleo protocol before, and then all of a sudden he goes and breaks the biggest rule there is. The girls around here are looking at you saying, why her?"

I slumped down in my seat as I tried not to feel decimated by what she was saying. She was voicing the exact thing I'd wondered ever since Ethan had confessed he cared for me the night of the Masks gala, *why me?* I didn't doubt his feelings, but I did wonder why he'd chosen me over any of the many other girls who would love to be with him.

Lou nudged my arm with her shoulder. "Hey, before you go and get all neurotic about what I'm saying, I want you to understand that's not how I feel. I knew Elizabeth, and even though you and I don't know each other that well yet, if you're anything like her, then I completely get why Ethan is willing to give all of this up to be with you. You can't worry about what anyone else thinks; they just don't know you, so they're quick to judge. As long as you and Ethan are happy together, that's all that matters."

Her words were kind, but it made me wonder something I hadn't wanted to even contemplate, and couldn't bring myself to ask Ethan. "Did Ethan and my mom ever ...?" I wrinkled up my nose. After Adam had mentioned asking Elizabeth out on a date, the thought had lingered in my mind.

Her eyes went wide. "No way! Honestly Hannah, you don't have to worry about that for one second. They were hardly ever around each other. As far as I know, Ethan never showed interest in any of the girls around here, especially not your mom. And Elizabeth, well Ethan wasn't really her type. I think you know by now she had a thing for bad boys; we had that in common." Lou laughed. "How is Adam? I guess you really were desperate to find Ethan if you climbed into the car with that guy."

My eyebrows shot up. How could she already know about my journey with the infamous former Hleo? "He was going to kidnap me either way. Convincing him to find Ethan was more of a stall tactic than anything."

"A gutsy move for sure." Lou sounded impressed.

"So you and Adam …?" I pictured him for a second, the way his brown eyes had softened as he'd almost admitted feelings for me, but I pushed the image away. He hadn't actually confessed anything, and now, well, now he never would. A wave of sadness hit me over how his life had ended.

"We never dated or anything. I was more of an admirer from afar while he was a Hleo. Then I was torn between my crush on him and my duty to chase him. I doubt he even remembers me now." Lou grinned and shook her head, her copper hair swishing around her shoulders. I thought of the story Adam had shared with me about the week the two of them had spent together in the Greek Islands. *He remembered you, Lou.*

Before I could tell her, she spoke up again. "I totally understood Elizabeth and Noah. She got what I wanted, in a way. Someone who would continually challenge her." She didn't seem to know how my trip with Adam had ended, and I didn't have the heart to tell her he was gone, especially when she was trying to make my situation with Ethan easier.

"You've been so nice to me. I feel really lucky to have met you."

"Knowing you is kind of like having a piece of your mom back, so I feel pretty lucky too." Lou squeezed my arm.

"Thanks."

Lou helped me back to my feet and we walked out to the garden to meet Ethan. He was standing on the stone veranda staring out over the landscape, but shifted to face us when we drew close.

The grounds were just as beautiful as I remembered, actually more so now that the flowers were blooming. The clear blue sky in the background accentuated the beauty. It was almost like looking at a postcard.

"I'll leave you two alone, but come find me after and let me know how it went." "I will," I promised.

She touched my hand. "And remember what I said, no one else's opinion matters."

I gave her an appreciative smile before she went back through the entrance doors.

"Everything okay?" Ethan led the way to the stone railing that ran the perimeter of the terrace.

"Yeah. She just wanted to give me some friendly advice." I concentrated on the stone terrace, seeking out solid places to dig the end of my crutches into. "Do you want to check out the garden?"

"Are you sure?" Ethan wrinkled his forehead.

"I told you, I'm good." I straightened up, trying to make myself look competent. It would be a bit challenging to get down the narrow stone staircase, but with the cool reception we were getting from the Hleo around Veridan I wanted to be somewhere secluded.

"All right." Ethan waved his hand in an 'after you' motion.

We made our way slowly into the garden. Ethan stayed at my side with an arm out, ready to catch me if necessary, but I made it to the manicured greenery unscathed. A quiet path that looked as though it didn't see a lot of action led into the woods. Brush and leaves were swept across it, and the flowers that lined the edges were starting to push in on either side, threatening to overtake it. I hobbled down it.

The two of us settled onto a wrought-iron bench under a large maple tree about halfway between Veridan Manor and the woods. I had to fight the urge to slip my fingers through Ethan's and grasp on tight. We'd been separated for so long, all I wanted was physical connection with him, but until we had pled our case to The Three it was probably better to keep our distance. Ethan slung his arm casually around the back of the bench and, by extension, me, but then he frowned and changed positions, leaning forward with his elbows resting on his knees. *He's thinking the same thing I am; we need to deal with this.*

"Who were you protecting in Lafayette?" I slid my foot across the dirt path, trying to find an angle that would stop it from throbbing.

"Grayson Hamilton. The older gentleman you saw me with at the Hamilton Center," Ethan replied.

"So what happens to him now?" I let a wide green leaf that hung over the arm of the bench slip through my fingers.

"I made some calls while I was on my way to the Bana trap house. I got a Hleo in the area to take over until someone else can be assigned to him. There hasn't been any activity on him in the time I've been there, so I'm not too worried." Ethan looked out across the flowerbeds. He was preoccupied, and truth be told, so was I. I had no idea how our meeting with The Three was going to go, but I knew Ethan well enough to know that he hated having to choose between me and obeying his superiors.

We settled into silence, listening to the hum of bees, the chirp of birds, and the breeze rustling through the leaves.

Ethan checked his watch. "It's time." He stood up and held out a hand to me.

My nerves kicked into overdrive. "Sure." I allowed him to help me up, then extricated my fingers from his and grasped my crutches. My armpits ached from supporting my weight on the pads. We ambled out of the garden and back to the manor. The massive library was as impressive as I remembered, but its solitude only added tension and gravity to our situation.

Bridget was waiting by the doors that led into the same meeting room where I'd first met with The Three, an unreadable expression on her face. "You can head on in; they'll be with you shortly." She pushed the door open and held it so we could enter the formal meeting space.

"Thank you, Bridget," Ethan replied. Bridget nodded and let the door shut behind her, leaving Ethan and I alone to wait for our judgment.

I settled into one of the leather chairs, while Ethan propped an elbow on the sill of one of the long windows that ran across the side of the room overlooking the grounds. *What are you thinking, Ethan?*

"They must be really mad to keep us waiting like this." I slid my hands back and forth along the smooth grain of the table. Ethan looked as though he was about to respond when the door opened and in came Gabriel, Victor, and Miriam. They filed into the room on the opposite side of the table I was on, the same reserved expression on each of their faces.

They chose chairs across from me with Gabriel in the middle. Ethan moved to stand respectfully behind the chair beside me, waiting for his superiors to sit. With graceful movements, they all settled into their seats. Once they were done, Ethan followed suit.

We were all silent for a moment. *Who's going to speak first? Should Ethan? Should I?* I threw a sideways glance at Ethan. His gaze was locked with Miriam's, and my stomach lurched.

"Good afternoon Ethan, Hannah." Gabriel nodded at us as he said our names. "I would say it is a pleasure to see you again, but under the circumstances I think you understand why I'll refrain from that comment." My shoulders slumped with the weight of the guilt I felt.

"We do." Ethan exhaled slowly.

"We are somewhat at a loss. Once again, we are presented with a situation that has never occurred in the history of the Hleo. And once again, you are at the center of it Hannah, my dear." Gabriel folded his hands on the table. "There have been incidences in the past of this rule being broken, but never has a Hleo then continued to defy the rule and our orders, and insist on reuniting with the protected again."

"I found Ethan, I went to him." I leaned forward. It was my fault rules had continued to be broken, not Ethan's. If only I could make them see that.

"We're aware of your journey, Hannah, but it's our understanding that you wouldn't have been able to find Ethan if he hadn't left you clues to his whereabouts." Victor's blue eyes were solemn, without the usual boyish gleam.

Gabriel sighed. "Ethan, I thought we had made the weight of your indiscretion clear to you. It was only because of your excellent service record and your incredible history of loyalty with the Hleo that we were able to give you a second chance, but I don't know how we could in good conscious let you continue on as a Hleo after another flagrant disregard of the rules." The words sounded like they came from a heavy heart; none of The Three looked as though they wanted to carry out this punishment. They didn't seem angry at all. They seemed sad.

Ethan swallowed. "I want to apologize for what must appear like heinous disobedience. I know it seems unexplainably defiant that I would behave in such a way. My only excuse is that I love Hannah completely and irrevocably; to deny being with her is the same as denying myself breath. I understand you have to do what you feel is necessary, but before you make your decision I want you to know that, no matter what, Hannah will be my last protected. If you would consider allowing me to stay a Hleo until her life is her own again, I will then walk away from the society with her." Ethan kept his gaze on The Three. My eyes widened. He had said the same thing in the Jeep on the way to Veridan, but to voice such a decisive assertion about our future to The Three gave me goosebumps.

"But Ethan, to reject your purpose, your reason for living ..." Gabriel raised his hands to appeal Ethan's decision, and I realized that, no matter what rules Ethan had broken, The Three didn't want to lose him.

"Hannah is my reason for living and my purpose now." Ethan straightened in his seat, and my heart swelled.

The Three looked at each other, obviously digesting Ethan's declaration and proposal. Victor's face was drawn, a strange contrast to his amiable personality. Gabriel's eyes betrayed that he was perplexed, while Miriam's expression remained stoic. *What do you think of all of this, Miriam?* I worked at controlling my breathing; the waiting was killing me. Why couldn't they just tell us if they were going to allow us to be together or not?

"Ethan, we would like to converse with you privately." Gabriel stood and motioned to a closed door in the wall behind him. Victor and Miriam also got up.

"Of course." Ethan rose and joined them. They slipped through the door into the smaller chambers. Ethan paused and glanced back at me before he walked through the doorway.

The door shut behind the four of them, leaving me alone at the long wooden table. *How will I go on without ever looking into those beautiful green eyes again if The Three make us separate permanently?*

I drummed my fingers on the table. It probably wasn't a good sign that they had wanted to keep me out of the conversation. I kept glancing up at the ornate wall clock, willing the four of them to reappear. Ten minutes passed without a single sound from the other room. I debated getting up and pressing an ear to the door, but with my luck that would be the moment it would open and I would be standing there looking like an idiot.

After twenty minutes I dragged myself out of the chair to stretch. I hobbled to one of the windows and gazed out over the gardens that stretched across the entire back part of the property. A flock of small blackbirds soared above the scenic rolling hills and forests, blissfully unaware of the emotional torture I was currently experiencing.

The door handle jiggled. I whipped around and managed to make it back to my seat without incident. I tried to appear nonchalant as Miriam, Gabriel, Victor, and then Ethan emerged through the doorway. Their expressions were pleasant, but gave away nothing. I bit the inside of my cheek. *Just tell me what you've decided.*

They all settled back into their seats; I glanced from The Three to Ethan expectantly.

"Thank you for your patience, Hannah." Gabriel's tone was warm.

"No problem." I smiled, but I wasn't capable of entirely wiping the anxiousness off my face.

"After careful discussion, and weighing in all the available details, we have decided to let Ethan stay on as your Hleo, and allow the two of you to continue in the relationship you have begun." Gabriel clasped his hands on the table. "We have grave concerns with this arrangement, but Ethan has agreed to follow certain terms while he remains your protector. He can discuss those with you at a later time. Understand Hannah, it is with great reservation that we sanction this connection, but it seems that Ethan is determined to be with you no matter what, and from the dangerous cross-country journey you took, it appears you are quite determined to be with him as well."

Happiness bubbled up inside me. No matter how negatively they viewed the prospect of he and I being together, ultimately they had given us a green light and that was all I needed. "Thank you for your understanding; it means a lot that you've tried to see this situation from our point of view."

"All we ask is that you be careful, both of you. A Hleo and a protected have never been allowed to be together before, and the bond you share may very well turn out to be a weakness as much as it is a strength," Victor warned, a trace of his carefree grin returning to his face.

"We will." Ethan nodded.

It was poor timing, but there was something else I wanted to ask The Three while we were at Veridan. "I'm not sure if Lucy kept you apprised of her work with me in East Halton, all the mental exercises she conducted with me."

The Three exchanged wary glances before Gabriel answered. "She did."

"Well then, you should know that, no matter what she tried she didn't get anywhere in trying to crack the mystery of why it is that I can do what I do."

This time Victor spoke up. "That's true Hannah, she was unsuccessful, but—"

I leaned towards them. "I think you should reconsider letting me into the circular room." This time, instead of shock from Ethan, he sat motionless, as though waiting to see what they would say.

"No Hannah." Miriam shook her head. "It's not time for that."

"But someday it will be?" I frowned. Was that what she was saying?

"There will come a day when everything you're experiencing will make sense, a day when your ability will no longer perplex you. I know it's challenging, but please try to be patient." Miriam's eyes met mine, saying far more than her words had.

I swallowed. The centuries of wisdom I could see in them were a lot to take in. "Okay." It was on the tip of my tongue to bring up what Ethan had found out about Elizabeth and her training to take over for Miriam, but I hesitated. We were already pressing our luck getting their approval as a couple, I didn't want to get Ethan in trouble all over again for digging up information he wasn't supposed to. I couldn't help but study them, though, curious about why they were keeping this information from me. Was it because Miriam was no longer in danger, or because they didn't believe it was time yet to let me know that Elizabeth's purpose had been passed on to me?

Thirty-One

The Three dismissed us shortly after. I was eager to get back on the road and home before Dad or Katie did something drastic out of their concern for me. I hadn't been able to recharge my phone, and could only guess what the message count was up to. I tracked down Lou and gave her the good news that Ethan and I were allowed to stay together, then said good-bye.

It felt like weeks since I'd been home instead of only four days. I hadn't realized how much I missed my dad, my friends, and my bed. I couldn't wait to flop down and have a long nap, wrapped in my own blankets.

As we drove back to East Halton, Ethan and I held hands, quietly content. I couldn't believe we could finally be out in the open with our relationship, no more secrets or sneaking around.

"You might be more comfortable stretching out in the back seat," Ethan suggested after I had shifted my leg for the fifth or sixth time. I couldn't seem to find a position that kept it from aching.

"No, I'm good." I shook my head. All I wanted was to be close to him at the moment, even if that meant a little discomfort.

"Hey, when Gabriel said terms we had to agree to, what did he mean by that?" I'd been so excited that we weren't going to have to secretly flee the country that I'd momentarily forgotten about that, but as we put some distance between us and the Hleo's headquarters I was curious to know what Ethan had agreed to.

Ethan winced slightly. Had he been hoping I wouldn't ask? "The first was that we keep our relationship as quiet as possible, particularly if we are around other Hleo. They're expecting a lot of resistance from my colleagues, who will feel that a very important rule has been bent for me, and The Three aren't entirely sure how they're going to respond to that criticism yet." Ethan slid his hand along the steering wheel. Personally I wanted to hit up every social media site I could think of to let the world know that Ethan and I were in love, but I could respect that we had presented The Three with a huge conundrum.

"The next is that I leave the Hleo society once this assignment is over, as I said I would." Ethan casually glanced over his shoulder to make sure it was clear to pass the sedan in front of us.

He sounded so cavalier. Had he really thought things through? The Hleo world was all he had known for so long. How could he be so nonchalant about the fact that he would be out of it as soon as his task of keeping me safe was done? "Are you sure about your decision?" I studied our clasped hands, suddenly feeling a trickle of doubt.

He squeezed my fingers and I could feel his eyes on me, beckoning me to meet his gaze. "Never question my devotion to you. You are all I will ever want."

"I just want to be sure you've really taken the time to consider everything."

"I'm done weighing everything. I'm ready to start living my life, with you."

"That sounds perfect." My cheeks warmed at his affectionate words. "Is that it for conditions?" The Three had been quite reasonable if it was.

"No, not quite. The last one was a bit complicated for me to agree to, because it involves the two of us." Ethan glanced over at me. "I had to agree that we wouldn't sleep together until you're no longer considered a protected." He bit his lip, clearly not sure how I would respond to this news.

I blinked. "How can they possibly demand something that?" My grip on the door handle tightened.

"Hannah, it's not something that was a big deal for me to promise them," Ethan said calmly.

"Why not?"

He slipped his hand around the back of my neck. "Trust me when I tell you that I want to be with you as much as any man has ever wanted to be with a woman. You are beautiful, radiant, loving, and I am privileged to have you in my life. Agreeing to their third condition had nothing to do with a lack of desire for you.

"This is probably hard for you to understand, but when I said I feel the way The Three do about you, I meant it completely. I see you as sacred, and I would never be comfortable with ignoring that belief to satisfy my own longing. Plus, I was born and raised in a tradition that believed that step of intimacy comes *after* marrying someone, not before. That's what I meant about rushing things, that people rush into sex before they've committed to each other in a meaningful way."

My throat tightened. Was he saying what I thought he was saying? "So, you want to wait until we get married?"

He glanced at me. "I know it probably sounds strange and old-fashioned to you, being raised in the culture you have been, but it means a lot to me."

"You want to marry me?" A smile spread across my lips. In the time we'd been together, constantly thinking and looking towards the future, marriage hadn't entered my mind. Being together as a couple, absolutely, but not that ultimate big step of the white dress, rings, and vows in front of all our family and friends. I guess I felt that we were too young to think that way. *Except that Ethan isn't young.*

"Of course." Ethan's eyebrows shot up. "Don't you want to marry me?"

I lifted my shoulders lightly. "I've never really thought about it."

"I guess, as young as you are, why would you? But I've known for a long time that I wanted to be joined to you in every way possible, and for me that means in marriage."

"I would be honored to marry you someday." My cheeks warmed, and I looked at him to see my own happiness reflected on his face.

"When all of this is over, we'll find our moment." Ethan repeated the words he had said that night at Veridan when we'd almost slept together, and my heart skipped a beat.

I gazed out the window at the lush, green scenery. We passed by forests and fields, small towns and farms, making our way closer and closer to home. Everything was new and fresh, in full bloom and brimming with life. *Like our relationship.* I looked over at Ethan and he winked at me. For the first time, we didn't have to hide or pretend we were just friends. There was no need to stay in the shadows for fear of being caught; we could finally grow and evolve into a real couple.

As we discussed how we would explain why I was with Ethan, and why he had returned, where I had gone, what had happened to Adam, and how I had hurt my leg, my mind drifted to thoughts of becoming Mrs. Ethan Flynn. An image of being in a small country church, walking down an aisle towards Ethan in a simple flowing white dress, a bouquet of wildflowers in my hand, came to mind. It wasn't a flash, simply my imagination, but the vision filled me with hope.

Thirty-Two

Relief washed over me when we pulled into my driveway. My house had never looked so welcoming, and I was glad to be surrounded by the familiar security of East Halton again.

Ethan scrambled out of the Jeep and came around to my side to help me with my crutches so I could totter into the house. My father stood in the hallway, his arms crossed and a deep frown of anger mixed with worry on his face. His eyes drifted from mine to my casted foot and the lines on his forehead deepened.

"Dad." I bit my lip, not sure how to begin to explain my disappearance. *He is so mad.*

"Hannah, where have you …? How could you …? Are you okay?" Dad hauled me into a fierce hug as he fired unfinished questions at me until sighing and landing on the one he appeared to want answered most.

"I'm okay, Dad, really." I pulled away from the hug. "This is not nearly as bad as it looks." I swung my foot a little to downplay the injury.

"Uh huh." Dad eyed my cast. "And I suppose this is welcome back, Ethan?" My father leveled a cold stare at Ethan.

"Yes, sir." Ethan nodded cautiously.

"Let's go into the living room and you can fill me in on exactly what has gone on the past few days." Dad motioned to the couch. Ethan and I exchanged an apprehensive look before complying. We'd already decided there was no sense lying to Dad. We were going to have to make excuses with so many other people; it would be a welcome change to actually share the details of our trip honestly with someone.

I slid into the armchair and Ethan plunked down across from me, letting Dad have the couch to himself. I launched into my explanation, beginning from the moment Adam had shown up on our front porch, to convincing him to find Ethan, all the way through to our trip to Veridan to see The Three. Dad's face remained expressionless as he listened and absorbed what I was saying.

I swallowed hard when I finished. Was it a good thing or a bad thing that he hadn't reacted?

He was silent for a long moment and my stomach twisted and turned in a knot. Would he ground me for life? Would he tell Ethan to get lost? Were we still going to have to hide our relationship if Dad was so mad he told us we couldn't be together? He leaned forward, studying me closely over the top of his glasses. "And this Adam fellow?" He sounded weary and my stomach tightened.

"He's gone," I assured him, still not exactly sure how I felt about that truth. I hadn't allowed myself to give Adam another thought since Lou had mentioned him, it was too strange. After all those months of hating him and fearing him, he had managed to form a connection with me, and in the end his sacrificial act of taking on Paige so Ethan and I could escape only added to my confusion about how to feel towards him.

Dad's shoulders fell, as though a weight had been lifted from them. "I think, all things considered Hannah, you are extremely lucky. I can't believe you just went off with that risky character in hopes of tracking Ethan down."

"I'm sorry, Dad. I never would ever have chosen to do if I thought I had another option. I hope you'll be able to forgive me." Guilt pricked at my chest.

"If anything ever happened to you ..." Dad wiped at the corners of his eyes.

I clamored out of the chair and sank down beside him, wrapping my arms around him. "I love you too, Dad."

Dad cleared his throat and turned to face Ethan. "And you are here for good this time?"

"I will never leave Hannah's side of my own volition again," Ethan solemnly vowed.

Dad sighed, and rested his hands on his knees. "I suppose I should just be happy that you're back and in one piece and try to focus on that. You should really get in touch with Katie, though. I'm pretty sure she's about to send the National Guard out after you."

"I can only imagine." I pulled myself up off the couch, anxious to get to my room. She'd been super skeptical about my decision to go with Adam, and that's when she thought I would only be gone a day. "I guess I'd better go call her." Before I could take a step, Ethan was at my side, ready to assist me up the stairs.

Dad stood too. "I'll be in my study if you need me. And in case you weren't sure, I am very glad you're back."

"Me too."

Ethan and I headed upstairs. As soon as my door swung shut behind us, I grasped Ethan and pressed my lips against his in a deep, relief-filled kiss. We were finally home and able to put the last month and a half behind us. His arms circled my waist and he held me tightly against him, kissing me back with equal fervor. After a minute or so we pulled away from each other, reluctantly.

"Can I just say, I missed you," I exclaimed, trying to catch my breath.

His green eyes sparkled. He pulled me in close again, brushing his lips softly across my forehead. "I'll leave you to call Katie. I should try to get a hold of Simon anyway, see if he's interested in working with us again." Ethan's grin was wry at the mention of his amusing colleague. He touched a finger to my cheek, then headed for the door. I had no doubt we would be seeing Simon again very shortly. *I wonder what he's been up to.*

"Do you have any idea where we should begin?" I hadn't bothered bringing up the subject after The Three had once again denied me access to the circular room, but after everything he had shared on our way to Veridan, I was curious to know whether Ethan had any thoughts on re-starting our quest to figure out my ability.

Ethan stopped in the doorway and pressed one palm to the frame. "As a matter of fact, I have."

"And?"

"The Three aren't going to give you any answers, that much we know. And I'm positive your ability is linked with Elizabeth's training. She was learning how to wield the power of the circular room, but The Three won't give you access to that room, so the way I figure it, there's only one thing left for us to do. We need to go after the Glain Neidr. It's made of the same material as the room, so maybe finding it will allow you the same control the room would have given Elizabeth."

My eyes widened. Had I heard him right? Was Ethan finally agreeing to go after the mythical stone with me?

"Yes, you heard me right. We're going on an adventure."

I laughed. In spite of, or maybe because of, our time apart. Ethan and I were closer than ever. He was even reading my thoughts now.

He pointed at my phone. "Call Katie. I don't have the energy to deal with the National Guard tonight." He winked at me before pushing away from the door frame and disappearing into the hallway.

After leaning my crutches against the wall, I flopped down on the bed, grateful to get off my ankle. I punched in Katie's number. When she answered, it took a couple of minutes for her to calm down enough for me to explain at least enough of what had happened to satisfy her. As soon as I got to the part where I could tell her that Ethan and I were officially dating and not keeping it a secret from everyone anymore, her tone changed from extremely upset to wildly enthusiastic and it took me another five minutes to convince her I was too tired to talk about it and we'd catch up at school the next day.

Finally I was able to disconnect the call and flop back on the pillow. I stared up at the ceiling and grinned. Ethan and I were together again, finally free to tell the world about our relationship. And now we were going on an adventure. The memory of Milton Cambry's office, broken into and torn apart, drifted into my mind and my grin faded. It would be dangerous, going after the Glain Nadr. If Ethan was right and the Bana had the relic, we'd be walking right into the lion's den. The same lion that had ordered Adam to abduct me and bring me to him.

I turned over onto my side, grimacing as pain shot up my leg. We didn't have a choice. The Three had ensured that we had no option but to pursue the mythical stone on our own. It was the only way that I could get my life back, and Ethan and I could begin ours together. And we'd be fine. Ethan and Simon were incredibly strong, smart, and skilled. And they knew the Bana. They were perfectly capable of keeping me safe, weren't they?

I pressed a fist to my lips. I guess we were about to find out.

Glain Neidr

The final book in the Hleo series

By

Rebecca Weller

Check Out the Exclusive Sneak Peek

Ethan and I wandered the ship, until we came to a set of stairs leading down a level. We descended into a glassed-in observation area that must have been used as a dining room. A bar area sat at the far end of the room, while round tables and chairs were set up in the middle. Plush navy benches lined both sides of the boat under the windows. Jill Nesbitt and Dylan Torino, two classmates, were making out in the corner of the one closest to us so I crossed over to the far side of the boat.

I plunked down, waving to a few girls from my art class who stood in line for the bathroom. "I should tell Heather this is where the action is." I nodded to one of the tables, where a group I recognized as the math club was playing poker at one of the tables.

"I've seen her in action her. She'd clean these guys out." Ethan watched as one of the guys threw down his hand in frustration. "Besides, I don't think Ryan would appreciate it."

"There does seem to be a little something sparking between them tonight, doesn't there?" I grinned. The two of them were an awkward pairing, and yet they worked somehow.

Before Ethan could respond, his phone buzzed in his pocket. He tugged it out. "It's Simon." He stood and crossed over to a dark hallway that appeared to be off limits. Someone had tied a rope across the entrance, but Ethan casually stepped over it.

I twisted on the bench to look out over the calm water of Lake Pocotoa as I waited for Ethan to return. Why would Simon call? He knew about our plans for the evening, so he must have had an important reason. Although knowing Simon, it could be just as likely he wanted to know if there was any leftover pizza in the fridge.

I drummed my fingers on the back of the bench for what felt like a long time, until Ethan dropped back down beside me. His forehead was creased and his jaw tight.

"What was that about?" My stomach churned.

Ethan ran a hand through his hair. He seemed hesitant to begin the conversation. "He found Alexander."

I forced myself not to react in a way that would garner attention from the other partygoers in the room. "Where?"

"In New York. He's meeting with some political figures tonight before heading back to France in the morning."

"New York," I breathed. The Glain Neidr could be close, only a few hours' drive away.

"Yeah." Ethan nodded.

Are you thinking what I'm thinking Ethan? "What does that mean?"

"It means, if you want to do this, if you want to go after the necklace, we have to do it tonight." Ethan studied me, as though trying to read my thoughts.

"Let's do it." I stood up and crossed over to the stairs that led to the main deck, with Ethan close behind. I whirled around to face him just before my foot hit the first step. "Wait, we're on a boat. How do we get off?"

"According to the schedule, we should arrive back at the dock within the next half an hour. We can wait that long. I'll call Simon and tell him to get ready. As soon as we disembark, we'll be on our way."

"Okay, we'll have to stop by home first. I don't think my outfit is all that practical for retrieving a priceless artifact from some of the world's most dangerous bad guys." I smoothed down the front of the shimmering strapless dress with both palms.

"Maybe not, but it is a pleasure to see you in." Ethan gave me an affectionate smile.

I pressed my lips to his briefly. "Thank you." I scrunched up my nose. "What am I going to tell Katie and everyone? She is going to be so disappointed if we don't go to Kristen's cottage. It's supposed to be the last official thing we do as our group." How would I break the news to my best friend?

"You could tell her I got us a hotel room for the night." Ethan's eyes were on his phone. My face grew hot. When I didn't say anything, he glanced up. "It's an explanation that wouldn't lead to a lot more questions, and would keep Katie from trying to contact you while we're gone."

I tapped my hand along the stair railing. "I guess that's true." Was I okay letting Katie believe that Ethan and I were taking our relationship to that level? Especially when we weren't? "It is the least complicated explanation, isn't it? Okay, well, I'm off to lie to my best friend."

Ethan grabbed my wrist, halting me. "Hannah, if we go through with this, you might not see your friends again for quite some time. If by some miracle we do get the necklace, we'll be hunted by some of the most dangerous people on this planet. And if we fail, well ..." Ethan gently tucked a stray strand of hair behind my ear.

"We aren't going to fail. I know you wouldn't let that happen. We're going to be successful." I straightened his tie and rested my hands on his chest. "We have to be."

He studied me for a second before giving me a slight nod. "I'll meet you upstairs in a minute."

"Okay." I went off to try to find Katie, and everyone else. They had congregated at the bow of the boat. Ryan, Heather, Kristen, and Mark were all dancing, while Katie and Luke leaned against the railing facing the water. Luke's arms were wrapped around her waist and I hated to interrupt. *What if this is the last time I ever see these people who mean so much to me?* I tried to capture the moment, to tuck it away somewhere in my mind so I would always remember the happiness my friends had brought me through the years.

"There you are. I was just about to come find you." Katie turned so that she was leaning back against the railing as I came up beside them.

"I'll go get us some drinks." Luke winked at Katie before strolling away, leaving the two of us alone. I rested my arms on the railing beside her and gazed out over the lake.

"So, this is it." Katie sounded thoughtful.

"This is it?" I glanced over at her. *What does that mean?*

"Yeah, we're done. We've finally reached that point when our time in East Halton is coming to an end." Katie bumped me with her shoulder.

"I hadn't really thought about it that way, but I guess you're right Kate, our time here is coming to an end." I bit my lip. She had no idea how true her words were. After tonight, I didn't know when I would be back in East Halton, if ever. A wave of sadness mixed with fear washed over me as I contemplated what Ethan, Simon, and I were about to attempt.

"At least we're heading out together." Katie turned around and slid her arm around my shoulder.

"Yeah." I plastered a smile on my face. *Oh Katie, you have no idea how much I hope that's true.* Was a future with Katie at Stanford even possible anymore?

She straightened up. "So, I've been thinking about the bedroom situation at the cottage and–"

"Actually, I have to talk to you about that." I pulled away from the railing and clasped my hands together in front of me.

"What? You aren't going to bail on us, are you?" Katie crossed her arms.

"I had no plans to bail, but Ethan sort of just told me that he, um, well, he kind of booked a room for us tonight, at a hotel." I stumbled over the words; they caused me more than a little embarrassment, especially since they weren't true.

"He what?" Katie grabbed my arms.

I winced and she released me then stepped back and stared at me. I smoothed back my hair where I had tied it back. "So ..."

"So go." She waved a hand through the air. "Don't even worry about it. I mean, his timing isn't perfect, but hey, we have most of the summer to hang out. Why don't you come over tomorrow morning and join us, unless you're still busy, that is." Katie wriggled her eyebrows.

"Thanks, Kate." I rolled my eyes. As Ethan had predicted, my excuse wasn't going to get a lot of flack or questions from her.

"Wow, are you ready? I mean, I know you've been thinking about it for a while, but do you think you're ready to take that step?" Katie's tone had grown serious.

She's such a good friend to be concerned for my emotional wellbeing instead of teasing me for my inexperience. "I think I am. I love Ethan, completely, and I know that I want to be with him forever. I'm ready for that to mean being with him in every way." My words were true, even if it wasn't going to happen that evening.

"Awww, that is so romantic. You guys are the cutest couple ever."

"Thanks. Don't say anything to anyone though. He wants it to be a secret just between us, but I had to tell you."

Ethan appeared at the top of the stairs and made his way over to us. He had a smile on his face, but there was tension in his eyes. He had been right about the timing. We were almost back to the dock we had shoved off from. Nervous butterflies started to flutter in my stomach. How would our evening go? *Ethan's the best at this. Everyone thinks so. We are going to be triumphant.* I swallowed hard. Even though stealing the Glain Neidr from the evil head of the Bana had been my idea, now that we were about to implement the plan, I couldn't help but worry.

The boat docked in the harbor again, and passengers in varying degrees of dishevelment from partying made their way off the boat. I turned and grabbed Ethan's hand. "This is it." I looked up at him, echoing Katie's earlier statement, quiet enough that only he could hear.

His forehead creased. "Are you ready?"

I simply nodded and tried not to bite my lip; I didn't want him to see my trepidation, or he might change his mind about us doing this. Or maybe he'd leave me behind.

Once we were back on dry land, Ethan and I said our goodbyes to everyone. I gave Heather and Kristen hugs, saving Katie for last.

"Thank you for being the best friend I could ever have hoped for." I held her tightly.

"Back at you." She leaned close and whispered in my ear, "And by the way, I'm going to want non-graphic details tomorrow." She pulled away and climbed into Luke's car. I slipped into the passenger seat of Ethan's Jeep and buckled my seatbelt. *This is not the last I will see of my friends.*

In spite of my assertion, something about the taillights of the Lincoln Continental disappearing into the darkness had a certain finality to it.

Glain Neidr

The conclusion to the Hleo series

Hannah is done. Done with high school, done with East Halton, and done waiting for answers. She and Ethan set off on a quest to find the elusive Glain Neidr necklace, believing it will give her the ability to regain control of her life.

When tragedy strikes, the pressure to get their hands on the mystical stone intensifies, leading them further and further down a rabbit hole in hopes that the Glain Neidr and answers about Hannah's destiny will be waiting at the other end. But whose rabbit hole is it? The Hleo's? The Bana's?

With their sights set on freeing Hannah from the entanglements of the Hleo society and the threats of the Bana, Ethan and Hannah plunge into a journey that will take them across the globe and make Hannah question whether her freedom is really what she wants.

With Ethan by her side, any future seems possible, but as their mission grows more complicated and dangerous, will they survive long enough to find their happily ever after?

Coming Soon

Acknowledgments

I can't believe I've made it to three books. Feel honored that you are the reason for this, without the amazing support of both my local and online community there's no way I would have had the courage to keep this endeavor going.

I'm always so amazed when total strangers are willing to give the *Hleo* series a chance. There are so many book options in the world these days and I want to thank the bloggers, the Inkitt writing community and Facebook pages like I Like YA Books and I Cannot Lie for giving *Hleo* a chance. I hope this next installment of Hannah and Ethan's journey will delight you just as much.

To my local support system and fan base, I wish I could personally thank you all by name. You have humbled me with your faith in this story, and as I watch you take it out and share it, helping it to spread further than I ever could I feel incredibly blessed. Aliege has a special place in my heart, and I hope you will feel the same.

Sara, once again your editing skills astound me. Thank you for continuing to shape the *Hleo* series into something truly special. I appreciate your honesty, your loyalty to the characters, and your gift at finding the words when I am struggling to do so.

David, what more can I say, but thank you. Thank you for your suggestions, your beautiful artwork for the covers, and most of all for believing in me. I'm so glad I get to go through this life with you.

Again, a big thanks to you. I appreciate your support so much!

About the Author

Scribbling down whatever her imagination could conjure, Rebecca Weller has been writing stories most of her life. Her hope is to inspire, and to use writing as a way to help others beyond the Canadian borders she currently lives in with her husband and two children.

Check Out: **https://hleoweller.wordpress.com** for more.

Reviews are Always Welcome and Encouraged! If you could take a moment to post a review to any of the following websites I would greatly appreciate it!

https://www.amazon.com/ - search for Hleo

https://www.goodreads.com/book/show/29571063-hleo

https://www.inkitt.com/stories/romance/150248?started_reading=true

https://itunes.apple.com/us/book/id1080233500

Made in the USA
Columbia, SC
08 December 2017